One Drum

Earth Songs, Book 1

Patricia Jamie Lee

Jamie Lee

Many Kites Press

Many Kites Press
Box 711
Cass Lake, MN 56633
www.manykites.com

ISBN 978-0-9618469-8-5

Printed in the United States

Then I was standing on the highest mountain of them all, and round about beneath me was the whole hoop of the world. And while I stood there I saw more than I can tell and I understood more than I saw; for I was seeing in a sacred manner the shapes of all things in the spirit, and the shape of all shapes as they must live together like one being.

~~From Black Elk Speaks, by J. Neihardt

Prologue

February 27, 2003

Cuny Table, a tabletop mesa in the heart of Lakota country, is an unlikely place for a restaurant. The mesa itself is a survivor, having held its ground as thirty-five million years of wind and rain eroded the land into what is now the Badlands of South Dakota. On its high top are a few scattered ranches, fields of winter wheat, and a view so wide it feels like the floor of heaven. Sketched along the skyline to the west are the Black Hills; and on the northeastern edge surrounded by a few rough buildings is the Cuny Café.

Agnes Stands Alone, the owner of the café, has been there as long as anybody can remember. She is an old, square-bodied woman with short, coarse hair and eyes like dark marbles that seem to see straight through you. The regulars call her *Unci*, or Grandmother in Lakota. Most of them wander in not so much for the food (although the food is good) but for her company and the unusual tea she brews from plants gathered down in the Cheyenne River breaks. The old ones, especially, find Agnes's tea eases their aching bones and makes the blood flow more easily to the toes. Oh, she makes no claims about her tea, but everybody who walks in gets a steaming cup slapped down before them with a brisk command to, "Drink up."

The café, an old thirty-foot trailer, has been gutted, insulated, and made into one open space except for a back bedroom which nobody but Agnes has ever been in. The front has a single booth, two tables, and a plywood counter top covered with blue-flowered contact paper.

1

Some strangers think the poor old trailer looks like a dislocated train car hooked to nothing, going nowhere.

Agnes never hesitates to give advice—or a solid scolding—when needed. But, more than the tea or Indian tacos or advice or whatever is on the menu that day (everybody eats the same daily special), the locals go to the café for Agnes's stories. She knows all of the old Lakota stories. She knows the creation stories, the stories of *Iktomi* the trickster and the Seven Sisters who can still be seen winking down from the sky on a clear night. Her favorite is the story of the Second Cleansing when *Unci Makah* grew tired of the antics of her warring human children and tossed all but a few off her powerful body. According to the story, those She sheltered later emerged from Wind Cave as The Lakota People.

Agnes, however, doesn't just tell old stories. Sometimes she tailor-makes the story especially for the person hearing it. For instance, once J.J. Runs At Night had a new colt so sick it couldn't stand. Agnes told him a story about how a grove of young willows withstood the mightiest of storms by forcing their roots further into *Unci Makah*, Grandmother Earth. "Such smart, young trees," she said, "to know just what to do." By the time J.J. got home, the colt was running across the corral on four sturdy legs.

Another time, June Player's daughter tried to die by cutting her wrists with the top of a tuna can. The poor girl nearly bled out before they found her. For this dangerous moment Agnes told June about a small ant who had lost his place in line—until the wind blew a single grain of sand across his path, forcing him to turn another way. The next day, June's daughter woke up from her deep, uneasy sleep talking about needing to find her place—before it was too late.

A while later, the girl began writing poetry and gave Agnes this poem written in a smooth, pretty hand:

In the greater scheme of things
Only she who sings,
And learns to play the wind,

Will ever grow wings.
Now I play the wind.

Agnes took a pineapple-shaped magnet, stuck the poem to her fridge and said, "Good."

Of the nearly forty thousand residents of The Pine Ridge Reservation, at least half of them have been in the Cuny Café at one time or another, not to mention visitors from Japan, Switzerland, Germany, and many other places. Agnes keeps a guest book and feeds them all tea and stories.

On slow days, Agnes sits in an old rocking chair on the rough-lumber porch that the regulars had built for her five years earlier and lights her pipe. When it's not in use, she keeps the pipe in a small, beaded bag hanging on a nail beside the screen door like a good omen. The bowl is carved red pipestone from a quarry in southern Minnesota. This particular stone, Agnes says, was once part of the Black Hills until it broke away and floated off during some ancient upheaval.

Agnes fills the pipe with a dried version of her tea and, while she smokes, she prays. Sometimes the praying takes her far off to what she simply calls "the other place." The first time she visited this other place she had been only seventeen and drunk. Her uncle, a medicine man, had found her puking her guts out beneath an old cottonwood tree and taken her home and made her pray for three days straight without food or water. That ornery old man—he'd cut straight through her young spirit to the old woman already living there, and Agnes had never again been able to return to her ordinary young life.

Now, when the locals drive up Cuny Table to grab a bite to eat and find her sitting so still with the pipe in her lap and the spirit absent from her eyes, they know not to disturb her and simply tromp up the steps to help themselves in her kitchen. Occasionally, the praying is so complete, so pervasive, that they find it impossible to cross her threshold and simply get back into their trucks and leave.

3

Agnes sees many things in the smoke curling up from her pipe; she sees the land, she sees distant places, she sees the beating hearts of the people, the breaking hearts of the people, the loving hearts of the people; and, sometimes, in the hazy curl she sees the old ones who once walked the earth but now watch from other realms. The old ones have stories of their own to tell, but Agnes never tells these stories to anybody except Bill Elk Boy.

It was one of these days, on the edge of winter, when Agnes cast her inner eye outward toward the weathered lands north of Cuny Table and saw the change coming. There, on a single square foot of dry, deserted earth in the Badlands, a thin line of dust rose up from a single needle-mark in the sand. Agnes watched the whorl of dust curl upward like the smoke of her pipe. It had no discernible color unless she used the very edges of her peripheral vision—and then she saw the palest of pink light rising from a dark horizon. As she watched, the pale moving spiral seemed to take shape, as if Creator was conjuring something from nothing, dancing dust into form.

When the dust settled, she saw the form of a woman asleep in the sand, and Agnes knew she had returned at last, the little one . . . the lost one.

Two young boys were walking toward the sleeping woman.

When the glaze cleared from her eyes and she again entered this ordinary realm, Bill Elk Boy was beside her. He took the pipe, the bowl now cold to the touch, tapped it clean on the edge of his chair, slipped it back into the beaded bag, and said, "It begins, Agnes. Today it begins."

Chapter 1

The two boys approached cautiously. From a distance Jed Forrest thought it must be a dead deer or that someone had dumped a pile of clothing out here in the middle of nowhere. He got closer, and his heart started thumping hard when he saw it was a person laying there on the ground—a lady. He and his little brother, Pete, had seen a lot of strange things out here in the Badlands—but they'd never found a body before.

Pete hurried ahead and was on the ground reaching out to touch the lady. Jed caught up to him and whispered, "Don't touch her,"

"Why not?" Pete asked.

"Because she might be dead, murdered maybe, and we'd mess up the crime scene."

"Oh," said Pete. "But Jed, what if she's just sick and needs a doctor? We got to do something."

"I know that. Let me think a minute."

Jed didn't know what to think or do. The lady was curled into herself as if she was cold. She wore nothing but a light jacket, jeans, boots, and no cap. He resisted the urge to touch her even though he'd told Pete not to. His dad was maybe fifteen minutes away—too far to hear them if they yelled—but Pete was right; they needed to do something. He reached for her wrist to see if he could feel a pulse. Her skin was warm and relief washed through him—she was alive. He pressed his fingers into her wrist and felt the thump, thump of her heartbeat. "She's not dead, Pete."

"Look," said Pete. "She's waking up. Maybe you brought her back to life."

"Shut up, Pete." Jed dropped her wrist just as the lady blinked her eyes once, twice and then looked up at him. It was strange, the way her eyes wandered, looked up and down, and then finally focused on him. She shook her head and rubbed her face. Jed said, "Are you okay?"

"What?" she said quietly, still blinking and rubbing her eyes.

Pete squatted down and said, almost yelling it out. "She's alive."

"Hush, Pete. You'll scare her. " Jed stood up and looked down at the woman. "Are you hurt?"

She moved slowly feeling her arms and shoulders and then pushed herself up into a sitting position. "I don't think so. No, I'm fine. Everything seems to be working."

Jed looked around for something to explain her being asleep in such a strange place "What the heck are you doing here?"

"I . . . I don't know. Where is here?" she asked.

"Sheesh—you don't even know where you are? This is the Badlands. We thought you were dead." Jed couldn't believe it.

She smiled. "Well, I don't appear to be dead since I'm sitting up. Who are you guys?"

"I'm Jed. This is my little brother, Pete. But who the heck are you?" Cripes, he thought, she looks like she just woke up from a little nap in her own bed.

"Give me a minute here, boys. I need to get my bearings. It's been a very long night, maybe the longest night ever." She planted her palms on the earth and dug them into the sand, as if the sand was going to tell her something she didn't know. Jed waited.

The lady finally dusted off her fingers and said, "To tell you the truth, I don't know who I am."

Pete sat down beside her and crossed his legs. "She's got nesia, Jed. You know, like when you can't remember things."

Jed said, "The word is amnesia, Pete."

Pete nodded, focusing all his attention on the lady. "Or maybe you got picked up by aliens, and they dropped you here from their spaceship."

"Aliens? Come on, Pete." Jed poked him with his toe.

"Well, I saw a show once and there were these creatures from another planet and . . . ."

"Not now, Pete." Jed tried to explain it to the strange lady, "My brother is—"

"Sweet. Your brother is sweet," she said. "No, Pete. I don't think it was aliens who left me here."

"What's your name?" Pete asked.

She rubbed her face and then scanned the earth around her. "Terra. My name is Terra."

Jed wondered if she was playing some sort of strange game with them "If you can't remember who you are, then how do you know your name is Terra? What are you doing here? And how did you get here?"

"So many questions for one so young," she shook her head and shrugged. "I don't know how I know, and I don't know what I am doing here. Waiting for you guys, I guess," she said. She looked around again and seemed to really see where they were for the first time. "This place takes my breath away. It's so beautiful." She gave her fingers a wiggle and then looked down at them as if surprised to find them working. "This is amazing, incredible really."

"What? What's incredible?" Jed tugged at his long, dark hair—hair he had not cut since his mom died.

The lady watched him, seeming to notice him for the first time. She looked from him to Pete and said, "Are you guys Indians?"

Jed nodded, "Lakota." He was beginning to not like this game or this lady or the way Pete was staring up at her as if she were the moon and sun combined. "Pete—quit staring at her."

"She's pretty, Jed."

"Oh cripes." He resisted the urge to kick sand at his stupid little brother.

"Pete. Jed." Terra said quietly, as if the names were sacred sounds. "It's okay, Jed. Everything is okay, don't you know?"

"What? What don't I know?" He was beginning to dislike this word game. The lady reached out as if to touch him but he pulled back.

"How old are you, Jed?"

"Twelve."

"Ah, such a good age." She turned to Pete. "And how old are you?"

Pete grinned. "Seven. Almost. Next month."

She nodded and said, "Perfect. Now, quit worrying, Jed. Never mind that I can't answer your questions yet. I'm just so happy to meet the two of you. Really I am." She stood up, pausing a minute as if to make sure her legs were working, and then she said simply, "Come on. Let's go."

"But . . . but where are you going?" Jed asked.

"With you and Petey, of course, since I don't know where I am, and it wouldn't make sense to just stay here all alone." She took Pete's hand and then started off down the draw in the same direction from which they had just come.

Jed shook his head as he watched the strange lady and his little brother walk off like who-do-you-know. His head felt funny, tight and full, and he couldn't figure out what was going on. There was no car or truck, no motorcycle or campsite, nothing to explain what she was doing passed out under an embankment, no clue of who she was or what the heck she was doing sleeping in the Badlands.

Jed didn't like strangers, and he most certainly didn't like strangers who called his little brother "Petey." He let Terra and Pete get ahead of him. He was thinking about how, when they'd first found her, he'd thought she was dead, lying there not moving, like something tossed away. He'd felt for a pulse and just when he'd been about to run for his dad, she'd opened her eyes and blinked up at them. Cripes, that had given him a scare—like a movie—the dead one getting up again and again.

Except they didn't all get up.

8

His mom hadn't gotten up again. Sometimes they were just plain dead. He felt the familiar plunk in his belly that always came when he thought of his mom. "Dang," he muttered aloud.

Now the lady and Pete were walking ahead of him like old buddies, and he had to hurry to catch up. He closed the distance between them. When he caught up, Terra put her hand out; and without thinking he took hold of it like it was a stick and he was drowning in a creek. The lady just smiled at him and suddenly his cheeks felt hot.

Something crazy is going on here, he thought, now totally conscious of her hand in his. In an eye blink, everything had changed. He looked at her, but she was staring forward, marching along like a soldier. When they topped the rise, he tugged his hand from hers and said, "My dad is this way." He pointed off in the direction of the truck and they walked soundlessly down the dusty wash and up over the bluff.

She looked at him and said with a wink, "Lead the way, my man. Wither thou goest, there go I."

"What did you say?"

"Relax, Jed. I'm only having some fun with you. Are you always so serious?"

"I am not so serious." The lady stared at him like she could see right through him, and that made him mad. He turned and walked off.

Staying ahead of them, Jed led the way over the bluff and back down into another wash following the tracks that he and Pete had made just a little while ago when the world still seemed together and they were just going off to collect sticks or cans. He could see their tracks pressed into the sand like fossils—yet it didn't seem like the same path they had come down. Suddenly nothing seemed familiar. He looked around and it seemed like a movie with the volume turned up, like there was more of everything: more color in the sky, more softness to the sand, more insects buzzing in his ears, more yellow in the morning sun . . . more, more, more. It made him dizzy.

9

He headed toward his dad's truck shaking his head, fighting a sudden weird urge to laugh and wondering what his dad would say about her.

Let him figure it out, Jed thought. Let him just go figure.

Chapter 2

Across the Black Hills and Badlands, shy animals raised their heads and sniffed the air, their noses twitching. It was time to seek their own kind, to gather in circles and caves and wait to see what would happen next. The animals scurried for miles finding first one and then another of their brothers and sisters and banding together. The birds caught currents of air and went east, west, south, and north in search of their own. Even the insects, barely awake and moving after the long winter, rustled with activity. They were traveling—traveling and gathering.

Agnes thumped up the steps of the Cuny Café with Bill close behind her. She stepped behind the counter and picked up the pot that held her special tea. There were no other customers—it was still too early for much activity. She poured herself and Bill a cup, threw some bacon into the pan, and popped the gas flame beneath it with a match. "A lot of movement out there, Bill."

He nodded and took a sip of his tea.

"I've never seen quite so much movement."

Bill nodded again. "I told you. It begins."

Agnes looked at him. "Or it ends."

"There is that, too," he said.

Chapter 3

John Forrest looked out across the Badlands for a sign of the boys. Pete and Jed knew not to get too far away from the truck, but there was no sign of them. They'd be back soon, he thought, forcing himself not to be anxious. He pulled his sunglasses out of his pocket and studied the horizon. The world seemed strangely quiet, and he felt small and vulnerable out here all alone, as if he were only an insect crawling on the giant earth.

Long ago the broken gullies and ragged tops of the Badlands had been the floor of a great inland sea swimming with life. Now, it was dry as dust. He'd been six the first time his parents had brought him fossil hunting our here. He smiled. As a boy, he'd thought he landed on the moon—the land cracked, dry, cratered. He'd loved this place when he was only six years old, and he loved it now. At home a pine shelf in his bedroom was still loaded with stones and fossils of all shapes, size, and colors that he'd collected over the years. The last time he'd roamed this land with his mother, she'd said, both in warning and in jest, "A person could cook their brains if he somehow got stranded out here in July."

He never forgot the way she had looked that day, bending low over the earth, her hair loose in the wind and wearing a smile as wide as the land, calling out to him occasionally. A year later—she was gone, dead of a brain aneurysm. Since then, he'd always associated this place with his mother.

The Badlands were in his blood.

Pulling a water bottle out of his pack, he leaned his backside against the truck and let the dreamy land take over his thoughts. He'd pulled the boys out of school and driven out at sunrise to capture the shadowy land as the sun crept up over the horizon. Producing a documentary on the Badlands was like being asked to eat chocolate for breakfast. He smiled at the circumstances that had brought him to this place: all the endless meetings, the jockeying for position in the rugged politics of The Pine Ridge Reservation. All along, he knew he'd get the contract.

He looked eastward to where the boys had walked off. No sign of them. No animals either. May as well pack it up for the day, he thought. He unscrewed the Sony Digital camera, collapsed the tripod, and packed his microphones stowing all the equipment in the waterproof shell attached to the back of his truck. Nearly finished, he brought his head up and rubbed his moustache, a habit he'd had since college. His ears tuned into the sound of the wind coming across the Badlands. It was a gentle dry wind, but suddenly it smelled as ripe as a Wisconsin deep woods when it rained, filled with a mossy scent not even remotely connected to sand, and swirling dust, and loneliness. The big empty land made him think of Mae Jo.

Three years earlier his wife had died leaving him and the two boys to fend for themselves. Just like that—a dark road, an icy highway, and crash—that was it. Since then, he'd awakened every damn morning wondering why? Why her? Why then? But there were no answers.

In truth, he sensed Mae Jo's spirit had always pulled in the direction of death. One night when Pete was just a baby, he'd found her alone in the living room, tears running down her cheeks. When he asked her what was wrong, she'd said, "I think that I won't be here to see them become men."

Why was he thinking of her now? After three long, painful years, he thought he'd at last accepted her death.

Where are those boys, he wondered. He walked in the general direction he'd seen them go earlier. He was about a hundred years from the truck when he heard them, their voices carried by wind. Within minutes he saw them still a quarter of a mile away looking like small clay figures

14

crossing a clay land—except they were not alone. A woman was walking between Jed and Pete—and she was holding Pete's hand. John peered out from under the brim of his black felt cowboy hat wondering what the knot in his belly meant. He noticed that her hair was almost the color of the Badlands, the strands layered in colors from white to palest earth red. She smiled down at Pete, and her hair brushed the top of Pete's head in the most intimate way, like mixing beach sand with farm soil. The sight made him uneasy and he couldn't shake the eerie feeling he'd seen this woman before, smelled this odd forest scent before.

Jed spotted him and ran ahead of Pete and the woman, closing the last three hundred yards in a burst of speed. "Dad!"

"Hi, Jed. Who the heck is that with you? You guys usually come back with rocks and sticks. What have you found today?"

Jed was still trying to catch his breath when the woman and Pete walked up to the truck.

"Her name is Terra," said Pete. "We found her taking a little nap down at the bottom of the wash."

He fully expected his youngest son to start in with, "Can we keep her dad, huh, can we, can we?" like he did with every stray cat, dog, lizard, turtle, and wounded bird he found. He eyed Terra. "Sleeping in the wash? Isn't that a bit dangerous?" He knew he sounded paternal, almost scolding, but didn't care—although she didn't look at all like other scruffy humans he'd found camped out here at various times. This desolate land was a magnet for lost souls. No, this woman looked sparkling clean, like a window. "Where's your gear?" he asked. "Are you hurt? Did your car break down?" The woman looked up at him and her eyes widened almost as if she recognized him— but he'd never seen her before, he was sure of it. "I asked you a question."

"Three," she said.

"Three what?"

"Questions. You asked me three questions. I have no gear. No, I'm not injured and no, I did not break down."

He wanted to call her a smart ass but he held his tongue. "So what is the story?"

"I don't know. I can't seem to remember where I am or how I got here. Your boys found me." She dropped Pete's hand, and he smiled up at her as if she was his very own goddess. She rubbed a hand across his head and said, "He's sweet, like a marshmallow, all light and fluffy. She stretched a hand out neatly and said "My name is Terra."

Like a robot, he automatically extended his own to meet hers. "John. John Forrest. I guess you've met my boys already." The air around his head suddenly went still and silent, and the forest scent filled his nostrils, almost overwhelming him. He pulled his hand back abruptly.

"Nice to meet you, John Forrest."

The moment lengthened. He was acutely aware of the boys staring up at him, waiting to see what he would say, what he would do. He turned to them and said, "Jed and Pete, run on back to the truck and wait for me there. I'll be right along." Reluctantly, they turned and headed toward the truck casting frequent glances back at Terra. When they were out of earshot, he said, "Okay, the little ears are gone. Tell me what is going on here. Did you get dumped off by a boyfriend? Take a few too many drugs last night? What the hell are you doing out in the middle of the Badlands with no wheels and no gear?"

The woman almost physically backed away from him. The smile was gone and her eyes looked distant. A full minute later she said, "Honestly? I don't know. I don't even know if that is my right name—it just popped out of my mouth when they asked."

"Are you saying you actually have no idea? Like amnesia or something?"

"Yes. I don't remember anything beyond your two boys standing over me when I opened my eyes. Quit looking at me like that."

"Like what?"

16

"As if I'm some kind of criminal or doper. I don't remember. That's all. I'm just happy they found me. At last."

John paused, letting her words register. "What do you mean—at last?"

She looked cornered, like one of the animals he'd hoped to capture on film earlier that morning. He tried to relax his interrogation. "You said they had found you *at last.*"

"Did I say that?"

"You did. I'd like some answers." Her dumb act was beginning to bug him. "So?"

She seemed to shake off her confusion and regain her composure. "Look. Can we not start out this way? Please? I was lost—and now I'm found. Can we just leave it at that?" And then she turned and walked away heading toward the truck.

No, he thought, we cannot just leave it at that. Angry now, he turned and followed her to the truck. When he got there, Terra was saying to the boys, "Looks like you are packed and ready to go. You're probably starving by now—I know I am." And then she opened the door of the truck and bent from the waist, sweeping her hand toward Jed as if she were the chauffeur. "After you . . . ," she said.

Jed looked up at John, a puzzled look on his young face, and then with a shrug, he hopped into the truck. Terra slid into the front seat beside him, helped Pete in, situated him between her legs, and then closed the door.

"Son of a . . . ," John muttered aloud as he stood outside the truck, the small hairs along his forearms lifting. His skin was first hot and then cold as if he'd been slapped with a damp cloth. "Shee-it," he whispered aloud, hearing Jed's favorite expression in his own voice. "This is too damn weird." A part of him wanted to jerk the stranger from his truck—and his sons—and find out who she was and what she was doing sleeping in the Badlands. "Later," he said aloud, and then took the keys from his pocket, pushed the brim of his hat away from his damp brow, and walked a circle around the back end to make sure he'd secured his equipment.

17

When he opened his truck door, Terra was singing to the boys.

> "One little, two little, three little Indians,
> Four little, five little, six little Indians,
> Seven little, eight little, nine little Indians
> Ten little Indian boys."

Pete interrupted her. "Dad doesn't like that song. He says it's a bad song because all the Indians disappear in the end."

Terra eyed John cautiously but then laughed and said, "Oh no, Pete, they don't disappear. Not the way I sing it."

"How do you sing it?" Pete twisted his head around to look up into her face.

She leaned down and made her voice a whisper. "When I sing this song, the Indians just keep multiplying—ten to twenty to thirty and on and on. They come from everywhere—millions and millions of them."

"Really?"

She wrapped her arms around him and said, "Really." She began singing her own version of the song again, and Pete laughed and sang along as the Indians became more and more.

John slapped the steering wheel in confusion and started the truck with a roar leaving a trail of dust very much like the tiny cloud that, only that morning at sunrise, had swirled and spun from a needlepoint mark in the Earth's surface.

He drove toward Porcupine Village concentrating on the road and trying not to listen to the boys laughing and playing with this strange woman. Terra. Her voice sounded as clear and melodious as a wooden flute, as if the vocal cords themselves had been cut from a thin branch of dry ash. She appeared to be in her mid-twenties, not exactly a teenager but with a nice, soft look about her, pale blue eyes, skin that looked like if you touched it . . . damn it, he thought. He kept his eyes on the road and beyond to the rolling pine-topped ridges and greening slopes, but his

18

throat tightened. Suddenly, for some inexplicable reason, he wanted nothing more than to be Pete, embodied innocence, parked between the legs of a strange woman. I must be nuts, he thought. He had no idea what to make of this morning's work. And so he drove. He'd get to the bottom of this soon enough.

Terra finished singing the song and then stared out the truck window amazed at the wide, stretching beauty of this place. The road was little more than a shabby, black ribbon of asphalt cutting across the miles of prairie. She dropped her nose to sniff the top of Pete's head, and the small boy smell and soft downy hair made her feel drunk. She felt as if for all eternity she'd been liquid in a bowl and, suddenly, here in this open land, riding in this truck with these men, she had gelled.

Sliding her eyes to the left, she took in the frowning man. John Forrest, his knuckles whitening on the steering wheel, was staring straight ahead as though sheer force of will would make her disappear and return his life to normal.

Normal. She wanted to laugh at that one. Here she was alone in a truck with strangers and no idea of herself . . . except that she had the strangest feeling . . . of rightness. She opened her palm and realized she was holding the small piece of pink quartz in it that she'd found when she first woke up and had stuffed in her pocket. Pink quartz— for the heart, she thought and then wondered how she would know something like that but know nothing else. She shivered although the warmth of Pete's body was like a blanket over her.

I am awake, she thought. Alive. She glanced at John again. He feels it, too, she thought, this vivid sensation of seeds cracking and bursting, of life springing forth. Her senses were humming, wide awake to every nuance of energy in the truck cab—especially between her and John. She recalled the way he'd looked as she hopped into the truck with Jed and Pete. He looked the way she felt inside—unsure of what was happening but compelled to step forward.

Terra really had no idea what she was doing here or even who she was; only that this was where she was supposed to be. A remarkable calm filled this body she had awakened to. "So, where are we?" she asked John at last, breaking the silence.

"On the Pine Ridge Reservation in South Dakota." John turned his head briefly to look at her. "How is it that you don't even know what state you are in?"

She laughed aloud at that and said, "Did you just say the state I am in?" The man didn't seem to appreciate her little play on words. She wanted to say she was in the state of confusion, the state of bliss . . . the state of extra-ordinary, but the truth was she couldn't tell him much of anything. She smiled to herself, turned away, and began singing the song again, pulling Pete close and smiling at Jed as he reluctantly sang along.

John concentrated on the road. He was relieved when the hum of the truck engine and the rough reservation road lulled them all into silence. He needed to think. He didn't know what to think. When they got to the trailer, he'd call the authorities and see if he could find out anything about their visitor. A person doesn't just land in the Badlands from nowhere. Maybe she had been abducted—raped or traumatized in some way—and that was why she couldn't remember anything.

Ten minutes passed and they were nearing the turn off to his friend Danny's trailer when Pete finally broke the stillness by squirming around to look at Terra and announcing, "We don't have a mother."

Jed nearly lifted off the seat as he turned to glare at his brother. "Shut up, Pete. We do, too, have a mother. Everybody has a mother."

Pete's eyes widened and his lower lip started to quiver. "No, we don't."

"Yes. We do. Sheesh, Pete, what are you doing?"

"I was just going to tell Terra—"

Jed punched his brother's arm and growled. "Shut up, Pete. Just shut your big, fat mouth."

John put his hand firmly on Jed's knee, but his own heart had skipped a beat at Pete's words. "Jed, don't talk to your brother that way. He's just a—"

"Yeah, yeah, I know. He's just a kid. But he doesn't have to tell Terra that we don't have a mom."

Terra looked sideways at John. He caught her glance. "She died in a car accident. Three years ago," was all he said. He reached up, grabbed a bag of Planters Peanuts off the dashboard, and made a big display of opening the bag and passing them to Jed, who'd frozen both arms across his chest like a statue. "Have some peanuts, son." When Jed kept his frozen position, John gave him a strong nudge to unlock his rigid arms.

Jed took the peanuts, tipped a handful out, dumped the pile of nuts into his mouth and then, refusing to look at his brother, passed them to Pete.

John glanced at the faces of his two sons, amazed at how quickly their day was unraveling. "Come on, guys. We're almost there." He turned left off the highway into Porcupine, drove past the clinic and small convenience store, and then followed a dirt road to the right leading up toward the white bluffs above the town. Pulling off onto a drive, he stopped the truck before a cattle gate. "Jed, hop out and get the gate. We don't have much time. I need to be at the cemetery in an hour."

Still angry and silent, Jed opened the truck and got out. He yanked the crude wire and pole fence across the road and waved the truck across. After he'd closed the gate again, Jed turned and, without a backward glance, marched up the quarter-mile driveway.

"Jed doesn't like to talk about it," John said, putting the truck back in drive and heading up to the ancient trailer house. He was struck again at how homely and out of place the trailer looked against the stark bluffs.

"This isn't our place. It belongs to Danny Elk Boy, a friend of mine. Danny lives in Rapid City but does a lot of work out here, so he keeps the trailer." He parked, pulled

21

the key from the ignition, and faced Terra. "We live in Rapid, too. I brought the boys with me to film the Badlands and the anniversary events this weekend. Maybe you came for the Wounded Knee anniversary?"

She was about to answer but was interrupted by Pete squirming to get out. Terra opened the door and let the seventy pounds of wiggling boy fall out of the truck.

Pete screeched, "There's Skid! Come on, Terra, we have to go see Skid!"

"Who is Skid?" she asked John.

"Danny's dog," he said. "Go on, Pete but be careful. Skid isn't always the friendliest mutt in the world." Pete ran off leaving the door hanging wide open. "Taking care of Skid goes along with the use of the trailer for a weekend, but the boys don't mind the chore. He's a mangy mixed-breed lab, skinny as a coyote, but the boys are crazy about him."

The warm, late morning air bathed the cab. John stared out the front window feeling awkward now that the boys were gone, and he was alone with Terra. "Jed still has a hard time with his mother's death. Mae Jo left one night to go to the store and never came back. A freak accident. Black ice, the highway patrolman said. She died instantly." He glanced at Terra and saw tears gathering in her eyes.

"That's tough," she said.

"Yeah, it is. Shit happens." A spear of anger and pain jabbed his heart with an intensity that surprised him. And the tears in the stranger's eyes didn't help. "Sorry. I still have a hard time with it myself. It's been three years, but I still don't get it." Great, he thought to himself, now I'm unloading to a complete stranger, some nut my sons found in the desert. "Never mind. It's over. Come on." He opened the truck door and got out abruptly leaving Terra sitting alone in the empty truck.

She got out just in time to meet Pete and Skid running back across the yard toward her. Jed was close behind them. In less than a minute his boys and Terra were bouncing off toward the grassy meadow behind the trailer leaving him still wondering what the heck was going on. "Don't be gone long," he called after them.

Jed and Pete flanked her sides and the three of them, plus the mutt, raced off behind the trailer. Skid had even licked Terra's hand as if she was his beloved mistress. John stared after them shaking his head. That dang dog was slow to like any human being—so why do I feel like the stranger here?

He walked across the yard. The old trailer had a new redwood deck attached to it, and the fine wood only made the trailer look more demolished. He tromped up the steps, unlocked the door with a key on his ring, and went in. He had just enough time to throw a hasty lunch together and get the boys fed before he had to be at the site. They'd eat—and then he'd make a few phone calls.

He crossed the living room to the kitchen and filled the sink with soapy water, submerging his hands in the warmth. He washed the breakfast bowls and cups and, with that small chore done, heated what was left of the morning coffee and stood at the window over the sink. It was only the end of February, but the day was already warm. The air in the trailer was stuffy and dead, so he opened the jalousie window over the sink and sipped his coffee. A breeze eased in carrying with it the odd scent of moss and old forest. Inside, John felt restless, itchy, off center but couldn't name the source.

She'd given him nothing, no information, not a single clue as to who she was or why she was here. For all he knew she could have wandered in from anywhere, a confused schizophrenic maybe or a rich college girl off on a little reservation adventure for spring break. Unbelievable, the way she'd hopped into the truck and taken over his boys. Still, he caught himself scanning the backyard for another sight of her like a teenage boy in heat. "Man, I need to get a life," he said to the empty trailer.

Jed felt blasted—as if somebody had just run over him and laid him flat. He couldn't figure out what was

23

going on and why it was making him so mad. He watched Pete and Skid racing around the yard with Terra, and he felt like throwing rocks at them.

They did too have a mother. Everybody had a mother. He didn't need anybody saying they didn't—not even Pete.

He went to the open frame of the sweat lodge and sat down. Uncle Danny had taken him into the *Inipi* ceremony once after his mom died—to call back his spirit Danny had said. Jed remembered the total darkness in the sweat lodge, the circle of half-naked men, the sad singing, the sage and cedar smoking up the stuffy place. His eyes stung now but there was no smoke—only memories.

Jed watched as Pete threw a stick and Skid chased after it. Terra left them playing and came over to where Jed was sitting and asked, "Mind if I join you?"

"No, I don't mind." But he did mind. He was still angry and felt like somehow it was this strange lady who was causing it all.

She took a place on the ground beside him. They were sitting on old, dead carpet pieces. An ant was making its way across the dirty rug. He stared at it.

"I'm sorry about your mother, Jed. That must have been very hard."

He couldn't say a word.

"Do you want to talk about it?"

"No. What's to say? She's dead. Dead is dead."

Terra didn't touch him, didn't do anything but lean a little closer and say, "But dead is not gone."

"What's that supposed to mean? You see her walking around here? Gone is gone."

"Close your eyes, Jed."

"What the heck for?"

"Humor me. Just do it. I want to show you something. Close your eyes and think of any memory you have of her. Any one at all."

He didn't want to do what she said, but it was like his mind skipped right past his own anger and there it was—a memory of his mom standing at the kitchen sink,

24

humming a song, turning around to laugh at something he'd just said. He could see her—even with his eyes open.

Terra said, "See, there she is."

And then the strangest thing happened. A slight breeze rose up in front of him and lifted the hair off his shoulder, and he remembered his mom pulling his hair back from his face. She'd done that a lot. "I want to see that handsome face," she'd say. Tears blurred his vision and he opened his eyes, wanting only to jump up and run away.

Terra whispered in his ear, "Close your eyes again, Jed. See her. Let her see you."

His eyes closed almost automatically. He heard Pete come over and whisper something to Terra, but she shushed him and told him to sit down beside her.

Jed thought it was weird, the way they just sat there, all three of them, not saying a word, not doing anything; and yet he couldn't get the image out of his mind of his mom reaching out to pull back his hair. He opened his eyes but the image was still there. And almost like an echo of his thoughts, Terra raised an arm and moved her hand as if she were pulling back somebody's hair.

Pete said softly, "What are you doing, Terra?"

"Making the wind dance."

"Really? What for?"

She laughed softly and said, "Because it wants to dance. The wind always wants to dance. It brings the spirits with it."

Jed heard them whispering, but suddenly the wind took all of his attention. He felt it dancing, moving around him. He felt it on his head and the place where his hand sat on his knee. Finally, he looked at Terra and said, "You're weird."

She laughed again. "I know. I am weird. But I'm a lot of fun, too." She took Pete's hand and held it, and then took Jed's and said, "Jed, maybe it isn't your mother's death that has you worried—maybe it's your father's."

Pete looked startled by her words and said, "Our father is not dead. He's alive."

But somehow her words made sense to Jed. "He works all the time, Terra. Even when he's with us, he doesn't seem really with us."

She nodded. "That's what I mean. He's not free to follow her—and he's not free to stay. It's a problem."

Pete nodded. "Is that why you came?"

Terra shrugged her shoulders. "I wish I knew, Pete. I'm in a cloud, unsure of what is happening. Will you help me figure it out?"

Jed looked at her. "You really don't remember anything?"

"I really don't. But I remember songs, how to talk and walk. I just don't know who I am, or what I'm supposed to do here. It feels like we are all supposed to do something. So, will you help me figure it out?" She addressed her question to both of them.

Oddly, Jed knew what she was talking about. He had this strange feeling that he knew more than he actually knew. Crazy. "Okay. We'll help," he said.

"I want to help, too." Pete said. "We could even ask Dad to help us figure it out."

Terra smiled. "Somehow, I think your father doesn't quite know what to make of me. I'm sure if I just have a couple of days to figure things out, it will get clearer."

Jed felt like they were talking in riddles and yet it made sense somehow. He couldn't remember feeling this good—not for a long time, and he couldn't remember feeling this bad—not for a long time. He caught Terra looking at him and she winked.

John picked up the backpacks—they were still in a jumbled pile from their chaotic arrival the night before—and carried them to the back bedroom. They'd been here one night and already the place looked lived in. His boys could carve a space for themselves within five minutes. Drawn once again to the window, he kneeled down on the bed and gazed out across the backyard. Behind the trailer, the land looked like two worlds had collided. On the left was a ramshackle shed held up by a rusted old car body;

on the right sat the sturdy willow frame of the sweat lodge. The area around the shed was cluttered with junk—but around the ceremonial lodge the space was immaculate.

He looked again and saw Terra sitting cross-legged on the floor of the uncovered sweat lodge. She was staring out across the bluffs and on either side of her, sitting perfectly still and silent, were Jed and Pete. There were no rocks, no heat, not even a canvas cover over the lodge. The sight of his ever-busy boys sitting so still only compounded his uneasiness. He felt as though he was spying on them, and the longer he watched, the stronger the restless itch grew. He yanked the curtain closed and went back into the living room, wishing Danny were there to explain away this strange morning's events.

Danny Elk Boy was a traditional Lakota medicine man who frequently ran sweats and ceremonies for the Lakota people. This land had belonged to his family since the Allotment Act had drawn invisible lines across the plains breaking it into parcels and doling it out to the families. John envied Danny. His friend was a Sundancer, a drummer, and a traditional singer. He also taught physics and biology at the local Oglala Lakota College, had a degree from Harvard and had traveled half the world only to come back and submerge his life back into Indian country. John, on the other hand, was nothing, a *wasicu*, a white man—a lost man. His own father had owned a small newspaper in eastern Minnesota. His mother had been an anthropologist who was passionate about the relationship between people and the land they lived on. "The land flows in our blood, son," she'd once told him. He never forgot.

His parents had met while his father was doing a feature about an ancient, serpent-shaped rock formation on a hilltop above the Missouri River. Within a month they had married and set off on happily-ever-after—except his mother had died when he was ten. His father remarried and life had gone on.

His mother had had good friends on the reservation, and they'd spent several weeks here every summer before she died. Something about this land always seemed to crack him wide open. This was where he'd learned to ride a horse, toss hay, wear jeans, and stare at the moon. And this was where he'd met Mae Jo while doing a video on the reservation. He'd married her six months later forever fusing his white trunk with her Lakota roots.

Mae Jo had been almost full-blood Oglala Lakota, a descendant of those who survived the Wounded Knee Massacre. That made his sons "survivors" as well, hooked into that painful event for all time, it seemed.

He went back to the kitchen window and looked out at the sweat lodge. When he'd first married Mae Jo, he'd tried to adopt her lifestyle as his own. But the one time he'd done a sweat with Danny, he nearly didn't make the four rounds. It was pitch black inside with boiling hot steam rising from the rocks. The mumbled prayers, the pipe moving blindly from hand to hand confused and disturbed him. And although the heat was intense, he'd suddenly gone ice cold. He'd felt as though he was suffocating—or freezing to death—and all he'd wanted was out of that canvas grave, out of Lakota country, out of . . . what? Even back then he didn't know jack about what he wanted.

No, that wasn't exactly the truth. He'd gone into that sweat lodge because he wanted to see something—a bit of magic, a spirit or two. Maybe it was his own disappointment that had nearly suffocated him.

Not much had changed since. Except Mae Jo was dead and . . .

He'd never gone back into the sweat lodge. He attended reservation events and kept the boys in touch with their relatives and Danny, but he no longer believed in magic and preferred the ice to the heat. Now, he did the job he was hired to do, paid the bills, and moved through each day like a stone man.

By the time the boys came in for lunch dragging the woman and Skid along with them, John was more determined than ever to find out who she was and what she was doing here. Unfortunately, he had only minutes to get the boys fed and out the door or he'd miss the opening events at Wounded Knee.

Lunch was ready to put on the table, and Pete sat down, his hands ready to snatch at whatever food was set before him. Terra caught him playfully by the collar and held him firm. "Oh no you don't, little guy," she said. "Come on. Show me where the bathroom is. Your hands will do no honor to the food you're about to eat. Time to wash."

Pete made a face, but he slid off his chair, took Terra's hand, and led her down the hall to the bathroom.

John was stunned. Getting Pete to wash was not an easy task. He laughed and asked Jed, "What did she do? Put a spell on him?"

"I don't know, Dad. She's awful weird, in a nice sort of way. She makes it okay to want to do weird things . . . fun things."

"Like what kind of things?" John asked.

"You should have seen her out there." Jed took a deep breath. "She said she could make the wind dance, and she did, Dad. I swear it."

For some reason, he didn't want to hear about this woman making the wind dance. It made him feel unsteady. "Come on, Jed. You can wash at the kitchen sink. We have to get over to the cemetery. The folks in the Four Directions Walk are supposed to show up before noon. I need to have my camera ready to roll." While Jed stood at the sink letting the water splash between his fingers, John stacked egg salad sandwiches on a paper plate and set out corn chips, cold beans, and sodas.

Besides the Badlands documentary, he had also been contracted to film the events surrounding the thirty-year anniversary of the occupation of Wounded Knee Village by the American Indian Movement. He'd been looking forward to it all month. In 1973, the year of the occupation, he'd been younger than Jed, living over the state line in Minnesota. Since then, he'd studied the Red Power Movement, the history of AIM, and the sixties in

29

great detail. There had been something about that era that held such promise . . . such energy for change. He hated that the rabble-rousers and hippies were now old men with pot bellies and thinning hair—and that he'd been too young to have any part in it. "Come and eat, Jed."

"Sure, Dad. Is she coming? To the reunion?"

"You just eat your lunch and let me worry about Terra."

When Terra and Pete came back from the bathroom, they sat down together to eat lunch. Terra bit into a sandwich and looked at him. "So, tell me about your work. Pete tells me you make movies?"

He chuckled. "Yeah, a regular Steven Spielberg. No, actually I'm an independent producer and do mostly contract work, program videos, for a lot of the non-profits around here. You know, folks trying to convince the foundations that their organization is worth the dollars."

"Videos?"

"Mostly. Oh, once in a while I get funding to do a documentary on something that really grabs me, but it's mostly bread and butter work—their bread, my butter, I guess."

They finished eating lunch and all John could think about were the unanswered questions hovering around the trailer. Finally he sent the boys to wash up again and get their day gear together. He turned to Terra and said, "I think you should stay here until I get back and then we'll contact the authorities. I'll take you to Rapid City later. They can help you figure out what happened." He looked up from the table and saw her ashen face. "What?"

"Please don't take me to the authorities. I'm sure if I just have a day or two to figure this, out my memory will come back. I could come along—help you with the boys. Please, John?"

"Darn it, Terra. I don't even know who you are. You could be a criminal—a crazy person. Why would I let you take care of my boys?"

"Listen, I know this sounds strange—but something is going on. I don't know what or why but I was supposed to be found by Jed and Pete."

"What are you talking about?"

She shrugged her shoulders slightly and smiled up at him. That smile sent a white heat flashing through him and, for a moment, he thought he was back in the *Inipi* again and Danny had just splashed water on hot stone. She was staring at him, her eyes bright and pleading, her hair framing her pretty face, and the deep woods scent emanating from her skin . . . man, he thought, I'm in big trouble.

Chapter 4

According to ancient Lakota history, *Paha Sapa*, the Black Hills, contain the heart of the universe. It is here, buried behind the needled, stone ribs of Mother Earth, that all energy must come in and go out like the human body's endless pumping of blood through the heart. The Black Hills, which rise from the prairie floor like an ancient city, were and still are the center point of life for the Lakota people. The stories hold their history.

It was to Harney Peak, tallest mountain of *He Sapa* that Black Elk soared in the great vision that would rule his life and, in the end, break his heart. It was here in the hills that legend says a great race was run between all the children of *Unci Makah* to see who would rule. A ring of red earth was burned into the ground, and it is still called the racetrack today. And it was at Bear Butte, the sacred mountain, that all the plains Indians gathered together to pray. And the Badlands? Who knows what tales those striped and weathered veins could tell?

Finally, in the southern hills there is Wind Cave. It is said that here the Great Mother, at last weary of the violent ways of her people, took only a few inside of her and then shook off the rest. It was called the second cleansing. Those who later re-emerged from the cave called themselves The Lakota *Oyate*—The People.

On a warm, breezy day dangling at the end of February, Agnes told the story of the second cleansing to all who ate at the Cuny Café. The customers came and went and nobody noticed the repetitive nature of Agnes's stories that day. She told it not to their ears, or even to their minds, but to their spirits. She knew that, like the Buffalo Joe sandwiches which were the special today, so this particular story was on the menu. She reminded them all, young and old, what the Elders had taught.

As above, so below—no event occurs on Earth without a corresponding event in the heavens above. She reminded them that this is no strained and uneasy alliance between the human being and the other forces of nature but a living relationship between heaven and earth. As above, so below. If you scatter the stones, you scatter the stars.

Unci Makah knows this. The stones and the stars know this. Even the trees and the fish and the ants remember. Only the people have forgotten. Or most of the people.

Danny Elk Boy was a tall, husky Lakota man, with a thick dark braid trailing down his back. When he spoke, his voice was surprisingly soft for such an imposing form. Since 1995, he'd taught physics and biology at the college centers around the reservation and in Rapid City. He was also a medicine man under his Uncle Bill. In public he was traditional Lakota wedded to the ways of his people. In private he studied David Bohm, Joseph Pearce, Pierre Tielhard de Chardin—even Edgar Cayce. Had the people known, they wouldn't exactly have him fired, but life could become difficult.

Danny drove up Cuny Table to have a talk with Agnes. For the past week he'd been disturbed by dreams of sun-scorched prairie, forests burning, and terrorist attacks. That morning he'd awakened drenched from head to toe as if he'd crawled out of the sweat lodge. The dreams were so disturbing that he desperately wanted a cup of Agnes's tea—and a story—to help him understand. He'd learned never to discount what he saw beyond the boundary of ordinary perception. It was a lesson he'd learned on his fourteenth birthday thirty years ago—the night that had changed his life.

34

He thought back to that night. His parents had driven from Pine Ridge to Rapid City to see a movie, a common family outing—ninety minutes to town, do a little shopping, grab a quick supper, and settle into the chosen movie by 7:00 p.m. But this particular Friday night turned out to be anything but common.

They'd arrived home in Porcupine just after midnight, and his parents had sent him off to bed along with his two younger brothers. After the entire household was asleep, Danny had bolted straight up in bed and watched a full-length movie in his mind without aid of screen or projector. As scene after scene unfolded, he was both paralyzed and wide-awake. He saw cars pulling into Wounded Knee Village. He saw helicopters overhead, soldiers carrying guns, and trucks rumbling over frozen ground. He saw frightened people huddling and angry people fighting. He saw gunfire and death. And he had seen all of this sitting rigid as a rock, eyes focused on a spear of twisted sage hanging from the window frame in his bedroom.

When the movie ended, the sky was pink with morning light. Exhausted, he'd flopped down into the pillows and disappeared into sleep for eighteen hours. Only later had he heard the details . . . .

The next morning his mother couldn't wake him up. Unable to find any reason for Danny's death-like sleep, his frantic father had called his brother Bill, a medicine man, to come and see to him.

Later, Uncle Bill told Danny that he'd shooed the others out of the room and lit sage, running his hands slowly up and down Danny's body to see what there was to see and whispering, "Danny . . . my boy, where have you gone?" Bill had noted his nephew's shallow breathing and gray pallor, but there was no fever, no shivering, and no hidden wounds from snake or spider. Finally, Bill had begun a low droning song that went on for nearly an hour as he followed his nephew into other places, places few had visited.

At midnight, the boy had finally opened his eyes and sat up.

Danny still remembered that moment of coming back, of opening his eyes and seeing his uncle smiling down at him.

"Welcome back, son. You've been on quite a journey, haven't you?"

The note of laughter hiding in Uncle Bill's voice had reassured him. "What happened, Uncle?"

"Someone came and took you away for a while, probably to show you something important. Tell me about it, Danny boy."

Bill made him describe exactly what he'd seen over and over until his stomach growled with hunger, and he was exhausted once again. Finally, at three-thirty that morning, Bill slipped out to the kitchen and fixed him a ham and pickle sandwich.

"Here, eat up." His uncle had handed him the plate and a glass of milk to wash down the sandwich.

Danny remembered eating that sandwich as if he hadn't eaten in weeks. Never had a ham sandwich tasted so good. And it had felt special to be sitting in the quiet bedroom in the middle of the night whispering to his uncle, sharing secrets, telling him all that he had seen. "What does it mean, Uncle?"

"We don't know yet, son. You passed through something. We don't know what or why. Let's keep this between us and the Creator for a while, okay?" Danny had nodded and finished the milk, feeling sleepy again. Uncle Bill had finally scooted him over, stretched out beside him, and they'd slept the rest of the night side by side.

They told no one of his vision but, after that night, Uncle Bill asked his brother to let Danny come and live with him. His parents, sensing the importance of the request, agreed to let him go.

Three months later a caravan of cars filled with villagers and militant AIM members drove into Wounded Knee Village. Scene by scene the inner movie Danny had

36

experienced that night unfolded in real life. Uncle Bill cautioned him to remain silent about the vision—its contents were strictly between them and the Creator. Only time would tell what it meant.

Now, Danny drove the last few miles to the Cuny Café thinking about those years with Uncle Bill and smiling. He'd been hungry for knowledge, his mind as ravenous as his body had been the night Bill handed him that ham sandwich. He'd stayed with his uncle until he was nearly twenty.

Uncle Bill was an unusual teacher. He'd insisted Danny learn not just the traditional Lakota ways but the new ways as well, and so he learned math, science, neurology, physics, and psychology. Bill had only two rules about Danny's education; he had to study something he didn't already know—and it had to be a strong interest, not something dictated by a weak but well-meaning teacher.

He'd learned like a pony grazing across a field in search of the sweetest grass. He also grazed at the Cuny Café. Whenever he felt overwhelmed with thoughts, he'd walk over to Agnes's place and shovel snow, or rake the yard, or help her pound nails into boards. She was always patching up that beat-up old trailer. She never said much but, somehow, whatever he was struggling to absorb went in better around Agnes. He figured she was like some special tonic that helped him digest things. Of course, it might have been the hard physical work she made him do, which forced him out of his mind and flopped him back into his body. She always made him work.

When it came time for college, it was Danny's own idea to go to Harvard. Bill made him leave the box indicating "race" blank on the application saying that Danny would have to get accepted, or not accepted, based on his own merit and not coddled along because he was a poor Indian. Bill had strong ideas about what the colonial mindset had done to the people, said it made them small and dependent—married to their captors—and Uncle Bill had other ideas for his nephew.

37

Now, at forty-four years of age, Danny still fed his mind on the intersection between physical and metaphysical, between science and spirit; but he hid his scholarly nature with a cowboy attitude, a thick Lakota accent, and a rich sense of humor.

Uncle Bill still lived down the road from the Cuny Café in the same cabin that Danny had grown up in. Bill and Agnes were never far from each other—or from Danny. He'd never figured out if they were lovers or married or just good friends. As the years tumbled by, the two never seemed to age or change. "Where would I be without them?" Danny thought aloud to himself. Being a kid on Pine Ridge had been tough—being a strange and smart kid with visions on Pine Ridge was even tougher.

When he turned right and pulled up in front of the tin can café, he saw Agnes sitting on her porch, a peculiar light surrounding the trailer like a mirage on a hundred degree day. He blinked and then blinked again, but the illusion remained. He parked his truck and got out.

Agnes, pipe clutched in her hand, was in one of her prayer places. She didn't move when he approached. Rather than disturb her, he took a small bench from the porch, planted it beside her and sat. He automatically mirrored her posture, his breath joining hers in a rhythmic cadence. It was a technique he'd discovered for locating a person's soul in relationship to the body. He tended to slide into other people's energy fields unwittingly; it had caused him a great deal of pain until he learned to put it to good use. With practice, he could slide in and out of other people without joining their inner turmoil.

Sliding into Agnes's energy field was oddly different. Her energy was not closed within the body but diffused, spreading out like light through a prism. He saw a spiral of rose light moving like aurora borealis in full daylight. Spinning and dancing in the midst of the light, he saw his two godsons, Jed and Pete. How strange. He concentrated, trying to go more deeply in, liking the sweet feeling the image contained.

"Stop that, Danny, you stupid, foolish boy."

He blinked and found Agnes, now fully out of her trance, glaring at him. "What?" he said.

"I said stop it. If I wanted you in here, I'd bring you in myself. You got no business just busting in without asking."

Danny grinned. "Sorry, Unci." Agnes was not his grand-mother, but sometimes he used the kinship term out of respect.

Agnes leaned forward and rocked herself up out of the chair. "Come on. I'll get you a cup of tea. We need to talk, Danny boy." Both Agnes and Bill had always called him Danny Boy, dropping the powerful "elk" out of his name in a way that kept him small and in his place. He grinned and followed Agnes as she turned and marched into the trailer letting the screen door bang behind her.

Seated across from him now, with the sun slanting across the table and the tea sending up a sweet, green scent from the steaming cup, Agnes fixed him with her eyes. "Time is short, Danny. Pay attention now. I have something to tell you."

An hour later Danny left Agnes and walked out the door and straight past his truck, shaking his head to clear the spots from his eyes. Something strange had happened back there, and he couldn't for the life of him even recall what it was. He remembered Agnes putting the cup down in front of him and telling him she had a story to tell him about the Second Cleansing—a story he'd heard a hundred, maybe two hundred, times.

Agnes's tea must have been a mite strong this morning, he thought. All he remembered was her opening comment about how the people had gotten it wrong about the Second Cleansing. And something about how people had to quit thinking prayer alone could make it happen—a call to action, she had said, and everybody had to get up off their butts and answer the call. Beyond that, Danny had little idea what she had said to him.

He thought through the story now, about how *Unci Makah*, Grandmother Earth, had grown weary with the violence and antics of her human children. The story said that she had taken a few and sheltered them inside of her body and then shaken the rest of them off the Earth. Later the people had re-emerged as the Lakota people from the mouth of Wind Cave in the southern Black Hills and repopulated the earth once again. The story had always reminded him a bit of Noah's Ark, but the Elders said it stretched further back in time than the Bible.

So what did she mean—the people had gotten it wrong? He forced his mind to focus through the fuzz. She'd said humans acted like helpless victims, as if they had had nothing to do with getting tossed off. "As above, so below," Agnes had reminded him. "What happens in the heavens corresponds with what happens below, and what happens below corresponds with what happens above. The time has come again, Danny."

His mind had gone blank then until he came back to himself and Agnes was grinning at him and saying, "Well? What do you think? Will it work?" She must have seen his empty face because she laughed then and said, "Danny boy, have you been listening to anything I told you or have you been just snoozing all this time?"

He'd just shook his head. "I don't know, Agnes. What the heck have we been talking about?"

"Forget it, boy. I'm not telling you again. For someone with a Harvard education you sure can be dense sometimes." She had laughed then, a full belly laugh. He couldn't remember ever hearing Agnes laugh like that. When she caught her breath, she'd poked a finger beneath his nose and said, "Remember. Look to your friend—the stubborn one. What's his name?"

"John. John Forrest."

"Yes, that's right. Johnny Forrest. The one who makes the picture shows. And my girl."

Danny had been stunned to hear John's name pop out of his mouth as if he did know whom she'd been talking about. "What girl, Agnes?"

"Ah, I guess you'll find out soon enough. Go now. There is much to be done."

40

He'd pushed the cup of tea away, wondering again if she had spiked it with something, and said, "I'm going. I'm supposed to be at the cemetery by 11:00."

No, he had no idea what had just transpired with Agnes. Had she gone off her rocker, he wondered and then laughed at the cliché—no, she seemed firmly planted on that old rocking chair. Maybe I need to quit watching the news, he thought, still trying to frame the nightmares. He hadn't even had a chance to mention that. His despair with local and world events was deepening, yet something in him felt urgent, alive, a readiness he'd never felt before. He started the engine and took a last look at Agnes sitting on the porch of the café smoking her pipe still smiling and nodding at him.

Patience, he reminded himself. Sometimes events have to play out before we can see what they mean.

John wiped off the table while Terra washed up the few dishes from their lunch. Her plea for a few days grace time before turning her over to the authorities was hovering in the air like an odor. He hadn't answered her— he didn't know how he should answer her. The boys were still clowning around in the bedroom, and he hollered down the hall, "Hurry it up, guys. And take your jackets. The weather can change fast." He turned to Terra and said, "I don't know what to do with you."

"What do you want to do with me?" she smiled.

"Don't be coy. You might have hypnotized my boys, but I'm not so easy. I don't trust your amnesia story. Tell me how you ended up in the Badlands."

She tugged at the bottom corners of her jacket. She looked like a schoolgirl, her cheeks a pale pink. "I don't have an explanation, John. Not yet. You know how sometimes you wake up and forget your dreams in the first minute? My problem is just the opposite. I feel like I'm dreaming and have forgotten my life."

He watched her search her mind for what didn't seem to be there, and he felt just a pinprick of pity.

41

"There is nothing sinister here, John. How can I make you believe that?"

He was saved from having to answer when Jed and Pete ran back into the room carrying their jackets and wearing small day packs. Pete stood next to Terra and asked, "Are you coming with us?"

She looked at Pete, and then looked up at John, and for the life of him, he couldn't say no to the need he saw written across his youngest son's face. Man, how is it that he had never seen that need before? Pete needed a woman in his life. The boy wanted to play, to be petted and loved . . . to be mothered. He felt as if he'd been standing on the edge of a forest fire for three years and the smoke was clearing for the first time. Pete had grown taller. He'd missed that, too. Where had he been? And Jed—the kid was more man than boy, just a few inches shorter than I am, he realized.

The boys and Terra were still staring at him as if the fate of the world rested on his next words. He said, "Got any plans for the day?"

She said quietly, "Not that I know of."

"Want to join us . . . just for today?"

"Yes, I do."

"Yes!" Pete shouted. "It's going to be so fun, Terra. There will be horses and a pow wow and lots of food. Have you ever ridden a horse? Or maybe you don't remember, but I can show you. I'm a good rider."

John looked at Jed and saw his son smile at Pete and then at Terra. He felt like he was an army of one trying to resist whatever this stranger was bringing into their lives. Two days, he thought. I'll be too busy to mess with figuring out what to do with her anyway. Two days.

Chapter 5

The Wounded Knee Cemetery rests on a gentle slope of land that curves up to the pine-topped ridge that gives the reservation its name. To the south is the site of the massacre. Although the reunion was actually marking the 1973 AIM occupation, nothing ever took place here without bringing to mind the massacre, a frigid moment in history that cost the lives of nearly 300 Lakota men, women, and children at the hands of the Seventh Calvary. Wounded Knee is a password for pain in this part of Indian Country.

Danny Elk Boy stood on the edge of the cemetery eyeing the sunny sky, grateful the day was clear and warm. Five years earlier, a blizzard had made the twenty-fifth anniversary miserably cold—but he wanted so much more from this reunion than a sunny day. For just one moment he wanted the focus to not be on the massacre or the resistance movement or the problems that were still thick as mud on the reservation—but on the strength of the Lakota People.

His mind buzzed and his lips still felt thick and swollen from Agnes's tea. Shaking off the remnants of his odd encounter with Agnes, he turned his attention to the reunion.

The day before he and a couple of guys had set up a tipi to act as a command post. He made several trips back and forth now unloading his truck, spreading pieces of carpet on the dirt floor, and setting up camp chairs and two cots. He lugged a cooler full of ice and soft drinks and set it just inside the flap. His body was going through the motions, but his mind was elsewhere, still pondering the big questions. He shook his head. I'm pretty damned good at asking the big questions—but not so good at finding the little answers. His mind was humming with ideas while he worked.

What good were all his study, ceremonies, prayers—a Harvard education—if he couldn't shift his people away from a painful past and toward the future? And it wasn't just the Lakota people who suffered. Pine Ridge simply magnified the experiences of the larger world—a world so out of touch with what matters that it seemed hell-bent on destroying itself.

Mitakuye Oyasin, we are all related. He believed that ancient Lakota teaching, believed that all beings are hooked into an energetic web, and he'd found nothing in science or quantum physics but evidence which supported that belief. In fact, his inquiry into science had led him straight back to the sweat lodge. In the realm of the mind he could ponder spiritual theory and practice, but in the sweat lodge he could experience it directly.

Still, he'd not managed to make the translation into practical steps, a way to lift his people up out of poverty, early death, and ceaseless, senseless violence toward one another and toward the white race.

Wave, particle, form, formless—somehow the words circled his mind like a snake swallowing its tail. That image, of a snake swallowing its tail, had been found carved in stone, painted in pigment, expressed in earthworks, tattooed on skin, and scratched on papyrus leaves throughout the history of indigenous people. To him, the image spoke of life—that life itself must be swallowed and consumed. We have to eat life, he thought, in order to live life.

And then wash it down with Agnes's tea, he grinned to himself.

Later, when all his preparations were complete, Danny stood beside his truck looking across the open land. It was late morning, and already the site buzzed with activity as people gathered to meet the riders coming in

44

from the Four Directions Walk. Many bystanders wore red jackets, red hats or feathers tucked here and there. They carried red banners.

Red was the color of the red power movement which had grown out of the relocation programs of the nineteen fifties, a period of time when native people left the reservation—courtesy of the U.S. Government—and went to the cities in search of work. This sudden shift of lifestyles had collided with the sixties and erupted into the militant, and sometimes violent, movement. He'd heard an Elder call it "the awakening of the sleeping red giant."

The cemetery road was edged with pickups, campers, and a string of cars. The walkers would be coming in from Manderson, Pine Ridge Village, Denby Road, and the junction of Highway 18 south of Wounded Knee. They would all converge on the cemetery about noon.

When John Forrest and his boys pulled into the parking area, Danny waved them over to the space near the tipi he'd reserved so John would have easy access to his equipment. He went over to greet them. "Hey, guys. You're just in time." His curiosity spiked when a sandy-haired woman climbed out of the truck with Jed and Pete. He offered her a hand and said, "I'm Danny Elk Boy, chief madman around here."

She laughed at the introduction and took his hand. "I'm Terra."

Her voice made him think of a meadowlark sitting on a fence post. She was short, maybe five foot five, a pale curtain of hair falling almost to her shoulders. Not a glamour girl but nice looking. How long had it been since he'd seen his buddy with a woman, he wondered? A frigging eternity.

"Terra showed up unexpectedly," John said. "She offered to watch over the boys while I'm working."

Danny smiled and asked, "Showed up from where?" He turned to Terra and said, "My friend never shows up with a woman in tow."

"Danny . . . not now," John said.

He caught the cautionary tone and backed off. "Well, any extra hands are much appreciated. There's plenty to do. You boys prepared to help out around here?"

"Sure," Jed and Pete replied in unison.

"Good. Get on over there and help the guys clean up the site. There's a strange wind blowing across the land today, and it keeps blowing the tumbleweeds and trash in with it. We want this place looking good. The trash bags are in my tipi. Grab a couple and pick up any trash and put the bags in the back of my truck."

Jed and Pete walked to the tipi and disappeared inside. The woman stood in silence, an odd, distracted look on her face as she scanned the land around the cemetery and the sky above, as if looking for something. At last she turned to John and said, "I'll go with the boys."

Danny was dumbfounded by the look on John's face, as if he couldn't decide whether to trot on after her or run the other way. Agnes's words echoed through his mind—watch out for your friend . . . and my girl. "Who is she?" he asked.

"Good question." John told him about the boys finding her asleep in the Badlands, how she had just walked out of nowhere and into the middle of their lives. John shook his head. "That's it. One minute I'm shooting some footage and the next minute the boys come up the wash towing her along like a stray puppy. I can't tell if she has amnesia, is just plain crazy. or got dumped by a boyfriend and is too embarrassed to say so. She wouldn't answer my questions—or couldn't."

The boys and Terra were already walking the grounds, gathering trash and laughing together under the tepid sun. Danny watched them. "It's strange. When I first spotted you, I thought for a second it was Mae Jo, but she doesn't look anything like Mae Jo—she's about the whitest woman I've ever seen." He laughed aloud, but then grew quiet again and said, "I guess it was seeing you all as a foursome again."

"Do me a favor, Danny. Don't start building a fairy tale out of this. That's all I need. I brought her because there wasn't time to do anything else. As soon as we get finished here, I plan to call the authorities."

"Easy, my friend. I'm just making an observation, that's all. You're such a monk, John. You haven't looked at a woman since Mae Jo died. It's not natural and it doesn't make any damn . . . . "

"Leave it alone, Danny." John said. "I mean it."

"Hey, all I said was that you look good with a woman nearby. Hell, you know I'm no good at watching from the sidelines."

"Knock it off."

"All right. I'm off," he said, but John's reaction only sharpened his interest in the strange woman.

"Sorry, man," John apologized. "It's been a strange morning. For some reason I've thought more about Mae Jo in the last two hours than I have in the last month. I don't know what's going on. I'm just making the moves, doing the next thing, all right? Can we just leave it at that?"

Danny resisted the urge to knock him closer to the edge, but gave it up. He again thought of Agnes's words, "Look to your friend." He intended to do just that. "Come on, let's go to the tipi and get an iced tea. I'll fill you in on who's coming to the reunion so you can get started with the interviews."

"Sure. Let me get my pad. I'll be right there."

John went back to his truck wanting to kick dirt and cuss. He hated it when Danny probed into his personal doings. And he hated it when Danny didn't probe. What a coil—and it wasn't even noon yet. He surveyed the cemetery site, deciding where to set up his tripod.

There wasn't much left of the landmarks of the original Wounded Knee Village or its famous occupation. The old church up by the graveyard had been a gutted concrete hole in the ground until recently. Somebody had filled in the hole since the last time he was here. The trading post was gone; only a concrete slab littered with trash and a dusty turn-off remained. Weeds had split the concrete giving it a softened appearance. Amazing the way grass can split concrete, he thought. Life is tough. He got his notebook from the truck and went into Danny's tipi.

The upward sweep of canvas and thinning poles of the tipi structure always gave John vertigo when he first walked in. He took a campstool and sat down to ground himself. Danny had already poured two plastic glasses of iced tea from a cooler jug, and he took a glass and drank.

Danny sat down on one of the cots. "I'm glad the weather is cooperating." He rustled around in a backpack and dug out some papers. "Here's the list of names. Ask around and see who else is here. You'll want to concentrate first on the walkers coming in. It'll be a long day, but I'm sure you can catch them all."

During the AIM occupation, John had been an elementary kid about to make the big leap into junior high. Although only fourteen, Danny had been in the thick of it. Like everything else in his life, John felt out of step with the greater movements of the world, moving half-time to everyone else's double-time.

They scanned the agenda. There was to be an Honoring Ceremony for those who died at Wounded Knee and for their living descendants. John said, "I'd like the boys to be at the ceremony if that's all right, Danny. Even though Mae Jo is gone, they're still her sons. They need to remember where they come from."

"Of course." Danny got up from his stool and reached high as if to stretch the kinks out of his arms. "When does it end, John? These events are always such a mixed bag. Yes, we need to remember—but at what cost?"

The note of despair in Danny's voice surprised him. He took a drink of the cold tea and nodded. "It's a tough call, isn't it? The boys and I are struggling with our own brand of remembering."

"What do you mean?" Danny asked.

"Jed. He pitched a fit earlier when Pete told Terra they don't have a mom. I think he still believes she's coming back, Danny. I don't know what the hell to say to him. I want him to remember Mae Jo—but not hold on to some crazy illusion that one day she'll drive back up to the house, and we'll all live happily ever after."

"That's just it. Time moves forward. Here on the reservation—and for you, too. Maybe if you'd get on with it, Jed would too."

"Damn it, I have gotten on with it. It's been two years since her memorial, Danny. We laid her to rest right here. She's there in the ground with the rest of them." He felt the turn of the blade in his belly. "And I'm still walking around on top."

"That's what I mean, buddy. You're not getting on with it. You don't let anybody, male or female, get within a hundred yards of you or those boys. You plant your nose behind that camera and watch life through a damn pinhole. Carol thinks . . . ."

"We're not talking about this now, man." He felt like punching Danny.

"Okay, okay, so I'm not your mother, you prickly son of a bitch." Danny shook his head and laughed. "I leave it to you. Come on, we've got work to do."

John left the tipi. He was still fuming but turned his attention toward the task at hand. Unpacking his camera and tripod again reminded him of that morning. Had it really been only a few hours since Jed and Pete had walked up the wash with a stranger? It felt like weeks ago. And where was Terra? Had she remembered anything yet?

Danny had a point. He was no monk. And his boys were not little monks. Maybe he was the one who believed Mae Jo was going to drive back up and bring a little happily-ever-after with her. The thought put a bad taste in his mouth.

John expected a couple hundred people would show up for the day's events. KILI FM Radio on Porcupine Butte had been putting out PSAs and playing the old movement songs by John Trudell, Floyd Westerman, and Buddy Red Bow for the past two weeks—stirring the slumbering red giant once again. A lot of the original AIM folks were now old men with less hair, bigger bellies, and a still-strong burning desire to right the wrongs doled out to

Indian people. A little red power would be good, John thought. A little any power would be good.

Danny watched as the trickle of cars and trucks winding their way up both roads to the cemetery became a steady stream. Uncle Bill was manning the turn-off and directing the traffic into the parking areas. He left the tipi and wandered down the road to check with him. His uncle was pushing eighty—what changes the old guy must have seen. Sometimes Danny wished that for just one moment he could see the world from his uncle's eyes, although his uncle's sight was more often turned inward now the way it does sometimes with age. Today, however, Uncle Bill's eyes seemed clear and bright. It appeared the world was once again interesting to the old man. He wore a black jacket with a bright, medicine wheel embroidered on the back and, on his head, a red baseball cap.

"Look at the cars, Uncle Bill. I didn't realize there'd be so many. We only had about seventy-five people at the 25th Anniversary."

"I'm not sure what's going on, Danny boy," said Bill, "but I got the feeling these folks are coming for some other reason."

"Like what? Food?" He laughed aloud. There was to be a feed following the ceremony over at Manderson School, and any feast in Indian country brought out the people. Many of the older folks even brought little *wotecya* bags or containers to carry some food home with them. Feeding the people was one tradition that hadn't died or changed in a thousand years or more.

"No, Danny," Bill said. "They're coming for more than food. I'm just not sure what. I got this feeling in my gut, like this is the kick-off for something else, something more than the reunion."

"I know what you mean, Uncle. I have the same feeling. What it is?"

Bill said, "Not to worry, son. We're ready for them. The feast will be just like those Christian fishes and loaves—the food will go around. Nobody will be hungry on this day."

Danny nodded and said, "Well, if you get tired let me know, and I'll send somebody to replace you."

"No, no, I'll be fine." Bill grinned, deepening the ridges and lines of his face.

He knew his uncle liked controlling the flow of people onto the land; that had always been his place, guiding and instructing the people, pointing a direction when no direction showed itself. Uncle Bill had been the one to show him the way. "Where's Agnes?" he asked.

"Not here. She had some other things to take care of. She may come later."

Danny thought again of the odd meeting with Agnes, the buzz she'd left in his mind. They were quite a pair, these two Elders. Without them, he doubted he'd even be alive. Gratitude welled up in his chest, and he said, "Thank you, Grandfather." It was only out of the deepest respect that he addressed his uncle in this special way.

Bill nodded and waved him on.

Jed felt strange. He'd worked up a sweat clearing trash and running from one end of the encampment to the other, but it was not sweat but the feeling of a fever inside that had him wondering. He had this frantic need to keep track of both Terra and his dad, as if an alien ship really would land and snatch them both away. His dad was setting up near the cemetery, and he ran over to talk to him. "Do you need any help, Dad?" he asked.

John was concentrated on setting up his camera and seemed hardly to hear him. "No, son. I'm almost ready. Danny says the walkers should be showing up anytime now."

Jed felt like clobbering his dad. That had not happened in a long time. He wanted to kick his shins and scream like Pete. What was wrong with him? Maybe it was what Terra had said, about being afraid his dad was dead too. What a weird thing that had been. His dad was clearly not dead, not a ghost but flesh and blood. He tried again to get his attention. "Dad?"

"Not now, son. I'm busy. Go talk to Danny. I asked him if you and Pete could be a part of the Wiping of the Tears Ceremony."

He never even looked away from the stupid camera, Jed fumed. Maybe I'm the ghost, he thought. Maybe I am the invisible one. He walked away from his dad and saw Terra and Pete sitting near Danny's tipi having a soda. It was like Pete had adopted her and that idea just made the fever hotter. He didn't remember ever feeling quite so alone. He thought, if I just walked off across the prairie and disappeared, it's not like anybody would even notice I was gone.

The thought was tempting. The thought was more than tempting. Jed walked down the road to where the cars were turning off thinking about just continuing to walk, to cross the road, go off into the prairie and never come back. When he got to the end of the road, he saw Danny's old uncle standing there in his shiny black jacket. He knew Bill Elk Boy from the times Danny had taken them to the Cuny Café for lunch.

He intended to walk past without saying anything, but Bill said something that stopped his feet.

"It won't work, Jed," Bill said, his eyes glittering beneath the red cap.

"What won't work?"

"Running away. It never works."

Jed was so shocked to hear Bill voice his inner thoughts that his tongue suddenly felt like a lizard in his mouth. "How did you know . . . ?"

Bill laughed. "Tried it once myself—when I was about your age, too, come to think of it."

He couldn't believe it. The old man is reading my mind, he thought. "You did?"

"Come here. Let me look at you."

He went closer, and, when he looked up, Bill's old eyes were full of tears. It shook him. "What?" Jed asked.

Bill looked at him again and said, "Yep. I see it all over you——your spirit is trying to fly off like an old crow. Just like I thought. Come closer."

He stepped right in front of Bill and the old man laid a hand on top of his head and held it there for a moment. It was the strangest thing. First the top of his head was burning, like it was on fire; and then it got cooler and cooler and cooler. He couldn't seem to say or do anything, couldn't even move. Finally, old Bill said, "Now, get back up there and do whatever you need to do. It's important."

Jed shivered. Whatever old Bill had done, he'd sucked off that alone feeling and left him empty as a tin can. He felt like crying. Bill seemed to see that, too, because he reached out, grabbed him by the shoulders and pulled him close in an awkward hug. Bill held onto him for several long moments and then whispered over his head, "You got to stay, boy. You just got to."

Jed finally pulled away from the old man and looked up at him. "I'll stay, Uncle Bill. I will."

Bill nodded. "Good. Now go. I got these cars here to tend to." He laughed and used the silly orange cone flashlight to wave him off back up the hill toward the cemetery. "No wait. You take this thing for a minute. I got to take a leak."

Jed took the cone and watched as Bill wandered off into some low bushes. A car drove up, and he pointed up the road like he'd seen the old man do. The car passed him, and somebody waved out the window at him. He waved back. Another car came and then another, and he had the feeling he was guiding the whole world onto that land. It was a weird feeling, like the orange cone had powers, and he could change things if he aimed it right. The longer he stood there, the more connected—and the less alone—he felt. When Bill came back, Jed was almost reluctant to hand over the orange thing.

"Thanks, nephew," Bill said with a grin. "I get the sense that you're pretty good at telling everybody where to go. You better get back up there now. The ceremony is about to begin."

When Jed was halfway back to the cemetery, he turned and looked back at Uncle Bill. How did he know all that? But the fever was gone, and the urge to run, and the anger. "Shee-it," he whispered. The whole world had gone crazy nuts.

Danny moved through the Honoring and the Wiping of the Tears Ceremony like a puppet, unsure of who held the strings. His throat was thick. So many tears—when would the tears dry up? It was what he wanted for the Lakota people more than anything; more than food or acclaim or great wealth, he wanted them to be at peace in their own hearts. He wanted it for all people. When he prayed over each of the survivors, he asked only for that.

When Jed and Pete, so solemn and wide-eyed, came before him, he ritually wiped their tears and prayed for them, too, that they would one day have a woman again to love them. He prayed for Mae Jo, that she watch over them from the other realms.

Following the ceremony, he introduced the speakers, a wry collection of AIM activists, once lean, long-haired Indians with grim faces and red arm bands who had aged and matured in the intervening years. Now they cracked jokes into the microphone about the Federal Marshals and the FBI, and told sobering stories about the nights of firefight, about cold frosty days, and not enough food. In spite of the jokes, Danny heard in their trembling voices the impact of this event on their lives. He knew—because he had been one of their youngest members.

What a powerful time, he thought. Justice had been the word of the day. He looked at the faces gathered there and knew that the need for justice had been so strong that, if tested, every one of them would have given their lives. He felt sure these AIM members had never again felt more vividly alive than during those seventy-three long days and nights.

54

There was also the recounting of old stories of the Massacre. In Lakota country, protocol dictated that each speaker be allowed to speak as long as she or he desires. It could be a challenge—some of these guys liked the sound of their own voices a bit too much; but today Danny was stunned by how short the talks were.

His wife, Carol, slid up beside him as he was listening. They had been married a long time. Once, during a dark time after she miscarried a second child, he thought he'd lost her for good. It had taken nearly four years to bring her out of the dark cave of alcoholism. Since then, he'd learned to never, ever take her for granted again. Every time he saw her, it was as if it was the first time.

"Hi, stranger," she whispered and took his hand.

There had been so much work to do to prepare for the events that he'd hardly seen her the past three days. Suddenly he was struck by the sheer presence of this woman who had tied her life to his. He leaned over and kissed her cheek. "You look beautiful," he whispered.

"I missed you, too. It's going well?"

"Yes, better than I expected." He slid an arm around her waist and noticed, for the thousandth time, that she was nearly as tall as he. Carol was slim and strong with long, dark hair that hung down her back like a black river. She was like the sacred tree in the center of his life. He needed her. She needed him.

"Who is the woman following Jed and Pete around?" she asked. "She hasn't left them for a moment since the ceremony ended."

He laughed. "Now, that's a story. Her name is Terra. The boys found her out in the Badlands this morning. She was sleeping under an overhang."

"Excuse me? Did you say they found her?"

"Yeah, found her. No gear, no car . . . nothing. It's got John a bit befuddled, that's for sure."

Carol laughed softly. "I can imagine."

Together they watched Terra sitting cross-legged on the ground in front of the lawn chairs with Pete tucked up close on one side and Jed not far away on her other side. She was stroking Pete's head.

"She looks so at home with those boys," Carol said. "What is John going to do about her? Did he say?"

"He plans to call the authorities as soon as he gets time." Danny laughed. "He says he brought her along to watch the boys while he worked. I say something is up, but I'll be darned if I know what it is. Something odd is going on here. I'll tell you more about it later." He was thinking about the destructive dreams, Agnes's tea, and the lost hour he had spent with her.

Carol pulled his thoughts back when she said, "Well, wherever she came from, it's wonderful to see somebody besides me mothering those little guys. I worry about them."

"I know you do. Fortunately, your heart has plenty of room for a couple of stray boys . . . and for me, too, thank the Creator." He leaned over and kissed the top of her head, patting her bottom lightly and lowering his voice. "You can mother me anytime you want." The sudden surge of desire surprised him. He bent closer and kissed her again, loving the scent of sage smoke still lingering in her hair.

Carol chuckled. "Watch your hands there, big guy. You are a wild man today—it must be the testosterone oozing out of all those old warriors."

"No baby. It's you. Only you."

Chapter 6

Danny watched the cemetery empty out as the people piled into cars and trucks and drove over to the Manderson School for more celebrating and feasting. Carol had left in her own car, and Danny waited until all the vehicles were gone so he could pick up Uncle Bill and take him to the feast. The long, trailing line of vehicles echoed the day the occupation began with a caravan of cars traveling from Calico to Wounded Knee Village.

By the time they reached the school, the feast was underway. Just as his uncle had predicted, the numbers had doubled and even tripled, but the food didn't run out. Some brought coolers of soda and salads, cakes and chips. Boxes of fry bread were passed around, and the big aluminum garbage cans of buffalo stew were dipped in and out of hundreds of times until all were fed. Young people circled the gymnasium bringing food to the Elders, and then later walked the room with large garbage bags to collect the trash when people were finished. He lost count of how many people there were.

Following the feed, a forum of speakers gathered to discuss the many issues still facing the Lakota people. The tribal president was running the forum so Danny was free to roam. By mid-afternoon, the crowd had thinned. Only the more politically minded stayed behind although he knew most would be back for the evening pow wow.

John stood in a corner, his camera aimed at the crowd, scanning left and right to record the discussion. He wasn't sure if John had eaten, so he filled a plate and crossed the gym to take him some food. "Did you eat?"

"Not yet. Thanks." John took the plate and tucked into it as if he was starving.

"Where is your hitchhiker? I still can't believe you found her in the Badlands. So strange."

"I know. Strange is hardly the word. She took the boys outside for awhile because they were getting restless and needed a break. Did you get a chance to talk to her?"

"No, I was too busy. Carol likes the look of it, though."

"The look of what?"

"Two boys in the care of a young woman." Danny saw the flash of pain cross his friend's face. "I know. Don't go there, right?"

"Right." John looked up from eating and challenged him with a stare.

He was about to pursue the conversation when he saw Bill enter the gymnasium with Agnes beside him. She seldom left Cuny Table these days. "I'll be damned . . . there's Agnes. I have a little bone to pick with her," he said, remembering the buzz he'd gotten from her tea and the strange comments she'd made that had been filtering in and out of his mind all day. "I'll be back later, buddy," he said. "I'll make it a point to talk to Terra and see what I can learn." He walked off thinking more about what he needed to learn from Agnes than from Terra.

Terra walked down the sidewalk in front of the yellow-painted school with Jed and Pete on either side of her. Some distance behind the school a long white bluff rose dramatically above the land. She resisted the urge to race across that open space to climb the hill. Somehow she needed to get above things, to see what she could see; but it didn't have much to do with the physical land. The boys ran ahead and when they came to the playground, they ignored the fancy equipment and raced, instead, for the gully beyond the school fence line. Her mind was overfull with all she'd seen and heard in the past few hours, and she didn't know how to begin to sort it out. She felt led to this place, to those boys—but for what purpose?

There must be a purpose. It was inconceivable that she would wake up in the dust and dirt with no idea of who she was or how she'd come to be there. There had to be some purpose. She felt it in her bones. She imagined a creative presence off somewhere delighting in the willy-nilly uncurling of events, God at play—or God playing a joke on her?

A part of her wanted to just sit down on a rock and refuse to move until she could remember who she was. She felt like she wore this body for the first time, as if some other part of her was living off in another place and time. She squeezed her eyes closed as if that would somehow force memory to return. The late afternoon breeze touched her cheeks and lifted the hair away from her ears. It was like a kiss—or like the wind itself had whispered the truth into her ear. When she opened her eyes again the confusion had evaporated into surety. She may have no memories—but she felt the absolute rightness of things.

She shook her head to clear it and then turned her attention back to Jed and Pete. They were weaving through the bushes at the bottom of the gully, and she hurried to catch up with them.

Jed walked over and asked, "Why didn't you want to hear the speakers, Terra?"

"It wasn't that. I just thought we could do more good out here. There is so much anger and pain. All of that emotion needs a good drain. Nature is as good as it gets for draining off bad feelings."

Jed said, "Dad tells us all the time that we must never forget what happened here. We must never forget our ancestors."

She smiled, hearing John's voice in the young man's words. "That's just the point, Jed. Sometimes staying angry or sad is forgetting the ancestors and what they suffered. It's complicated; but to truly honor them, we have to let them have the dignity of their own suffering. We're not allowed to carry it."

"Are you saying we should just forget about what happened to them? I don't get it."

"I know. It's difficult to understand." She resisted the urge to tousle his hair. He looked so serious, so much the young man and not just a boy. "Think of your mom, Jed."

Pete seemed to hone in on the word "mom" and walked over. Now they were both staring at her. For someone who didn't know who she was, she sure knew how to stick her foot in it. She fingered the buds on the bushes, buying time and trying to get the words right in her mind, feeling sandwiched by the intense need these two boys had to talk about their mother.

"What about our mom, Terra?" Jed prodded her.

"Well," she chose her words. "Think about how hard it must have been for your mom to leave you guys behind. Now she can only watch you from some other realm. Just think—when she peeks around the curtain of the other realm into this one, how would it make her feel to see you both suffering and sad? Would she be happy about that?"

Pete answered simply, "No."

Jed shook his head and said, "No, I guess not."

She went on. "That's right. It would break her heart to see you both hurting. She wants to look from the other realm and see you laughing, playing, and becoming strong young men. Isn't that right?"

Jed was silent for a long moment. She fought the urge to reach out to him but knew he needed to just consider this without her interference. Finally, he said, "You're right, Ter."

Pete nodded. She smiled, thinking how much easier it is for the younger ones to grasp complex concepts. "It's like a river flowing down a mountain—it can only flow down. Life is like that river. When somebody dies, life has to continue flowing. The living can't stop because of what happened."

She said nothing for a moment but began walking. Jed and Pete followed, and she took one of Pete's hands. She stopped, listened once again for the wind to whisper its secrets to her—she could swear the wind really was listening and communicating with her, mentoring her through this ripe moment. More confident now, she laughed softly and then walked on. "No, I'm sure of this. The ancestors want us to be happy. It's the only thing that would make what they suffered worthwhile, don't you see? They want to see us dancing and laughing, to see life going on in a good way."

A sudden surge of energy raced through her body. She felt as though the small path they walked was lined with ancestors, the boys' mother included and she said, "Come on. Let's run." She ran ahead and turned to the boys. "Come on. Run like it is a race to the far side of the gully. Run until you can hear them all cheering and clapping."

Jed and Pete caught the surging energy and ran, overtaking her in a few bursting paces."

"Yes," she called to them. "Run for it. Run for all of it."

When they reached the upper edge of the gully, the boys tumbled into a heap, giggling and rolling into each other. When she reached them she rolled to the earth with them, gathered them close, and hugged them. "Oh, you've made your mother so happy. Can you hear her laughing with us?"

Both boys looked at her, their eyes suddenly tearful, a potent mix of both grief and joy. She sat up straight, crossed her legs, and shifted to face Jed. "Look over at those high bluffs, Jed, and then say it out loud—Mom, I miss you."

Jed looked as though he'd swallowed a stone, but he straightened his body and said in a voice rough with emotion. "Mom, I really, really, miss you. I'll be happy—so you can be happy."

Terra gave him a firm nod of approval and then turned to Pete. "You, too, Pete. Tell her that you miss her."

Pete, still close to tears, swallowed hard and said quietly, "But I don't remember her too well, Terra."

She felt as if she'd caught the small boy's broken heart in her two hands. She wrapped an arm around his shoulders and said, "Oh, Pete, that doesn't matter. Not one bit. Every single cell of your body remembers her. Mothers can never, ever be forgotten. Just try it, you'll see."

Pete looked out across the wide sky, his chin tilted upward and he said, "Mommy." His voice caught on the word, but he straightened his body, swiping at the tears leaking down his cheeks.

She braced his shoulder with her hand and waited for him to go on.

"Mommy, I miss you. And I love you. And I will laugh and run and play—for you."

Terra leaned over and kissed his cheek. They sat together in the total silence, and a soft wind suddenly swirled up and seemed to wrap around them like a soft shawl. She nodded, smiled, and then stood up. "See, we remember only the love and we let the rest go. Oh, what brave, wonderful men you are to give her that." She sat a moment, savoring the fresh, friendly wind and wordlessly whispering her own prayer to remember who her mother was. Finally she stood up, brushed off her backside, and said, "Come on, I'll race you back to the school."

The boys raced ahead of her and she followed, letting them put a few yards between them. She looked again up at the bluff, the scrub pine topping it like whiskers, the sinking sun drawing gray shadows across the land. The time of sunset was drawing nearer. She thought of the ancestors and smiled, feeling as though she had just joined in the willy-nilly play of events.

Danny stood outside the school. He saw Jed and Pete and their new friend racing across the gully, outlined in the waning light. He felt huge, as if his chest was expanding to meet the melon-colored sky. He couldn't get the strange woman out of his mind. Who was she? Something told him she was more than a drop in—she was here for a reason. But what reason? He thought again of his earnest prayer to the spirits for this river of pain and suffering to reverse its course. Maybe they were listening . . . .

Vehicles were again pulling into the school parking lot. He watched the people tumble out of cars and trucks, laughing and excited. They looked good. Young and old were dressed in their finest regalia for the pow wow. The pretty girls tinkled in their jingle dresses, each step a musical one. The young men wore feather bustles, headpieces, or the swaying yarn of the grass dance regalia. Everywhere there was movement. The sheer numbers arriving signaled again that some tugging energy was at work in the world.

He looked across the land and could no longer see Terra and the boys. They must have dipped into the gully. Danny turned and went back into the gymnasium to watch the dancers gathering for the grand entry.

Inside the gym sequins glittered on collar-draped shoulders, arms danced with fringed shawls and beautiful braided hair twists adorned the heads of young Lakota girls. The older women wore the dignified beaded buckskin dresses of the traditional dancers. Drummers gathered in tight circles on metal chairs around the pow wow drum. All of the low wooden risers of the gymnasium were crowded with the Elders watching the dance floor and the young people clomping up and down the bleachers behind them.

The room quickly grew stuffy, but nobody minded. The master of ceremonies called for the grand entry, his voice squawking out through the lousy sound system. "Hoka Hey! Welcome to one and all." he cried, and the pow wow began with the sharp slicing thrum of the drum and the high pitched voices of the singers.

It begins here, Danny thought, and then wondered at the words forming in his head. What begins?

He had been asked to open the evening with a prayer so he took his place at the microphone. Speaking first in Lakota, in deference to the Elders, he prayed to *Tunkasila* to watch over the people gathered for this event, to guide and direct them, and to bring peace into their hearts. He repeated the same prayer in English and then sat down again, amazed at the depth of emotion swamping him. The drum took over, filling the gym with sound as children darted across the floor, turned somersaults, giggled, and chased each other to the beat.

He felt like a teenager, his skin as raw as an untanned hide. Something was alive in this night, something he'd never felt before. He saw Carol, her face shining like the North Star, and he resisted the urge to cross the gym, throw her to the ground, and make love to her right here and now. He saw John, the spiked legs of the tripod extended, looking like a friendly spider, his camera whirring—if cameras still whirred. He saw Jed and Pete now firmly planted beside Terra, who was scanning the crowd with bright eyes, her shoulder touching Jed's.

Just watching the woman gave him this odd buzz in his body. He knew it wasn't sexual attraction—only Carol mattered to him that way. No, it was more like being poked with a cattle prod or accidentally hitting the electric fence. That's it, he thought. The sensation was like an electrical energy surrounding her. Damn it, what the hell is going on around here, he wondered.

Carol spied him and began crossing the gym toward him. She looked like a warrior woman in her nearly 40-year-old body and again his body hummed. Yes, there was something electric about this night. Something was happening. Something good.

Terra could hardly breathe. Each breath she took pulled the night in closer; the sounds, the kaleidoscope of color—and the drum—how she loved the drum! If she could lay her heart out on the top of one of those drums, she would do it.

Just moments before, Pete had yielded to his own inner beat and joined the other children tap, tapping their feet on the edge of the gym floor. Jed was nearby. She couldn't see John in the crowded room but felt him near.

It begins, she thought, right here, tonight, with every name invoked, every tale told, every tear wiped, every toe hitting the gym floor. Something amazing was unfolding. A piercing sensation rose up in her that was both joy and incredible pain. It made her want to weep. She stared across the crowded gymnasium and replayed the events of the day, the long ceremonies, the brave talks, the shining faces of Jed and Pete, the stern presence of John. All of this filled her until even the missing memories seemed to no longer matter.

The heated room grabbed her senses and her eyes defocused. She could see the crowd but was seeing past the crowd as well. Her peripheral vision seemed to widen out until suddenly the words drifting off peoples' lips appeared to become tiny luminous orbs hovering near the ones who had spoken them. Tears and laughter also lifted off, joining other glowing orbs and illuminating the room with a peculiar light. In spite of the brightly lit room, she saw the tiny lights forming and moving. Each drumbeat strengthened the fragile spheres until the whole crowd appeared to glow. The sight stunned her. Even more amazingly—nobody else seemed to notice the phenomena.

She laughed aloud. I'm the only one who sees it, she thought. And it has something to do with me, something to do with why I'm here. The urge to move and dance overwhelmed her. Without thinking twice, she rose up from the chilly gym floor and joined the dancers in the center; her feet stepped into the snapping rhythms of the shawl dancers as if she were born to it. She saw an elderly woman grinning at her from the first row of bleachers. The woman nodded at her and then sent a tiny girl in pigtail braids across the floor with a shawl in her hands. It was a shimmering pale blue, the color of sky. She wrapped it around her arms, gave a little bow to the old woman, and then stepped again into the dance wearing the sky itself.

John walked back to his car, lugging his equipment under his arm. He'd shot enough footage for one day and was relieved to put the big camera away. He was bone tired, but now he could settle in and enjoy the pow wow. He didn't dance and didn't drum, but he liked the pow wow anyway. Although he'd married a Lakota woman, he still felt like an outsider in Indian country, even after twenty years working around Pine Ridge.

He stowed the tripod and camera on the front seat, and then unzipped the bag that held the small Sony he kept with him most of the time—he'd nicknamed it "little traveler." He locked the truck, and went back into the gymnasium. He stood for a moment outside the tight circle of bodies wondering what it would be like to truly belong. It was not a thing you could choose—you either belonged or you didn't. And it wasn't as if he wanted to belong to the people of Pine Ridge. He had no illusions. Living on Pine Ridge was no big picnic. The men of Pine Ridge often didn't make their 60th birthday.

He eased his way through the crowd keeping an eye out for Terra or the boys. The pounding drum struck his chest and it felt as though his heart was beating outside of his body. Someone came up next to him and he saw it was Carol, Danny's wife.

She looked up at him and said, "Hi, John."

She said something else but it was difficult to hear above the drum group. He leaned closer and said, "What did you say?"

She took his arm and pointed to the dancers. "Look at your new friend. She's no stranger here."

He looked where she was pointing and spotted Terra out on the dance floor with the other dancers. Her feet were flying and her loose hair was twirling about her head. She wore a shawl—he had no idea where it had come from—and she looked so sensuous, so alive that his belly tightened just to look at her. Almost without thinking, he flipped his small camera on and began to film her and the dancers around her. "Wow," he said, "she can dance."

Carol laughed. "It would seem so. In fact, she appears to be on fire. Look again, John."

Still holding the camera steady on the crowd, he looked up to watch Terra dance. Carol pointed and he saw a luminous gathering of light hovering above her. Even in the bright room, the small dancing lights were visible.

66

Carol said, "You see it too, don't you?"

"What is it?" He stared in disbelief at the woman dancing with small orbs of light lifting off her shoulders, hair, and fingertips. Suddenly the green forest scent was back and his underarms were wet and his belly hurt and all he could say was, "What the . . . ."

Carol left him standing there with his mouth hanging open. She'd never seen John so rattled—she found it both amusing and hopeful. Mae Jo had been her best friend and she missed her—but it broke her heart to see those beautiful boys wander around like little lost ghosts. And trying to be their replacement mom was equally hard. More than anything, she wanted a child of her own. She reached down and touched her belly; she had not given up hope.

The pow wow was in full swing and she had agreed to work the refreshment stand for an hour. She made her way in and around the crowd. Danny was right. Everybody seemed to be having such a good time. She knew he had prayed and worked hard to help people get beyond the unhappy history and take new steps into the future. Maybe there was hope there, too. The lights above Terra's head hadn't disturbed her—she'd seen enough mystery in the ceremonies to recognize the spirits at work. Danny was encouraging her to take a more visible role in the healing ceremonies—especially with the women. She didn't know how to tell him that she just couldn't. He often joked and said she was like a cotton ball, absorbing every tiny hurt and sadness into her self—and that was as close to the truth as she had come. She couldn't work with people and not have a broken heart. It was easier to stay in the background.

The women at the refreshment stand looked hot and tired. They welcomed her. At least I can pour out Cokes and hand out potato chips, she smiled to herself. No danger there.

Phyllis, her cousin, was running the cash register. When she spotted Carol, she said, "Oh, thank God. I so

67

need to go to the bathroom. Can you take over for me? I can't believe how many people showed up. It feels like the Oglala Fair and Rodeo." She hurried off, and Carol took over the money box.

She couldn't wait to get Danny alone and ask him about John—and the woman who had showed up in their midst. Unfortunately, she had an early appointment in the morning and wouldn't be spending the night. Tomorrow she'd catch up on the news.

Chapter 7

Sleep should have come easily by the time John's tired crew arrived back at the trailer. It was long after midnight, and they'd not stopped moving since early morning. He went into the back bedroom and made sure the boys were settling down to sleep. To his surprise, they were both dead to the world already.

The pow wow drum still pounded in his ears although the trailer was night silent, and he couldn't get the image of a glowing Terra off his mind. Other images of the day flickered through his mind, of Terra getting Pete to wash his hands, of her wiping the kitchen table, of her sticking like glue to his boys all day. Damn, it was like she really had planted herself into the middle of their lives in a few short hours. Aside from Danny's bantering, John hadn't had a moment all day to talk to him seriously about this strange encounter. His mind urged him not to trust, but his body was giving him another message entirely— and he didn't much care for that new development either.

When he went into the living room, Terra was awake, stretched out on the couch in the living room. Not knowing what else to do, he'd gathered dusty blankets and sheets from a back closet and made it up into a bed. Now he had an urge to tuck her in like a child, bringing the blankets up around her ears and kissing her forehead—but the feeling was not fatherly—far from it. He checked the feelings and stood in the center of the living room. He teasingly asked her if she would prefer to be taken back to her sandy Badlands bed.

"Was that really only this morning?" she murmured. "Man, this day has lasted a thousand years, I swear it."

"I wanted to thank you for helping with the boys. I do appreciate it," he said. "It was a good day."

"It was the best day. The best."

Terra had stood guard over the boys all day and into the night, stopping only after she'd led a sleepy Pete from the truck to the trailer and guided him gently to the bottom bunk.

He felt awkward standing there, staring at her sleepy face, so he sat down on the plaid easy chair and said, "We need to talk, Terra."

"I know."

"I want to know what's going on here. I don't understand the rules of the game."

"It's not a game, John. I honestly don't understand what's happening any more than you do. All I know is that I've come here to do something important with you and the boys, and I haven't a clue what it is."

"That's not an explanation." He leaned forward in the chair, and stretched his legs out. "What am I supposed to think? When you disappeared for so long with the boys before the pow wow, I honestly thought maybe you'd kidnapped them or something."

Terra laughed. "And where would I go with them? I'm no kidnapper. I wouldn't hurt you or the boys. You must believe that."

"I don't know what to believe. Give me something to work with here. You show up like a vagabond in the Badlands, you hop in my truck and take over my boys, and now you're about to spend the night on my couch."

She sat up, crossed her legs, and stared at him for the longest time. "Do you ever have a sense that larger things are unfolding around us, a divine force at work; but with our limited perception, we can't begin to understand?"

He flopped back into the chair, a thick, muddy sensation weighing on his chest. "Spare me. I gave up thinking a divine force was at work here long ago."

"Really?"

"Really."

"No magic for John Forrest, huh? Such a sad life."

"I don't know. It's my life. As it is." He could hear the resignation in his own voice. The magic had fled long ago, maybe when his mother died, maybe when his father remarried . . . maybe when Mae Jo died. Damn, but he felt a hundred years old.

He rose from the chair. "Good night, Terra," he said, unable to look at her again. It was clear that this conversation was not going to yield answers. Feeling bone tired, he went down the hall to get ready for bed.

In the small tin-can bathroom he stood before the mirror and washed the day from his face, wondering if the rugged brown washcloth would carry an imprint of this day. The warmth of the cloth relaxed his jaw, brows, and forehead. He wanted to bury himself in its wet warmth. No, if he were honest with himself, he wanted to bury himself in her warmth. Terra—he liked her. That was the truth of it. Being with her all day, then watching her dance and laugh with the boys, he felt as if somehow her pale skin and hair had darkened until there was no difference between her and the dark shining heads around her, until she really had become Mae Jo. "Damn," he said to his reflection, "you really are living in a fantasy."

She'd blended so easily into that room in a way he'd never been able to. It made him feel alone, and it pissed him off that he continually felt like a stranger in his own life. And this strange attraction he felt to Terra would have to end. He wanted nothing to do with some gypsy moth who could take flight at any moment. Losing Mae Jo had nearly killed him. No way would he take a chance with his own heart—or his sons' hearts—again. Not ever.

He slid into bed and stared at the ceiling, trying to sleep. Rolling over, he rested his head on an outstretched arm and looked out the window. There were no outdoor lights here and only faint moonlight illuminated the room. He envisioned the meadow at Wounded Knee sloping down toward the creek, the upper ridge topped with dark pines. Jed and Pete are Wounded Knee survivors, he reminded himself again for the thousandth time. The thought tightened the space between his ribs and made his heart ache. Pete was born with a jimmied-up foot that a whiz kid surgeon at Denver Children's Hospital had fixed up in a single surgery. He remembered clutching that poor twisted foot, and realizing that if this had been then, and not now—Pete couldn't have run from the soldiers. John pulled his knees up closer to his body and took a deep breath.

It hurt to love. It hurt to lose the one you loved. Fear shot through him, leaving only pain in his gut. If anything ever happened to the boys . . . he'd die. Plain and simple. No, there was too much to lose. Danny said he used his love to create a steel net around Jed and Pete—or a cage.

At last abandoning the effort to sleep, John got up, slipped on jeans and a deep purple sweatshirt and moved silently through the trailer and out onto the front stoop. He sat down and the cool night air surrounded him. There was no noise. Unlike the city where sublevel sound littered every night, here the night was completely still, the silence a sound all its own.

"Quiet as an Indian, huh?"

He heard Terra's voice behind him, yet it didn't disturb the presence of night around him.

"Can I join you for a minute?" she asked.

"Sure. Sit down." He scooted left to make room for her.

She sat one step below, and his eyes grazed the top of her tawny head as he looked out across the night. The night looked back.

"I couldn't sleep either," she said.

She wore Jed's dingy gray sweatshirt and had pulled it tight around herself to ward off the night chill. She planted her elbows firmly on her thighs and rested her chin in her hands. John thought she looked like a child, but her presence did not bring up childish feelings in him. No, he had to resist the urge to reach out and stroke her hair; it looked almost white in the dim moonlight. He thought of the odd orbs of light he'd seen at the dance. "What are you doing here, Terra?" he asked softly.

72

"Oh, I wish I had answers to your questions. When I woke up in my wonderful, sandy bed this morning, I couldn't remember a thing," she said, "Yet it feels like I know exactly why I am here."

"The Badlands can be dangerous. It isn't even March, and you had nothing with you, not even a bottle of water. Had it been July—or January—the boys might have found a dead body instead." The thought of her stretched out on the sand without even a sleeping bag made him shudder.

"I know." She ran her hands down over her knees and calves as if discovering her lower limbs for the first time. "How can I make you understand? I have this feeling that I'm supposed to meet somebody or gather with a family, like a reunion. Beyond that, I just don't know."

She fell silent again. He watched her stare out into the night just as he had been doing moments before. All day he'd been so self-absorbed, fearing what she might do to him or the boys, that not once had he considered what it was like for her to awaken in some strange place without memory or understanding. "You really have no idea?"

Terra laughed, the sound tinkling like thin pipe chimes across the night. "None." She leaned over her knees. "When I saw Jed and Pete squatting there and staring down at me," she chuckled. "I wanted to jump up and kiss them. You should have seen Jed's face. He looked at me like I was a rattlesnake."

He imagined his eldest son's reaction and smiled. "Jed doesn't warm up to people he doesn't know well."

"That's just it, John. I did know him. And he knew me."

He shook his head and said, "Damn. I don't get it."

She sighed. "Neither do I."

Her voice drifted off in the breeze and the green scent of deep woods returned. It intoxicated him, drugging his rigid resolve to stay distant. He shook it off, determined not to give in to some strange fantasy. "Terra, if you have amnesia or were abducted or something, we need to ask around, find out who is looking for you. You must have family somewhere, maybe a husband, somebody

73

who is worried about you." He was surprised at the spur of jealousy that stabbed at him. A husband? It was only logical that a woman in her late twenties would have a husband, maybe even a child or two somewhere. His reaction shocked him.

She looked up and smiled, as if reading his thoughts. "I don't have a husband."

She sounded so sure.

The silence grew around them until John could hear the sound of his own heart beating. He listened and thought he could hear ants burrowing beneath a humus soil, cocoons spinning, wings flapping—the sound of a night passing while unseen nocturnal creatures foraged for food and existence.

And he could hear the air passing Terra's lips as she, too, breathed the night in and out, in and out. Something about this woman made him want to turn inward, to ask big questions like why did he feel he was always reaching for something he could neither touch nor smell nor see? He half wished he was the one who had awakened in a sandy bed without memory or understanding.

For him, all potential for vision had died like the women and children of Wounded Knee, like his mother had died . . . like his wife had died . . . there was so much death around him. He sighed.

Terra shook her head slightly as if repelling the heavy thoughts drifting over her head. "There's no need for sadness. You carry sadness like the old ones used to carry food and water, as if you could live on it. The whole world is dining on sadness and grief—especially here. It is so senseless, don't you think?"

He resisted the anger that flared and said, "You're right. It doesn't make much sense. You've only lost your memory. I'd like to lose mine."

"And what would you put in its place?"

"In place of memory?" He laughed harshly. "Sometimes I'd like to just go get blasted drunk and forget it all. You don't get rid of memory, but it would be nice to believe in something."

"But what?" she persisted. "If you could choose it, what would you believe in?"

"You're asking hard questions. I don't know. Maybe I'd put Pete's brain into my head and believe that the world is a wonderful place full of magic and miracles.

"But you can—put Pete's brain into you're head, I mean. You were a boy once, full of the stuff of boys."

"Give it up, Terra. I am not some young boy who can fall under your fairy tale spell." He was not angry—more resigned. He stood up from the steps and said, "I need to move. Let's walk to the end of the drive and back."

"All right, but do me a favor first. Take off your shoes."

"Why?"

"I don't know. Humor me." She extended her legs to show him her own bare feet, wriggling her toes. "Take your shoes off and then we'll walk."

"But it's winter—in spite of the warm weather. The ground is still frozen." He stared a minute and then relaxed, smiling for the first time at Terra as he bent to remove his loafers. "Okay, but I'm kind of a tenderfoot."

"What? An Indian tenderfoot? Impossible!"

"I'm not Indian. My boys are half Lakota—from their mother's side." Even to his own ears he sounded rude and abrupt.

"Then you have the best of both worlds around you, don't you?" she said.

He pulled his loafers and socks off, amazed at how worn and weary his feet were after the long day. It felt good to free them in spite of the cold earth. He let Terra take his hand and pull him down the drive. A blanket of clouds drifted over the slivered moon, darkening the night even further. His feet felt vulnerable as they made contact with the cold ground, and he peered out to make sure there were no stones or roots lurking, ready to bite at his naked toes.

"Stop it!" She teased. "Do you trust only your eyes? Come on; relax and feel what is beneath your feet. You'd be surprised at what feet can see. They have little eyes on

75

the end of each toe, like headlights." She giggled and then strode confidently out ahead, leaving him alone and barefoot in a darkened driveway in the middle of the night.

Suddenly his attention was drawn down his legs to where his feet connected with the earth. His mind went still. The blood in his body surged downward, and then seemed to lazily turn and move up towards his heart. He knew right where his feet ended and the earth began. Then slowly, subtly, it felt as though the veins in his feet stretched root-like into the soil. Instead of ending at his feet, the flow entered the earth before returning the blood to his heart. He took a step. The rooting sensation intensified. His skin tingled and the hair on his scalp prickled with new energy. With several more steps, the dark road no longer felt threatening to his bare toes.

Terra turned and watched. "See? Isn't it wonderful?" She walked back and touched his arm.

Her touch didn't interrupt but seemed to join the energy field, intensifying the odd sensation of veins and arteries rooting into the earth.

Terra stared up, pointed at the sky and said, "Oh, look. Aurora borealis."

He looked up but didn't see anything but a sprinkling of stars against a black background. "We don't usually get any northern lights here. I don't see anything," he said.

She turned to him and said, "You don't see them."

"Them?"

Terra laughed. "Sorry, I'm just being a romantic. Did you know some northern tribes say Aurora Borealis is a highway the spirits travel between the living and the dead?"

He felt himself stiffen. "How is it that you would know something like that and not know who you are? It doesn't make sense. Maybe you are a trickster, *Iktomi* or something. Last night you were a spider looking for fun and games, and today—you found us."

"Could be. Who really knows? Maybe all of this is the work of a trickster and we just take his—or her—jokes a little too seriously. Like you, for instance."

"Me?"

"Yes, you. The boys told me more about their mom's accident, how serious and sad you've been, trying to be both mom and dad, probably blaming yourself for her death. I'm shocked I can even get you to go barefoot under the night sky."

With her words, the rooted-to-the-earth sensation suddenly shriveled, pulling upward toward the trunk of his body. "This isn't your business."

"Sorry." She went silent for a long moment, then said quietly. "I know it's none of my business, John; but you and the boys need to go on. You can't follow her, and you can't bring her back. She's gone."

"Don't you think I know that? And who are you to tell me what to do with my boys? Every morning when I wake up in my bed and she isn't there I wonder . . . how the hell can I go on?" He turned and walked back to the trailer steps.

She caught up with him as he reached the steps and said, "It's not her you remember. All you are thinking of is yourself—not her—and that's a selfish way to live."

Who does she think she is, he thought. Wandering in like a stray dog and suddenly has all the answers? "Oh sure, and you—the Badlands ghost—you know all about it?"

She leaned back against the smooth wooden rail post, looked at him cautiously, and said, "Think about it, John. You get hurt so you stop trusting people, and pretty soon your spirit is full of ugly little scabs—and you can't stop picking them."

He turned on her, fully aware that his anger could be both shield and sword. He wanted to hurt her, but it was the truth that hurt so much. "You don't know anything about my life. Well, I'll tell you something," he went on, angry now. "The highway patrol said she slid off the road, he called it black ice." He felt like punching something. "But damn it—there was no ice. It was forty degrees that night." He'd never told anyone of his belief that Mae Jo had left for other reasons, reasons he could never ever forget . . . or forgive. "She's gone. For whatever reason, she's gone. And I'll tell you something else, Terra Whoever The Hell You Are—you can't take her place—not with me and not with my boys." The soft look on her face dissolved, and she looked as if he'd slapped her.

"Don't be cruel."

She stepped away from him, tears beginning to slide down her cheeks, but the anger hummed through his body and he said harshly, "I'm sorry to burst your bubble, Terra, but the world is cruel." Unable to stop himself, he pulled her close. Her arms felt slim beneath his larger hands, thin and frail, as if he'd seized a child—but she was no child. She was a woman; and she was staring at him with wide, tearful eyes, and he didn't know whether he wanted to slap her or wrap himself up in her Badlands hair with the moon winking behind the clouds and the silent night surrounding them. He did nothing. He dropped his hands. "I'm sorry. Just go, Terra. Leave me alone."

She turned and soundlessly walked up the steps and went back into the trailer.

Jesus, I'm becoming a monster, he thought. What had just happened? One minute he'd wanted to throttle her and the next he wanted to kiss her—or make love to her. He plopped back down on the steps now disgusted with himself.

But the box was open and all the hidden feelings flew out like bats—the guilt he felt for not being enough of a man, his anger at Mae Jo for leaving him with two boys, his rage at this place that made staying alive harder than hell. Danny was right. He was not getting on with it—and he'd just taken it out on a stranger—a woman his boys had picked up like a pretty stone in the Badlands just that morning.

Terra pretended to be asleep when John came in and walked through the living room. She was not. She waited until she heard him move down the hall and crawl into bed, then she got up quietly, went back outside, and sat down. She stared out at the night sky, demanding answers, straining her eyes to see the stars and the answers she knew were hiding behind the light cloud cover. She felt raw, burned to the bone with the long day. All the energy of going along, being wise and bright, drained out leaving only doubt and fear behind. What am I doing here? She dropped her head and the tears started—there was nothing she could do to stop them. She was scared and alone, and John Forrest had looked like he wanted to beat her.

She wanted a bullhorn to call her question out to the smirking stars. Who am I?

She sobbed as she thought about those motherless boys and that lonely man masking his grief in anger and sarcasm. Their three faces swam behind her eyes bringing a painful ache to her heart. Some vague, anxious feeling urged her to act quickly—but she had no idea what she was supposed to do.

Finally she dried her eyes and pulled herself into an upright position. "Self-pity is never an answer," she whispered aloud. She looked up at the sky and saw a slim, wispy cloud slide in front of the moon—it looked like smoke or dust curling from nothing and taking shape.

She smiled at the moon and then, closing her eyes, she searched the surrounding landscape—and beyond—with her inner sight. Suddenly, it was as if she could see across the entire world. She saw the people of earth, their hidden desires, their dreams and fears. She saw tears forming in the corners of eyes, empty spaces filling up, overfull spaces emptying out. Her own breath stopped for a moment; there was no single word to describe what she felt. This energy was not of the material world but of the subtle world, where human language fails.

"What?" she pleaded. "What do you want me to do here? Tell me what you want me to do." The night was so still, so silent . . .

Chapter 8

On Cuny Table, Agnes was again on her porch, although the sun had gone down long ago. She watched the curls of smoke from her pipe against the moon and she saw, over the Black Hills, a strange illuminated energy seeping in.

She smiled at the moon and then, closing her eyes, she searched the surrounding landscape—and beyond— with her inner sight. Suddenly, it was as if she could see across the entire world. And what she saw made her ache with the terrifying richness of life. She did not know what was happening but she was comfortable with not knowing. The spirits often worked this way—beyond visibility. And in the distance, she heard the thoughts of another and thought, stay strong, my girl, stay strong.

Chapter 9

Danny was wide-awake and restless. Not for a decade had he felt so charged. Carol had an early appointment the next day and had just left for Rapid City—he'd almost gone with her. Something about this night made him not want to spend it alone. He smiled. Truth was, he did feel a little testosterone-charged.

He stood in the kitchen of his uncle's cabin willing his body into sleepiness but finally gave up all thoughts of a warm bed. Uncle Bill was snoring in the back bedroom. He must have been burning cedar earlier; the scent lingered in the air.

That smell. It took him back to the years he'd spent learning the medicine ways from his uncle. He'd been restless then, too. How many nights had he spent out under that moon roaming Cuny Table like a bobcat? How many nights sitting there in Bill's uglier-than-sin easy chair asking the hard questions? Then, and now, he felt young and randy and restless.

He slipped on a jacket to ward off the night chill and went out. The toes of his feet pointed him in the direction of the *Inipi* lodge behind the cabin, and he followed his toes. Just looking at that canvas-shrouded frame made him want to crawl in and offer it all to the Creator—all of his doubt and restlessness, all of this big uneasy energy. He squatted and stepped through the opening and sat down.

How strange to be here alone with no heat, no steam, no voices calling out their prayers to the spirits. A song came to him.

We are traveling, traveling,

From all the realms we are traveling.

He caught the unfamiliar tune in his mind and hummed it, the words forming in Lakota.

During those early years, Uncle Bill had made certain he was fluent in their language. Within the walls of the cabin, Bill had spoken only Lakota to him. He'd struggled and struggled to understand it and then one day, it had suddenly clicked and gone in. He remembered Uncle Bill saying that when we speak to the spirits of our ancestors, we need to speak their language so they will understand. Being a spiritual guide for the people was hard, especially when trouble was a deep trough too many of his people fell into.

He closed his eyes and prayed. The song entered his mind again and he sang it softly.

We are traveling, traveling,
From all the realms we are traveling,
On the rivers and on the wind
We are traveling.
Hear my voice when I call to you, Tunkasila.

The air in the *Inipi* lodge went still and thickened around his head. He heard nothing—no bird sounds, no insect sounds, no wind blowing—nothing audible entered that space. He closed his eyes and again hummed the tune running through his head. The tips of his ears felt hot as if from some potent drink.

When the first burst of heat rolled out and hit his body, he clamped his eyes shut and waited. There were no hot stones—and yet there was steam. He continued singing, a single voice in the night, calling out, calling out. The air in the sweat lodge got hotter. Still he prayed, eyes closed, his sight directed inward. The heat intensified. It nearly drove him back out into the restless night. When he could stand it no longer, he suddenly had the feeling of falling down into a well or a dark tunnel. He felt the outline of his own body dissolve, and suddenly he was in another place.

There was movement, like water flowing, but there was no water. There was a rushing, flowing-forward sensation but nothing to carry him, nothing to be carried. He saw nothing. His spirit flowed forward, and he swam with it like a silvery fish in a deep moving river. Time seemed meaningless. Then he noticed that there were others flowing around him, bright flashes and flickers of movement behind and beside him. The longer he swam in this deep, hidden current, the more a part of it he felt.

No words formed to describe what was happening— language failed him—and yet he knew with something outside of language that he was in a river of beings from all the realms, like a great underground aquifer of the sacred. The flash and flicker of this place was the essence of freedom. His body had disappeared, and he seemed to know the others who were flowing with him. Names entered his mind—of old leaders, of dead relatives, of holy men from many tribes—and not just his people, but all the people. It was a shimmering, silvery school of spirits, and he was swimming with them.

After what seemed like eternity, he suddenly felt his grandfather beside him. His sense of the old man was so clear that he felt the rough canvas of the old man's jacket, smelled the familiar tobacco the old man had liked, saw the turn of his head as he spoke. "Grandfather!" he cried aloud.

With a humming whoosh, the vision disappeared and he was, once again, sitting in the cold, dark sweat lodge. Across the fire pit sat his grandfather, in the flesh—not dead, not gone, but here. It was too much to hold after taking in the tears of the people, after sensing all that this day held. He bent over, crawled across the sweat lodge on all fours, put his head in his grandfather's lap and wept.

Chapter 10

Jed lay on the top bunk listening to Pete's even breathing in the bunk below. Outside his window, the birds were awakening. He saw the sky growing pink, but it was the sound of a drum that had awakened him.

He listened. Was it a dream drum left over from the pow wow, he wondered. If he'd been dreaming, why could he still hear it? And it was slow—so slow—not like the frenzy of the drum circle with the dancers tap, tapping, but slow . . . like a heart barely beating. . . like a call to come.

He sat up and tugged his hair away from his ears. Instantly chilled by the early morning air, he grabbed the t-shirt he'd discarded during the night and put it back on. Ever since he'd found Terra sleeping in the sand, something weird had been going on. He intended now to find out what it was.

In the dark, he crept quietly down the bunk ladder being careful not to wake up Pete. He slipped sweatpants on over his shorts, put on his jacket, and donned his sneakers. Moving through the house, he wished he could become a ghost and pass through walls instead of through creaking doors like an ordinary human being. Shivering with cold and excitement, he made it outside to the landing and heard the drum rhythm increase. He felt invited, dragged from bed in the early chill for some weird reason. Along the path near the back shed, he stopped to pee.

Skid was sprawled behind the shed dreaming his own dreams and barely raised an ear at him. In spite of the wash of light across the horizon, the path was still hung with night. He stopped . . . listened . . . then walked past the sweat lodge and into the trees that fringed the base of the low bluff behind the trailer. Oddly, he knew just where to find the source of the beating drum. He knew the trail.

He and Pete had played these bluffs like a video game, realizing over time that all paths led to the same place. Where the land rose behind the trailer there was a shallow stone bowl carved out of the side of the bluff. It wasn't really stone but the white, packed powder of clay and gumbo, but they liked calling it the stone bowl, as if it really were a pipe bowl carved into the earth, their own special fort.

Jed moved cautiously toward the bowl. The drumbeat grew soft and steady, as if the drum knew he approached. Shivering again, he half wished he was still hearing the drum from his top bunk instead of dampening his sneakers and racing his heart down this dark path.

The stone bowl was twenty yards up the bluff, an easy climb on a well-worn path fringed with low junipers and scruffy sage; distant pine trees stood like soldiers along the ridge top. He stopped. The drum was near. He felt it beneath his feet, smelled the smoke of a wood fire. The air crackled around his ears as if lightning had just struck the earth. He gulped, easing his way up to the edge, wanting to see—but not be seen. He crouched, staying in the shadows behind a juniper, and slowly peeked into the center of the stone bowl.

There in front of the fire sat two old Indians—one was beating a hand drum with a padded stick that looked like a beat up old cattail. Jed scanned the floor of the bowl looking for wine or beer bottles; but there was nothing, just two sober Indians sitting in front of a fire. He blinked, rubbed his eyes, and, when he looked again, a third person was sitting between the two old men, a woman. She wore beaded white buckskins and had a long shining braid. He patted his own long hair, remembering the way his mother used to stroke it. His strength, she'd called it. He'd not cut it since her death.

He stared, scarcely daring to breathe, and thought, Mom?

No, he scoffed at his own fantasy. It couldn't be her.

The men talked softly and quickly to one another and to the woman. Jed crouched down and wrapped his arms tight around his knees and listened. The old one without the drum was swinging his arms in wide arcs as he spoke. The woman was nodding and smiling as the old man talked. She laughed softly and the sound nearly knocked him dizzy. He knew that soft laugh as well as he knew his own face. Backing further into the shadows, he caught his breath. More than anything, he wanted to step into that circle and find out what the heck was going on, but he was afraid of being seen, so he rested his head against the cool embankment and listened.

The men spoke Lakota—he wished he understood more than a few words in Lakota. Several moments passed and the voices hypnotized him. He loved the sound of Lakota and hearing it reminded him of his grandmother. The voices lulled him and his eyelids grew heavy. His body felt curiously free, floating up and away from his mind.

All of a sudden the drummer brought his stick down with a final hard thrum and raised his head as if listening. Jed jumped. One minute he'd been almost asleep and now his heart was thumping so loudly in his chest he feared the old drummer would hear it. He saw the old man smile, dipping his head slightly as if giving him a nod. Does that old drummer know I'm here, he wondered. No, he can't see me. He pulled even further back into the darkness.

The old man set the drumstick in his lap and said, "It begins. She has called us back to help them. And we come." He picked up his stick again and began a slow rhythm, his voice joining the beat. Suddenly, Jed realized he could understand what was being said even though the old man was still speaking Lakota. The old man began to sing,

> We are traveling, traveling,
> From all the realms we are traveling,
> On the rivers and on the wind
> We are traveling.
> Hear our voice, Tunkasila,

We send our plea out to the universe,
The people suffer, Tunkasila.
Hear our plea.

The second man joined in the singing and then the woman joined the men's voices. When the song ended Jed heard only the crackling fire, yet the tune continued on in his mind.

The woman spoke. "So, she has really come? What are we to do?"

"She says we old ones have earned our rest; but the others, the living, they are trying to snooze through eternity, too. She wants us to wake them up." His voice made an odd whooshing sound, but low, almost like a growl."

"She won't shake them off again, will she? I mean, I worry about my boys, Jed and Pete, and how it will be for them. They have suffered so much already."

When he heard his name, Jed's head jerked up like a small startled animal.

The old man patted the woman's arm. "No, my dear, *Unci Makah* is never cruel—but they have to do their part, they have to act. She never did shake the others off. They lost their spirits and fell off." He laughed aloud as if he'd made a big joke.

The woman watched the two old men and then looked in Jed's direction. "I miss being with them. Jed especially—he is most like me, you know."

Jed's throat thickened and he thought he might cry out. His mom was talking about him, about how he was most like her. He tried to stand straight, lost his balance and plopped down on the ground feeling like he'd been hit with a rock. The beautiful Indian woman was his mother—or her spirit—or something.

He stood up again, his legs trembling all the way down to his toes, but he just had to talk to his mom. He forced his legs to work and walked out from behind the rock and into the shallow stone bowl.

It was empty.

90

There were no old warriors drumming and laughing and talking to his mother in Lakota. There was no fire— and the sun was brightening the horizon. Where did they go? He shook his head in utter confusion.

The remains of the fire looked old and dead. Without thinking, he squatted down and poked a forefinger into the black, charred bed only to jerk his arm back in relief and pain. The embers beneath the blackened surface were glowing red hot.

He stuck the injured finger in his mouth. "I didn't dream it. They were here," he said aloud. He squatted again and concentrated on the dying embers as if they could give him the answer. He fought back tears until he could fight them no longer. Wrapping his arms around his middle, he rocked and rocked, trying to stop the tears, trying to stop missing her for just one dang minute. When he could do neither, he spoke to her instead. "Why? Why did you leave? Where are you? I . . . I need you."

From around the corner of the stone bowl, the sweetest wind ever came to him; it felt like soft fingers. It stroked his cheek, dried his tears, and pulled his head up until he was standing again, chin raised, looking up and out. He pulled a deep breath into his lungs and stared out beyond the horizon, trying desperately to see the truth.

His eyes burned with fresh tears, but he grew still. Suddenly he no longer felt twelve but old and huge and powerful. He tipped his head to the sky, raising his palms as if he were tall enough to touch the very belly of the universe. He sang the lines of the song he could remember.

> *From all the realms we are traveling,*
> *On the rivers and on the wind*
> *We are traveling.*

The wind carried his song—and the earth took his fear. He gulped as if drinking deep. At that moment, something big unfolded deep within him, like flags unfurling, like mythical beasts growing wings. He raised his

91

hands higher and knew that whatever the old men had been talking about—he was a part of it. "It begins," he said. Jed shivered. The sky was getting light, and down the slope, he could see through the trailer, could see his father and little brother asleep in their beds. Pete was dreaming of large animals made of green air and of thin silvery fishes moving though mist—he could see Pete's dream!

"Shee-it," he said, and then turned and walked slowly back down the bluff to the trailer.

Terra heard Jed sneaking into the trailer. For the past hour she'd been wide-awake listening, just listening. She'd heard the drum—and Jed creeping past her couch earlier. All her fear and confusion had evaporated under a moonlit sky the night before after her clash with John. This morning she felt calm, almost amused. All she knew for sure was that she was to follow each impulse, large or small, and the picture would eventually emerge.

Jed was being so quiet, padding across the living room. She waited until she could almost smell his boy breath, then she snaked a hand out and grabbed his arm. "Gotcha!"

Jed nearly fell to the floor. "Sheesh, Terra. What are you doing? Trying to scare me half to death?"

She sat up. "Where are you going? Or should I ask where have you been? I didn't see any cows around here that needed milking, no early chores."

"You wouldn't believe me if I told you. Where I've been, that is."

"Try me."

"Well, I heard this . . . nah, never mind. I better get back to bed. Dad will skin me alive if he knows I went out."

"Come sit by me, Jed. Tell me about the drum."

His eyes got so wide she wanted to laugh. "I know what called you, Jed. I heard it, too."

He sat down on the couch, picked up a metal sculpture from the side table, and fingered the lines of the piece. In a whisper he told her all that he had seen and done, including the part about recognizing his mother. "It was her, Terra. I'm sure of it."

She saw that something had transformed the boy—perhaps "boy" was no longer the right word for Jed. His eyes looked sharp and focused, and his body seemed straight and firm. "They are making you ready, Jed."

"What do you mean?"

Leaning back into the couch, she considered the question. "I don't know. They are making me ready, too. We'll just have to follow the trail. See where it goes." She wanted to put an arm around him but comfort wasn't what he needed. The tiny lights flickering over everyone at the pow wow the night before were now enveloping the boy—a sight too beautiful for words. It reassured her that she was not in this alone. "Go back to bed now. I have a feeling we'll need our rest."

Jed nodded and, saying nothing more, went back down the hall.

She brought her legs up, sat cross-legged on the couch, and looked around at the small living room. It seemed an unlikely temple for such God-like things to be happening. Everywhere there were signs of Danny, the medicine man she'd met the day before. John had said he owned this place. She picked up the sculpture Jed had been holding. Cut from steel, it looked like a cave painting found in ancient Indian sites, an odd-looking warrior about seventeen inches high. The heavy figure had dark holes for eyes with hair or feathers flying off his head. In his extended arm was a spear or perhaps a pipe. He looked exactly like how she felt, odd and out of place, cut from nothing into some form. She touched the extended arm that held the pipe.

Setting the sculpture down, she took the blanket, wrapped it around herself like a shawl, and rested her palms on her thighs. She closed her eyes and picked up the funny warrior or shaman and tucked him against her torso.

Behind her eyelids she saw faces, hundreds of faces that reminded her of the glowing orbs of light. Each one awakened a sweet, gentle feeling in her heart. They were her friends . . . and relatives. She knew in her soul this mysterious event unfolding had something to do with the words she'd heard the day before during the ceremonies. *Mitakuye Oyasin.* John said it meant, "We are all related."

She tried to drift deeper and deeper inside, but as she sank into her meditation, she heard only an inner cacophony of sound that made her blink and straighten her spine. It sounded like wind and wailing and a badly-tuned radio all at the same time. What is that awful noise, she wondered. The sound made her stomach queasy. She sighed and gave up trying to peek into the mystery. She set the metal man down again, lay back, and closed her eyes.

She could not force the seeing. No, she would just rest in the pale shine of Jed and Pete instead—and John.

John Forrest. She thought again of the moving energies surrounding him last night out on the stoop. He'd looked first sad, then angry, then like he wanted to throttle her—or kiss her. Like a turbulent sky, she thought with a smile.

No, the mystery wasn't just about the boys—it was about John Forest as well. A part of his spirit had fled on a dark road the night his wife died. She was to help him call it back again.

He should have kissed me, she thought.

Chapter 11

At dawn, Danny awakened in the sturdy, army-issue oak bed of his childhood. His body felt wooden and immobile. Panic gripped his chest. He waited, forcing the breath through his lungs, calming his heart until sensation returned to his limbs. How strange to awaken again in Uncle Bill's small cabin on Cuny Table. He dragged his body out of bed and went looking for his uncle, feeling sure this rough, raw feeling had something to do with his experience in the sweat lodge the night before.

When he went into the kitchen, Bill was parked at the plain, plank table drinking a cup of steaming black coffee. A second cup was already poured, still hot, as if Bill had monitored the end of the dream and knew Danny would soon appear. The old man was uncanny that way, sliding into his head just like he'd tried to slide into Agnes's head the day before.

"Morning, son," said Uncle Bill.

"Uncle." He sat, took the cup with both hands and held it, pulling it to his mouth and sipping the warm liquid.

"Strange things are about, Danny boy."

"Tell me about it. After the celebration, I spent half of the night in a cold sweat lodge with my Grandfather. This morning, I couldn't move a muscle."

Bill stared across the table at him. His eyes were clouded again as if he had been off wandering the realms beyond this one. "Finish your coffee. We need to go talk to Agnes."

Danny took another draw on the dark liquid, allowing the warmth to chase the remaining woodiness from his limbs. "I'm ready."

John stood in the kitchen of the trailer sipping a hot cup of freshly brewed coffee. He stared out the window across the peach-lit land, bathing his senses in the early silence of the day. What does it really mean to be a human being, he wondered? The thought was not new, but this morning the question felt charged, rippling through his mind and body in a new way.

In the past, it seemed only heartbreak could result from any serious self-inquiry—but not today. Outside, the pine trees shimmered green against the bluing of the day. He cranked open the window over the sink, suddenly needing to smell this world—and not just catch a drifting scent, but to actually rediscover pine and earth and wind. In less than twenty-four hours, something had entered his body and left him raw and changed. He thought about the night before, walking barefoot on the earth, how harshly he'd treated Terra and guilt replaced the rippling excitement. It wasn't like him to be rough with a woman. And the other things he'd wanted to do to her . . . .

"What are you watching for, Dad?"

The sound of Jed's voice startled him, interrupting thoughts he shouldn't be thinking. His son's hair hung down his bare back and the shorts, his favored sleepwear, were riding low on his slim hips. Already John saw signs of the young man he would soon become. He smiled and said, "I'm watching for ghosts, son. Thought I saw one for just a second over there, on the path coming from the stone bowl." He pointed out the small window to the back shed, his mug still heavy in his other hand.

Jed's eyes widened, his jaw nearly sliding to his chest, and John laughed at the disturbed look on the boy's face. "Close your mouth, Jed. The flies are hatching." He smiled. "I was only joking."

"Some joke." Jed looked almost disappointed but moved to the sink to stand beside him. "What do you really think, Dad? About ghosts? Not cartoon ghosts but real ghosts? Spirits? Are they real?"

He studied his son's serious, handsome face, paying close attention to the urgent note he heard there. Carrying the mug to the table, he patted the chair next to him and said, "Come here, Jed. Sit down a minute."

Jed took the chair beside his father, folded his legs beneath him, and perched his elbows on the table.

"You thinking about ghosts, too, Jed? I don't know too much about these things. Our grandfathers tell us that when people die they don't really leave; they just go on to another world, to the other side. If that's so, then maybe the spirits can travel between the worlds."

"Uncle Danny says they do travel between the worlds. During ceremonies the spirits come and talk to him and tell him what to do. That's how he knows what to do to heal people or where a person's spirit has gone—but then he's a medicine man."

Ah, youth, John thought. How easy it is for them to believe. They take reality and color it with their own crayon. Not so simple for crusty old souls like mine. "Yes, he's a medicine man. He's also about the most truthful man I know." He thought of Danny telling him to get on with it. In the morning light, the words pinched.

"I know. But can ordinary people talk to spirits, too, or only medicine men?"

"Jed, what are you really asking? Is there something you want to tell me?" He thought about the night before, the rooting and branching energy moving between his feet and the earth. The small hairs on his arm rose and he shivered. Jed seemed caught in his own recall. What was he remembering? He stroked Jed's forearm and felt the soft, downy hairs rise on the smaller arm. "What is it, son?"

"I don't know, Dad. Strange things are going on. It started when we found Terra. But it's more than that now. Where did she come from?" Jed hesitated and then added, "And I'm afraid that she . . . ." Jed's words trailed off.

"Are you afraid she'll leave, too?"

Jed looked surprised and then nodded. "I like her."

John leaned his head down until it connected with the darker head of his elder son. "I'm afraid too, son," he

97

almost whispered. "I don't know who she is or how she got here or why she came. All I know is it feels like I was missing an arm; and now the arm is back, and I can't figure out how I could ever go back to living with only one arm again." He shocked himself with this honest admission. He slid an arm around Jed's shoulder, sat a moment, straightened up again and smiled. "So, go figure."

Jed laughed, and then got up and moved to the fridge. He opened the door and stared into its cool, barren depths for a minute, a youth's meditation. "Sheesh. Danny never has any food here." He clung to the handle of the fridge and then turned. The smile faded from his face and his skin paled. "I really miss her, Dad."

"Mom?"

"Yeah. Why did she have to die?"

Tears freshened in Jed's eyes, and John watched him struggle to blink them back. The kid had hardly mentioned his mother in over two years. Now, in less than twenty-four hours, they were all talking about her. One more indicator that something—some colored mist or drifting thought-form—had entered their lonely sphere. "I don't know. I wish to God I knew—but I don't. Maybe some mysterious thread stretching from the other side caught her and pulled her over."

Jed stared at him.

There was a new intensity about the boy he hadn't seen before. How can I explain death when I don't understand it myself, he wondered. But it had been so long since Jed had talked about his mother that he didn't want to screw this up. He lowered his voice and said, "I like to think she's near, son. Maybe she's like a good ghost now watching over us from some other place." He went to Jed and pulled his head close until their foreheads touched. Jed's eyes glistened, a clay pot overfull and spilling. John said, "I lost my mother, too, when I was about your age. I thought I'd never get over missing her." He thought of collecting fossils with her in the Badlands; the memory of her was as fresh now as it had been then. He smiled and put his hands on Jed's shoulders and backed off so he

98

could look into the boy's eyes. "Maybe I never did get over missing her, but the missing her eventually just went back to loving her. Whatever happens from here on out, I'll be here. You need to know that."

"I know. I do know that, but sometimes . . . ."

"What, son?"

Jed gulped. "Sometimes, I'm afraid you'll go, too. Sometimes it feels like you're living in one house, and Pete and I are living in a different house."

The words hit their mark. Danny was right. He'd not done a good job of getting on with it. There was nothing he could say to reinvent the past three years. "I know, Jed. And that is going to change."

"Maybe you should do what Terra had us do yesterday."

"And what did she have you do?" He didn't like the idea of Terra making his boys do anything.

Jed smiled and told him about the quick race, how Terra had them imagine all the ancestors clapping and cheering, including their mom. "Then she had both of us stand up and say out loud, 'Mom, I miss you.' Pete almost cried but he didn't. He just said, "Mommy, I miss you.' Try it Dad. Just say it."

Grief, loneliness, a wash of despair chilled his body as though an icy wind had stolen his breath.

Jed said quietly, "It isn't so hard, you know, to just say it out loud."

John looked at his son for a moment and then faced the small window opening out onto this giant land. His hands were trembling. He fought back tears himself; but finally he said aloud, "Mae Jo, baby, I miss you." He repeated it a little louder and felt the heavy pressure on his chest release. He took a breath.

"See what I mean, Dad? Terra says that when we suffer, they—the dead ones—are peeking around a curtain and crying, too."

"Why would they be crying?" He couldn't believe he was having this conversation with his son.

99

Jed smiled. "Because they want us to be happy—even if they can't be here."

Jed sounded a bit like "Duh, Dad", but he had to admit that the logic made perfect sense. He said the words again in his mind, sending them out the window in search of his lost wife. "We all miss you," he said aloud again for Jed's benefit. "It does feel good to say it out loud. We do miss her. And you're right—she wouldn't like it at all if she caught us moping around, feeling sorry for ourselves all day long." A breeze wafted in the window and made him smile. That wind was uncanny lately.

"Anything else you need to tell me, Jed?"

"No. Not now."

"Good. Go back and see if Pete is up. Terra, too. We need to get ready to go back to town. The way things are going, it could be another long day."

"Okay, Dad."

Jed went down the hall to the bedroom. He couldn't bring himself to tell his dad about the fire circle, about seeing his mom or about the drum or Pete's dreams or how later he lay on his back in the top bunk staring at the shadows forming with a filled-up feeling in his chest. He still felt that big feeling.

Pete was up and wriggling into his sweatshirt. Jed hadn't seen Terra on the couch and figured she must be taking a shower. The water was running in the bathroom. He stepped up and helped Pete get the sweatshirt over his head. "Dad says we need to get packed up."

"All right, Jed."

Most of the time, his little brother was just a pain in the backside. Until this moment, he hadn't really realized that Pete was a human being. He laughed at the thought.

"What's so funny?" Pete asked.

"Come here."

Pete looked at him as if he'd grown horns.

"I'm not going to bite you. I just want to look at you."

"What?" He came and stood in front of Jed.

Jed took his hand and measured the top of Pete's head against his own height. The kid came past his shoulder. "You're growing."

"Hello? I am almost seven, you know."

"You look good, Pete. That's all. You look good."

"You're weird."

"I am not."

"Are too."

"Am not." They laughed at their old game, and Jed said, "Let's go see what's for breakfast."

"Yeah. I'm starving," said Pete.

No, there were things Jed wouldn't say to his father about earlier this morning. Not yet. He was afraid too much talking would shatter the mystery and throw them all back into the way it was before. And that would suck.

John looked at the boys sitting at the kitchen table, one on either side of Terra. Pete begged her to sing the Ten Little Indians song, but she was focused on food. Breakfast was hot oatmeal, buttered toast, bursting orange segments, and dishes clattering. His sons' dark heads dipped toward Terra, and he thought, what should I do with her? He couldn't forget that they still didn't know where she'd come from. Somebody must be missing her. He needed to call the authorities—and soon.

My boys will miss her.

He didn't want them to be hurt again, to get attached to this stranger and then have her drive off in some Honda SUV with whomever she belonged to. He watched Jed toy with his toast, looking lost in thought. What a damn tangle. And her odd appearance seemed to coincide with this sudden unearthing of Mae Jo's memory.

"You're not eating," Terra said to him.

John looked at her and wanted to laugh at her motherly comment. Instead he nodded, picked up his spoon and ate, turning his attention to the day. "Here's the plan, guys. First, I need to log my interview tapes while things are still fresh in my mind, so after breakfast I want

101

all of you to head outside and give me an hour or so alone. Then we head for Rapid. But first—a few chores."

When the kitchen was tidied and the dishes done, the boys went into the bedroom to finish packing their stuff. John went into the living room and hooked the big Sony Camera to the VCR and arranged the tapes beside a pen and a blank legal pad. Logging tape was about the last frigging thing on earth he felt like doing this morning. All of his edges were raw and awake.

Terra came and stood by him. "The boys and I are going for a hike so we'll be out of your way. John, about last night."

"Don't say anything, Terra. I was way out of line. You didn't deserve to be treated that way." A fist of guilt punched him. Her actions the previous day had been nothing but generous and helpful. "I'm a beast when it comes to protecting my boys," he said simply.

"Right." She looked as though she wanted to say more but turned and went into the kitchen to pack a picnic lunch.

He heard Terra puttering around the kitchen, building sandwiches and stuffing them into a backpack. The urge to follow her and make amends was powerful, but he needed to keep his distance. She would be leaving again, probably as early as that evening when they returned to Rapid City. He wanted her gone now—before the boys got too attached to her. He could almost hear Danny's voice calling him a monk, telling him to get on with it, and he chuckled. He wanted her gone . . . before *he* got too attached to her.

Jed and Pete came back out, set their gear by the door and went into the kitchen to add what they could to Terra's picnic lunch from the slim pickings of Danny's kitchen. After a final search for Pete's shoes and water bottles, the three headed toward the bluff with Skid dancing in their tracks.

Chapter 12

Agnes watched Bill and Danny drive away from the Café in Danny's black truck. It was still early, but she'd been sitting on the porch when they arrived. These times required vigilance, and she'd slept only three hours the night before. Later she could sleep. Right now, they needed her.

Danny. He was one of the travelers—although he didn't realize it. She'd watched him the night before, flying off to far corners, inviting them all to come.

The old ones say life starts when a spirit begins his or her journey from the spirit world, traveling great distances to cross into this human realm. What the old ones don't say is that the spirit is always traveling. When it jumps into a body, the spirit is simply occupying that space for a little while. It wanders in and out and eventually returns home. In truth, it is this ordinary human realm we visit only for a moment.

She felt weary to her bones, as though she'd been holding a gate open, muscles straining. In all the many decades she'd been given, never had she felt a moment to be this ripe, this alive . . . and this precarious. All was not clear; but she knew she must hold the space, keep it open and moving.

The pipe in her bag felt heavy, a burden only she could carry right now. It was not the pipe she usually prayed with. This one was a gazing bowl, a *cannupa*, passed to her from her grandmother so long ago. The spirits had given it to her great-grandmother. How long had this bowl been smoked by the women in her family, she wondered, by the women who see, the women who hold the beating heart of the world in their hands. Her grandmother had told her that the bowl of a sacred pipe contains all that is and that they must hold the pipe for her, for *Unci Makah*, Grandmother Earth. Sometimes, it required great sacrifice.

She took out her cheap plastic lighter. One of her nieces had beaded a small pouch for it and now each tiny glass bead winked with pink and purple light. She lit her pipe and hummed the song that had been coming into her mind since early morning.

> *We are traveling, traveling,*
> *From all the realms we are traveling,*
> *On the rivers and on the wind*
> *We are traveling.*

> *Hear our voice, Tunkasila,*
> *We send our plea out to the universe,*
> *The people suffer, Tunkasila.*
> *Hear our plea.*

Chapter 13

Jed watched Terra walk up the sage-scattered path with firm steps. Excitement curled through his body. Ever since they'd left the trailer, the feeling had grown, a feeling of something coming, something big.

"Where are we going, Ter?" asked Pete.

"It's a surprise. I have some important things to get done this morning and have chosen you guys, and Skid of course, to assist." She turned and looked at them. "Are you up for it?"

Jed almost laughed. She sure didn't know his little brother. Pete liked nothing better than to be included in some big adult thing. It was funny how suddenly he could actually really see his little brother.

Pete nodded solemnly and said, "Sure, Ter. Just tell us what you want us to do, and we'll do it."

"Jed?"

He smiled and said, "Lead the way—with her ghost."

"What?"

"With her ghost—isn't that what you said to me yesterday when I took you to my dad?" He watched her face to see if she would get it. She did.

"You're playing with me, aren't you? Scamp. I said 'Wither thou goest . . . there go I. It's a quote—but I can't remember who said it." Terra laughed and said, "But I like 'with her ghost' even better."

Jed felt good about having told her about the old men in the stone bowl and about his mother. She understood. Whatever strange things had happened the day before, he somehow felt clear and sure of himself today.

105

Terra turned and walked up the path. Pete followed close behind her, his head dipped down as if watching the earth move beneath his feet. Jed was last in line. On his back was the backpack stuffed with sandwiches, water bottles, and Hershey bars. He was not surprised when Terra followed the identical trail he'd taken the night before in search of the mystery drum, but it still made him shiver. "Shee-it," he whispered aloud. His stomach felt empty although he'd just finished breakfast. The early sun felt warm and lazy on his back, and he thought again of how crazy he'd felt when he poked his finger into that fire and found it hot. He looked down and saw the tiny blister on his forefinger—proof positive it hadn't all been a dream.

"Here we are," said Terra at last. She was standing in the center of the bowl just above last night's mystery fire. "Here is where we need to do our work."

Jed shivered again. "Why here, Terra?"

"It's special. You guys know that already. Sit down and I'll explain the best I can."

A humming began behind his left ear as Jed sat down with Pete and crossed his legs. The sound was like bees swarming or machinery running. He heard again the song the old men had been singing, about traveling, traveling. He blinked his eyes and looked at Terra.

She had dropped to the ground and was patting the dusty earth beside her as if it were a pet. She scanned the bluffs and the sky around her and then caught his eyes again and smiled at him. That smile warmed him clear to his toes and he felt himself blush.

Terra looked at them and said, "We have all been in a mystery together. Ever since you found me, I haven't been sure what the mystery is about; but, somehow, I know what we are supposed to do." She smiled. "Do you trust me?"

Jed nodded and so did Pete.

She went on. "Do you know how, when babies are born, they have a little soft spot on their heads and you must never press or bump that soft spot?"

106

Pete nodded again but Jed just watched her.

"Well, it's a place on the baby's head where the bones haven't come together yet. Nature puts it there to allow the baby's brain to grow further. It's like a magical hole—and if you looked into that hole, you could see all that is possible for that baby. And here," Terra waved both hands to indicate all that surrounded them, and then she once again patted the ground fondly, "is just such a spot on Mother Earth's body."

Pete's said, "But it's just the ground, Terra—not soft at all."

She laughed. "No, of course not. That doesn't matter. Nothing is ever what it appears to be. But trust me, this place is a soft spot that opens right into Mother Earth's very brain."

Jed recalled how, every single time they came to Danny's house, he and Pete automatically (and as fast as possible) came to this place first. Even at dusk when the evening shadows seemed large and frightening, still they begged their dad to let them run up to the stone bowl before doing anything else. Dad always relented.

Terra looked at him and said, "You knew this already, didn't you, Jed?

He nodded. The buzzing and humming behind his ear intensified. What else do I know, he wondered? Today the world felt so bright he almost had to close his eyes to shut it out. Whatever was going on, he didn't want it to stop.

"Anyway," Terra began again, "Since this is just such a soft spot on the Earth's body, it makes perfect sense that we need to do our work in this place."

"Okay," said Pete. "So, what do we do now?"

"We need to do a ceremony. But first we should gather sage. Pete, Jed, go collect some sage. It is time to get started."

Jed wasn't sure how this stranger, this white woman from who-knows-where knew that all events in Indian country begin with cleansing, but his mind had slid beyond questioning every move they were making. Within five

107

minutes he and Pete had hands full of the fragrant plant, and he almost broke out laughing when Pete presented his bunch to Terra. She pulled it to her nose and sniffed as if it were flowers.

"You guys are the best," she said. Rummaging in a bag, she pulled out the tuna can she'd washed after making the sandwiches. Then she took several stems of sage, stripped the leaves, and rolled them between her palms until she'd formed a small ball. She dipped into her pocket for matches and lit the ball of sage, letting it burn a few seconds before blowing out the flame.

Jed watched every step, stunned at how familiar each movement looked, as if she had done it a hundred times. How does she know all this stuff, he wondered again.

Terra placed the smoldering ball in the tuna can, letting the billowing smoke drift up for a moment. The smoke rolled over her head and face as if it already knew her. Then she handed the smoking tin to him and said in a hushed voice, "Jed, you are very nearly a man now, will you cleanse this place for us?"

Oddly, her request made his throat thicken, as if he'd tried to swallow the ball of sage. Tears formed in his eyes, but he blinked them back and leaned over the drifting smoke. He used his hands to pull the smoke over his own head and face and then pulled it toward his heart. Then he took the tin reverently, turned slowly to offer the smoke to the four directions and then to the sky as he had seen Danny do. When his hands reached high he was again filled with the wide, powerful, scratching-the-underbelly-of-the-universe feeling. In a final move, he lowered the tin to the Earth and, as he squatted, something inside him burst open. Suddenly he did not feel big and powerful but weak and tiny, as small as a mouse. He knew he was nothing—and everything. For the longest time he could not rise, could not even bring his eyes up to look at Terra or Pete. His gaze froze on the scented smoke rising from a small tuna tin in the stone bowl, soft spot of Mother Earth, and he shivered.

The sage crackled a final time and the smoke withdrew from him. All he heard was the slight sound of Terra's and Pete's breathing enveloped by the larger sounds of the wind as the Earth, too, breathed in and out. A great sadness filled him and, unable to stop himself, he sobbed as the smoke withdrew and left him.

Terra hurried over and squatted beside him. She rested her hand on his shoulder and said, "It's okay, Jed. It is exactly okay. It's hard to be a man. You had to take it all into yourself before you could cleanse this place. Thank you. And Mother Earth is pleased, too. You do have a mother, Jed. Never, ever, ever forget that."

Terra's words felt like cooling salve on a burn. The sob dissolved in his throat as he brought his eyes up to meet hers.

She nodded, took her hand away from his shoulder and stood. "Good. Now for the next thing—and I expect this will take longer—so listen carefully. Out there on the land are several helpers we'll need to collect in order to continue with our ceremony. These helpers might take the form of rocks or sticks or pinecones, maybe a plant or a bit of glass. It doesn't matter. You'll know what to collect because they'll tell you. Just walk around as if you were hunting for shiny pennies or pretty rocks, and then bring back whatever says it wants to come with you."

The cleansing smoke had carried the humming and buzzing off and Jed's head cleared. Pete looked at Terra intently, listening as if his life depended upon it. Pete feels it, too, Jed thought—the big thing. They looked at her and waited for further instruction.

She gave them both a gentle shove. "No, I'm not going to say another word. I'll explain later. Just go. Listen within yourself. You'll know. I have to get ready here." She smiled at Pete and at Jed and said, "What are you waiting for? Go."

"Come on, Pete," Jed said, turning away from Terra and starting back down the path.

When they were a few yards down the trail, Pete said, "What's she doing, Jed?"

109

"I don't know. But she knew where to go, didn't she?"

Pete nodded, his serious eyes trained on Jed.

He looked at his little brother and said, "She knew where to go. She knew how to do the ceremony. I say let's do what she tells us and see what happens next."

"Yeah, okay. But I don't know what she means about picking up stuff. What's going to tell us what?" As the last words tumbled out of Pete's mouth, he stopped and stood still, staring off to his right at a little pile of rocks sitting all together like they were holding their own council meeting.

Pete marched straight over to the rocks and picked one up. He didn't hesitate, didn't sort them around, just plucked a rock up and carried it back and said, "Here's one."

"Sheesh, Pete. How do you know that's one? One second you say you don't know what she means and then you pick up that rock and say, 'Here's one'? What's up with you?"

Pete grinned. "Gosh, Jed. You don't need to be getting mad at me just because I found the first one."

Jed took the rock. It was dust-bone white, shaped almost like a tiny scull only flat. He had an urge to lick it. Weird, he thought. Sure, he could see a small head in the rock, a nose and a jaw. As he held it, the rock turned hot in his hand, so hot he finally shoved it back into Pete's hands. His heart thumped crazily in his chest. "Okay, so maybe it is one. It must be. She said we'd know. But she didn't say how many, so we better get started. Why don't you take the path down into the draw, and I'll go up that hill. Yell if you want me."

Terra felt a little like she imagined Jed must have felt when he did the sage ceremony. She wanted to flop down on the earth and let the tears come. She felt like a robot with someone else at the controls. Her body was moving, her mouth was talking strange talk; and yet she felt as if she were sitting in a back row watching it all unfold. If only I could remember, she thought. I must have had a life

110

before this moment, before these boys . . . before that man down the hill. Who am I? She desperately probed her mind for anything, any little tidbit that would put some reason behind her actions this morning.

She sat down, crossed her legs, and closed her eyes. An almost hysterical giggle formed in her mouth—I don't even know if I know how to pray, she thought. What a carnival this was, to be thrust into the middle of big events and not know the occasion. "Focus," she whispered. An image grew in her mind of a grassy hillside, not this one but another; and standing with her was a beautiful woman dressed all in red. The woman sat down and motioned to Terra to sit down beside her. She did. No words were exchanged, but the woman waved an arm to indicate the entire long view from their hillside. In her mind, Terra heard the same words she had just said to the boys, "Do you trust me?" And like Jed and Pete, she simply nodded her head, and just as quickly as it had come, the image evaporated and Terra was again sitting before a dead fire waiting for the two boys to return with their gifts.

While she waited, she thought about John Forrest. Yesterday, when he had said she must have a husband or someone looking for her, it was on the tip of her tongue to say no, you are my husband. And last night, when he had pulled her roughly into his arms, she hadn't wanted him to let go. She had wanted him to tuck her inside of that frozen heart until it melted. It was as if she had slipped into the spot Mae Jo had vacated—but that didn't make any sense at all. She was not Lakota, not the mother of those two boys. In fact, she was a stranger even to herself.

Do you trust me? The words floated back through her mind; she smiled and said aloud, "I don't seem to have much choice but to trust."

There is always a choice.

Terra heard the words but could not discern where they had come from. Choice. If she could choose right now, it would be that John not call the authorities and turn her in as if she were some vagrant. I want to stay, she said silently to whoever it was that had spoken. I want to stay.

111

For the next half-hour Jed walked up and down the dusty-white bluffs waiting to see what wanted to come with him, as Terra had said. All around there was a peculiar stillness. How did the birds know not to make a single sound, he wondered. And how did he know just what to pick up? He'd walk along slowly, following his feet, watching the ground—and there they were. They didn't speak, not with words—and yet he knew. Even the dark piece of glass still wearing a mucky, old Budweiser label wanted to come along. He even caught himself talking to the stupid piece of glass saying, "No, she doesn't want you. You're nothing but an old busted up bottle." But still, the little chunk of glass was riding in his pocket along with the other stones and cones and weird stuff.

The last thing he found was a spiky flower pod. He didn't push it into his pocket because it seemed too fragile. For some reason the ugly, dead plant made him feel tender and generous—even sad—so he carried it carefully upright, the stem firm between his thumb and forefinger.

When he got back, Pete was already in the stone bowl with Terra, proudly laying out all of his found objects, soaking up her praise and admiration for what he'd gathered. Pete was holding up an old chrome hubcap, dangling it like a shield. He looked like a midget warrior. Jed couldn't help it, he laughed. "Cripes, Pete. A hubcap?"

Terra giggled.

Pete grinned foolishly, clutching his prize. "I don't know, Jed. It wanted to come along to see what was going to happen here."

Still laughing, she took the old hubcap from Pete and laid it right smack over the black charred remains of last night's mystery fire. "Leave him be, Jed. He did just right. Now show me what you have."

Her face was like a bright light turned on his little brother, and Jed suddenly felt angry and jealous. He resisted an urge to turn and walk off in the other direction. Instead, he reached his free hand into his pocket and took out the things he'd found. She took them but stood staring

112

at the poor scrubby weed in his hand with a soft, girlish look on her face. He suddenly felt shy and dumb. She didn't say a word but gently pulled the little stem from between his fingers and brought the scratchy pod to her cheek and held it there for a moment. He was surprised to see tears gather in her eyes.

"Oh, Jed, she's perfect. Beautiful." Then she bent down and gently placed the spiky pod in the very middle of Pete's hubcap.

A place of honor, Jed thought, feeling pleased. Then he thought, I probably look as stupid as Pete with his hubcap. Everything was upside down, but who cares?

Terra quickly gathered the pile of stones and cones and bones and the bit of brown broken glass, smoothing out the mucky label. When all the objects were gathered into a little mound near the hubcap, she began selecting and arranging the objects, fingering each one for a moment, and then placing them evenly around the hub, leaving at least a few inches between the metal rim and each carefully placed object. When she was finished, she reached into her pocket and took a small pink stone and stuck it right on the edge of the center hole of the hubcap.

Pete squatted and whispered, "What are you doing, Terra?"

"Shh. Wait a second and I'll explain." She was quiet, intent upon her task, and, once again, a silence like none Jed had ever noticed wrapped around them. It felt like if he reached his hand out six inches away it would run into web and paper, like a cocoon sucking in all the sound. When finally the circle and all its distant points were completed, Terra sat down facing the south, motioning for them to sit on either side of her. They complied, saying nothing, just waiting in the hushed world.

"Terra?" Pete whispered. "I have to pee."

She laughed. The sound shattered the silence and Jed felt like he could finally breathe again. She said, "Go, Pete, and do what you have to do but hurry back. I have something very important to explain to both of you now."

Pete scurried off behind the rocks. Terra held her sides, still laughing, until Jed couldn't help but chuckle, too.

When she caught her breath, she said, "Your little brother, Jed, he is a jewel among men. You, too. You both got shine that just don't quit."

To his surprise, Terra leaned over and planted a kiss, plop, on his left cheek. Before he even had time to realize what she'd done, Pete was back sitting on her left waiting, all ears, for her promised explanations of the strange circle planted before them.

Terra spoke. "Yesterday, when you found me down in the wash, I could not for the life of me recall what I was doing there or how I got there. It was like I was just waiting. And then I realized I had been waiting for you, and everything was just right."

Pete said, "Yeah, it's like you never were anywhere else but with us, right?"

She bobbed her head at Pete and continued. "And then, last night, it was the strangest thing. I sat out on the steps under the moonlight and I understood. Then I heard a drum beating late, late in the night, and somehow I knew what we were supposed to do next."

Jed held his breath, anxious for her to go on.

"Yes, as soon as I heard that old drum beating, I knew what we had to do." Terra said. "And after Jed smudged with the sage, I saw more of it."

"What, Ter? What did you see?" Pete asked. He scratched his nose and leaned closer.

"Shush, Pete, so she can tell us." Jed thought she was going to explain about those old fire builders sitting in the stone bowl . . . and about his mother.

Instead, Terra had a whole different tale to tell.

Chapter 14

John stared down at his small stack of mini DV and DAT tapes. For the past hour he'd been shuffling notes and tape logs, but his mind was anywhere but on the reunion. After the crew had left for their picnic, it was all he could do not to jump in the truck and return to the bit of desert where Jed and Pete had found Terra. He needed something to go on, some bit of evidence—a discarded purse, tire tracks, a water bottle—anything that made some kind of logical sense, but he didn't have time to go back there, and he didn't want to leave his boys with a stranger—not under these circumstances. He was so damned restless he felt like Pete. He stood up and paced the limited length of the 55-foot trailer trying to identify the source of the raw, bleeding restlessness. He knew what he *should* do.

There is the phone. Pick it up, damn it. Call somebody and report that you found a body in the Badlands. Well, not a body exactly—a woman—a living, breathing woman. He wasn't sure if he should call the reservation police, the Rapid City police, or the state police. He went into the kitchen, picked up the phone, slammed it down again, and went back into the living room.

This is bull, he admitted to himself. Not knowing who to call has nothing to do with why you haven't called anyone yet. The truth was, he didn't want to find out that she was some schizophrenic off her meds—or that she had been dumped there by a disgruntled boyfriend. He didn't want to find out that she was . . . what?

Who the hell is she? The moment the boys had topped the rise tugging the strange woman along, his life had begun to flip over. He'd even admitted to Jed that it was like he had been missing an arm and the arm was back. Damn, none of it made any sense. Not the scent of forest, or the ripe feeling in his belly . . . or yes, admit it, the desire he felt for her. Am I falling for this stranger, he wondered, a woman I've known only twenty-four hours, a woman suffering from amnesia?

It was illusion—all illusion—like the Badlands, a pocked and rippling land that appeared to be solid stone, older than God, until you strutted out to test the truth of nature. In reality, it was nothing but dust and white clay powder. Anybody with a big enough baseball bat could level those rifts. Dust, all dust. Nothing new there, he thought. Love is dust, land is dust, and memory most certainly is dust. He moved toward the phone and then smiled to himself, realizing he knew how to report a missing person—but he had no idea how to report a found person.

Forcing himself to focus, he returned to the stack of tapes and began logging his interviews. He worked for a half an hour, and then he remembered the smaller Sony camera he'd had aimed at Terra when Carol pointed out the odd special effects. He sorted the tapes, found the one he was looking for, and popped it into the small Sony, the little traveler, and plugged it into the television. He clicked play. He'd not used that camera for anything but the remaining dance after he'd stowed the big camera in the truck. He shook his head in disgust when he saw his fingers were trembling on the remote. Man, I need a life, he thought, but he watched as the film showed Terra dancing amidst the crowd, the shawl dancing around her like the wind. God—she was so alive. He peered closely at the screen wishing he could close out all the light in the trailer. He looked again but saw no luminous orbs dancing above her head or around her body. Nothing. He unplugged the hookup to the television and replayed the bit of film, peering closely at the matchbook-sized screen.

116

Nothing. He clicked the off button suddenly angry at himself for buying into the smoke and mirrors once again.

He went to the kitchen and pulled open the fridge door feeling like Jed, meditating on emptiness with no idea of what he was hungering for. He slid into his shoes, intending to go find Terra and the boys. He tossed on his jacket and went out the door just in time to see Danny's black Chevy truck snaking its way up the drive. Maybe now he'd get some answers, he thought.

The truck stopped. Danny got out and extended a hand to him. "Well, white boy, how goes it?"

Danny always gave him a hard time about being white. Even though he had married into the tribe, he still felt like an outsider. "It goes well, Danny."

"Ha! The hell it does. That's why your face looks like rattling water."

John laughed. "Rattling water? Man, you missed your calling. You should have been a poet."

"What do you mean? I *am* a poet. Come on, John, I need a cup of your strongest brew. We need to do some serious talking. Strange things are about, my friend, some very strange things."

Inside the trailer they brewed a fresh pot of coffee. John smiled, thinking they were like rural wives—unwilling to open any conversation without the ritual brewing of some friendly dark drink. When at last they were planted across from one another at the table, Danny sipped from his mug and asked, "Where are the boys?"

"Out on the bluff showing Terra the sights. They packed a lunch and left an hour ago, whispering about some task they had to do. I was trying to work." He indicated the paper and tape mess scattered in front of the VCR.

Danny was silent for a moment and then said, "Ah, Terra, the mystery woman. We seem surrounded by mystery, my friend, starting with last night. Did you notice anything unusual at the gathering?"

"You mean besides the large crowd?" He was thinking about the orbs of light.

"Well, that, too, but something more. Remember how worried I was about another gathering focused on Wounded Knee? How I wanted to pull the focus away from the massacre and focus on the future—and not just our pain?"

"Sure, we talked about it the other day. I remember."

"I was determined to make this event not just another round of rehashing old history but a step in a new direction. I prayed about it. In fact," Danny laughed, patting his extra twenty pounds protectively, "I sweated so much in the last month—I was afraid I'd get skinny. The sweat lodge is better than Slim Fast, I always say."

John liked the way Danny draped his humor around this often screwed-up reservation life. The man was an odd blend of Harvard business graduate and homegrown Lakota.

"Anyway," Danny went on, "It didn't happen. That's what I mean about unusual."

"What didn't happen?"

"The bitching and complaining. In fact, I've never seen such a happy bunch of Indians in my life, at least not when two or more of them get together anyway. And there were several hundred, maybe more, yesterday. It was uncanny."

John couldn't help but laugh. He did a mental rewind of the day's unfolding, recalling the speeches, the Wounded Knee activists he'd interviewed, and the pow wow. "Okay, I get it. What do you make of it?"

"I don't know, buddy. At first, I didn't notice it—I was having such a good time." He laughed and then grew serious again. "But something about the whole day kept bugging me. I decided to ask the spirits what was happening, so, after the pow wow, I went over to Cuny Table to the sweat lodge behind my uncle's cabin."

He had seldom heard Danny talk in such long sentences. His face looked like Pete's, all wonder and awe.

Danny took a long sip of coffee. "I was alone in the sweat lodge. No heat, no steam, no sound, nothing. No cars, no birds, nothing. Just silence." He described the sensation of falling down the well and the expansive opening into the wide river of spirits and beings.

John listened, but part of him wanted to run straight out the door and not hear another word. His poor mind couldn't handle any more twirly bird twists of reality. "Go on," he said.

"The whole other world was there floating in this great river. Damn, it was incredible." Danny lowered his head; his voice dropped with it. "Man, the energy rushing through me—I thought I'd drown in it. And then I sensed my grandfather was near and I called out to him. Next thing I know, whoosh, I'm back in the sweat lodge and Grandfather is beside me."

John remembered Danny's grandfather, a full-blood Lakota with the biggest sense of humor he'd ever seen. He'd been dead for what? Ten years? "What did he say?"

"It was strange. At first I couldn't hear him, like my ears were stuffed with cotton. Grandfather scolded me for not listening deeply enough. Said it's a problem with all the people—they forget to listen. And they forget to act."

"What did he say?" John asked again, impatience humming in his body.

Danny smiled. "In a hurry are we? Like I said, rattling water. Grandfather told me that we are on the edge of a big event, on the edge of a third cleansing, and we need to listen with more than our ears."

"That's it? That's all he said?"

"Easy, John. I don't quite know how to interpret what he said. It was pretty cryptic, but he told me that we needed to prepare for a spring celebration like no other, that she was coming and bringing them all with her."

"She?"

"I have no idea what he meant, except that we need to trust her and go with the flow."

"Sounds like your grandfather—he did like to play with words. What else?" John felt like slamming his fist down on the table and demanding answers. Rivers of spiritual beings, luminous orbs, a dead grandfather sitting in a sweat lodge—my God it was like a Hitchcock movie

119

made in Lakota country—none of it made any sense. "This all sounds crazy," he said.

"It isn't crazy. And if you would crawl out of your armor for just five minutes you would know it, too. Something is going on, and we need to be aware."

"I'm sorry, Danny, but I don't talk to spirits—and they don't talk to me."

"Hah. Or maybe you just ain't listening, buddy." Danny took a deep breath. "Anyway, one minute Grandfather was there and then zap, he was gone." Leaning back in his chair, he folded his hands behind his head. He laughed at John. "Damn, but you can be a prickly son of a bitch. Come on. I have to get out of this tin can before I suffocate." He got up from the table and walked to the sink to rinse out his cup.

They left the trailer and walked down the drive to the cattle gate in silence. Finally Danny said, "My grandfather was a wild man, eccentric and unpredictable. Sometimes I'd come home from school, and the driveway would be bumper to bumper clunkers, the kitchen so full of people I had to go to the wood shed to do my homework. One day this guy came in bitching and complaining. Grandfather picked up a broken broom handle and bopped him. 'Be a man, George,' he said. 'Get out and don't come back until you can be a man.' The dude went slinking out the front door like a dog. I thought it was hilarious."

John thought of his own grandfather, a small-boned, quiet man who shuffled around his woodshop building furniture and carving chunks of wood. There had been no storytelling or teaching, just the older man beside him, but it had been enough. "What is really going on, Danny?" he asked finally.

"I wish I knew, buddy. I wish I knew," said Danny. "But I have to go with it, even if I don't understand it."

The dirt beneath their feet was dry and cracked. John thought of his bare feet rooting into the earth the night before. A sliver of envy pierced him once more—that the world Danny had traveled to was somehow closed to him.

120

When they reached the steps of the trailer, they went back inside, and John poured them each another cup. He was on the verge of asking what Danny thought about Terra when suddenly the screen door shot open.

Pete raced in breathless and flushed as if he'd run a long way. "Dad, Dad, it was so cool. We had a great picnic and we called them all to us. It was the coolest thing and Terra says there's going to be a mighty powerful celebration, a party even bigger than last night. Can we go, do you think?"

John and Danny stared, open-mouthed, at the childish rambling of the small boy. John planted his hands on Pete's shoulders and laughed. "Whoa, son. Slow down and take a breath. Yeah, that's right," he said, as Pete took a deep breath. "Now, what is this all about?"

"We went all around the bluff gathering stuff that talked, and things, and then . . ."

Jed tumbled in the door before Pete could finish. "Pete!" he said with a fierce look.

"She didn't say not to tell. Not really."

"She said not yet though, that things have to go slow."

"But Jed—"

"Shut up, Pete! Just shut up your mouth for one minute, will you?" Jed looked disgusted. "He's such a bubble head."

"Calm down, Jed. And don't call your brother names." John looked at Danny who was grinning like he'd just heard a great joke. Damn, the whole world had gone crazy. "Listen up, guys. Go and get packed. We have to leave soon. I've had about enough ghost stories for one morning."

Jed glared at Pete, straightened, and said, "We didn't do anything except play a stupid game. That's all. We went around and we picked up a lot of sticks and rocks and other junk, and then we pretended they were people. That's all. And we pretended all those people would come floating in on a giant river. And then we ate our tuna sandwiches and came home. Tell them, Pete."

He saw Danny's eyebrows curve up at the fierce tone of Jed's voice and his innocent revelations. His throw-away explanation, coupled with Pete's ramblings, was too eerily close to Danny's own vision the night before to be just the talk of a bubble-headed boy. "Where is Terra?" John asked.

Jed looked relieved to have the subject dropped. "Repacking the lunch things, I guess. She said to go on ahead of her, that she'd be down soon."

He hustled the boys off to the back bedroom to make sure they had packed everything. When they were gone, he said to Danny, who was grinning at him, "What the hell was that all about?"

"I'm telling you, buddy, we have to pay attention. I think I'll go have a chat with Terra if you don't mind."

"Go for it. I'm over my head here, Danny."

Jed jammed his sleeping shorts and other clothes into his backpack. He felt like punching it—or Pete. He was deeply superstitious and worried that if he hadn't shut Pete up right that minute, all the magic of the past twenty-four hours would pop and go flat like a balloon, and he'd never figure out what was going on. And without the magic, life would be just plain ordinary again.

Terra's long ceremony and her explanation up on the bluff had been like science fiction. All the stuff about birds and ducks and geese knowing in their hidden selves when it was time to gather and travel north, south, north again. And how, in the other world, the spirits were doing the same thing, gathering and traveling. How even boys and adults had a hidden self that would tell them things if they learned to listen deeply.

"Jed . . ." said Pete.

"Yeah, what?"

"I'm sorry. I wasn't going to tell about calling the spirits to us. I wasn't."

His anger at Pete drained away as if the wind came in the window and grabbed it out of him. He sat on the edge of the bottom bunk and looked at Pete. "It was something, wasn't it?"

"I don't know, Jed. I didn't know half of what she was talking about, but it was fun. Everything has been fun since we found Terra."

It made Jed ache a little inside to see his brother's bright face. Maybe Pete had lost more than he did when their mom died. He'd hardly gotten a chance to really know her. "You like Terra, don't you."

"Well, yeah . . . don't you?"

That was a hard question to answer. He did like her, but he couldn't get the image of the pretty Indian woman from last night out of his mind; somehow it felt like it wouldn't be right to like another woman—other than his mom. But he couldn't lie either. "Yeah. I do like her. She's kind of crazy, but nice. I can't help wondering where she came from."

Pete smiled. "I know where she came from."

"You do?"

"The Creator sent her to us."

"Oh, Pete. You really are a bubble head." He said it jokingly though, without any anger.

"Am not."

"Are too."

Danny left the trailer and headed straight up the path the boys had just come down. His feet, though a man's size twelve, still felt like a boy's size four when they hit this trail. He felt ten again, wandering out into the great, sunny mystery of the world. It was intoxicating, his senses pulling in grass, sun, pine, dust, sweat. The knowing feet took him straight to the stone bowl where he abruptly stopped and stared at the young, girlish-looking woman sitting so still and silent before the unusual wheel of objects.

Without so much as a hello, he sat down beside her, tucked his long legs easily beneath his body and said, "I can't remember a time when we didn't come to this place. My family has been on this land for over a hundred years. What a clan we were . . . and still are: cousins, uncles, brothers, sisters—and Grandfather." He paused, feeling the old man nearby, like last night in the sweat lodge. "So . . . how can I help?" He knew not what he offered or to whom, but the words dropped from his tongue like ripe berries.

"Hi, Danny." Terra sighed, and said, "Honestly? I'm not sure how you can help."

"What can you tell me?"

She told him, without hesitating, about all that had unfolded since the boys found her asleep in the Badlands, how strange and unfamiliar her body felt, how relieved she was to see those two boys, how each moment revealed some small clue, a piece linking like a chain to the one before it as if she were being pulled along one inch at a time.

Carol had told him about the luminous orbs floating above Terra the night before. He figured she was being guided, probably by the spirits. "Go on," he said, "I'm all ears."

She shook her head and sighed. "But I have no idea to what end. Where is this going? It's so frustrating. And John thinks I'm crazy or, worse yet, deceiving him somehow." She stretched a single finger out and drew small circles in the pale clay dust surrounding the hubcap medicine wheel. Then she looked up into his face. "The only clear memory I have is of a grandmother. I'm not even sure if it is a memory or a dream. In the memory she is crying, so very, very sad. I throw my arms around her and tell her I love her more than the sun and the moon put together. Then she gets up and starts wandering around, saying that I've given her the perfect solution. I had no idea what she was talking about."

Terra stood and began walking back and forth as if assuming the grandmother's role. "She rattled on and on about love and how humans can't resist their basic natures and how she intended to make them silly with love— foolish with love—until their dreary old hearts cracked open like coconuts, until earth was dripping with love. She

124

said love had the power to tame and soften even the hardest heart. That's it, all I can remember."

He smiled. Her grandmother sounded as eccentric (and wise) as his own grandfather with his broomstick teachings.

Terra sat down on the ground again beside him, pulled her knees up close to her chest and hugged them. "Earlier, I also saw a woman on a hillside. She was dressed in red and she said I should trust her and choose. I can't remember anything else of what must have been my whole lifetime. It's terrible. And I have no idea what to do next."

"Why don't you start by telling me about this circle here?"

"Oh, that. We already did that. Jed and Pete helped."

She was like a small child showing him a picture she'd drawn. The shapes and objects were perfectly clear to her, but his eyes didn't share the vision. "I realize that you already did *that*, but what exactly did you do?"

"Oh, we were just pulling the lovers out of the Great River, calling a circle."

Terra seemed oblivious of how odd she might sound to the disbelieving world, but by now Danny was beyond being surprised at the unusual events unfolding around them. Instead, he slid naturally into the kind of trance he used in prayer. He thought of the river. He'd never heard of the Great River before last night when he took his own little swim in it. "You pulled the lovers out?"

"That's right. We called all the lovers of life, of men and women and children, the lovers of ideas, animals, birds, Earth—anyone tied by the silver cord to the heart. It was the old ones' idea to help. So the boys and I were calling them out of the River."

Danny burst out laughing. He felt as if he'd been too polite to scratch the itch; but suddenly the itch was all there was. He laughed until tears pooled in his eyes and his belly ached. "Girl, you are either a complete psycho or you're telling me the tale of the century. And what is most unbelievable is that . . . I believe you." He stood and paced around her ceremonial circle noticing the hubcap. The laughter felt good in his belly. "I will certainly help you in any way that I can. Damn, if this don't beat all . . . come on, we better get back to the trailer before Grandmother catches us slacking off."

He got up, took Terra's hand, and helped her to her feet. She looked down at the circle, and he said, "Leave them. I like them right where they are for now."

Terra went back down the path from the Stone Bowl walking in front of him. He watched her choose each step with intention, not once crushing a tiny plant or overturning a stone. The Great River. Terra's innocent words framed his hazy vision of the night before. He saw the picture now as clearly as if it were hanging on his wall back at the trailer. Sure, it lacked detail and cohesion, but damn, it was the prettiest picture he'd ever seen. It linked up perfectly with the paralyzing dreams he'd had, the overwhelming sense of dread, his grandfather's report. Help had arrived.

The sun was already topping the sky and moving west when he and Terra walked up to the trailer. John was sitting on the stoop with his elbows planted on his thighs looking lost. Time to knock the foundation right out from under my good friend, Danny thought. May as well topple him once and for all. Since Mae Jo's death, he'd tried to get John to rejoin the human race but without much luck. Now—he may not have a choice. Danny walked over and, with the tip of his boot, knocked John's elbows off his knees.

"Son of a . . . " said John, recovering his balance.

"No shit. Hoka hey, my friend. It is a great day." He turned to Terra and said, "Why don't you go see what Skid and the scamps are doing. I need to have a word with my friend John." He intentionally made it sound like the nursery rhyme—deedle, deedle dumpling, my son John. Getting as witty as my grandfather, he thought. All I need is a broom-stick to wave around.

Terra took Danny's hand and shook it gently. "Thanks. I appreciate your help." She turned and disappeared into the trailer.

He turned back to John and said, "Walk with me, buddy."

"Sure. I'm ripe with curiosity," John said sarcastically.

Danny strode off toward the skeletal frame of the sweat lodge and chose a stump to sit on. It was a wide, cottonwood stump dragged from the Cheyenne River bottoms and deposited here. He liked it better than any plump, overstuffed easy chair anywhere. "Someday I'm going to turn this friendly old stump into a drum," he said, patting the wood. He'd built several drums during the last decade and loved the painstaking process of infusing the ancient wood with sound and rhythm and spirit, a true labor of love. Most drum groups these days opted for the convenience of the metal-framed bass drum, but something was definitely lost in the translation. The drum, in Indian country, in all ancient cultures, was the heart of that culture.

John didn't speak. He looked madder than a hornet but chose a second stump closer to the fire pit used to heat the rocks for the sweats.

Danny grinned. "You should see your face. If looks could kill, I'd be a dead man. Tell me what you know about your Terra?"

"She is not my Terra," John said.

"Easy, boy."

"I'm glad you're having such a hell of a good time."

"Stuff it, John. So she's a real mystery lady, huh? But how do you feel about her? Surely you must have some impressions after a day and a half."

"What is this? True confessions time?"

"Go ahead, John. Shock me."

"As if I could." John looked at him and then said slowly, "When they first walked up to my truck . . . I smelled a green, wet forest."

"What?"

"You asked. That was the first impression before the boys even topped the rise with her. Ever since, my mind has been all over the map. I've thought of Mae Jo, of the boys, of green forests and water and . . . bare skin and bare

127

feet. And I'm thinking of Terra." He said the final word as if it were a death sentence.

"Ha. That doesn't surprise me. How long has it been since you were with a woman, Mr. Martyr? Three years?"

"Longer. After Mae Jo was pregnant with Pete, she seemed to pull into herself. I couldn't get her to come back out. We never made love again after Pete was born."

He watched John descend again into the dark place that had captured his spirit since his wife died. He said nothing, just waited.

John looked at him. "What the hell does this have to do with anything?"

"It matters."

"No, it doesn't. The boys and I are doing fine."

"Sure, you and your boys—the three musketeers. You are a good father, John, but those boys need more than you're giving them. You've stuffed them in the same closet that you've closed yourself in. It's bad for them."

"Give me a break, man. It's only been three years since she died."

"Three years is a long time to a child. Besides, I can't give you a break," he said quietly. "We may not have time."

"What do you mean we may not have time? Time for what? Damn it, just tell me what is going on. My kids follow that woman around like puppies. For a split second last night at the pow wow I saw the three of them together and thought she was their mother. Christ, I wanted to fall at her feet and thank her. She makes me feel sixteen and so fully alive I'm afraid to stand up. Five minutes later, I want to thrash her or call the authorities and have her hauled away."

"Ha, so she does get a rise out of you . . . so to speak. Somehow that doesn't surprise me."

"Quit screwing around, Danny. What do you know?"

"An excellent question, my friend. I'm not sure how you'll react to my theory. I mean, we're talking high fiction, sci-fi, best picture of the year. We're talking fantasy of the most real variety. You won't believe me if I tell you."

"You sound like Pete. Spit it out before I have to thrash you."

Danny stood up, stretched, and tugged on his braid. "Shee-it, man." He imitated Jed and Pete's favorite cuss word, and turned to John. "Okay. I think she's Grandmother Earth. *Unci Makah.*"

"Oh right. Grandmother Earth?" John laughed aloud. "Good God, man, I think you've been dancing with the tooth fairy, smoking that good prairie grass maybe."

"Well, not Grandmother Earth, exactly, but sent by her. A granddaughter, maybe."

"You're serious? You really are serious about this?" John stood up and faced him."

"I told you, sci-fi of the most real variety."

"Let me be sure I get this straight. You think Terra was sent by Grandmother Earth? You're cracking up, man. What's the game, Danny?"

He got serious for the first time since they started this crazy conversation. "No game, friend. I'm telling you true—the spirits are involved in this strange appearance of your friend Terra. I think she was sent by *Makah* to do a little job for that great lady."

"Of all the lame-brained crazy, things I've ever heard. She can't be from Grandmother Earth. The world doesn't work like that . . . like myth or legend or Disneyland, Danny. And besides . . . she . . . she's white."

Something about John's perplexed, exasperated face, his incredulous disbelief that an emissary of Grandmother Earth could be white, was hilarious. Danny laughed so hard he had to hold his aching sides.

John, as though suddenly realizing what he'd just said, also burst into laughter, kicked Danny's stump and tipped it, dumping him to the ground. Danny grabbed John's foot and dragged him down. Soon they were rolling in the dust, tossing each other around like schoolboys on a playground.

At last Danny rested his back against the earth and looked at the blue sky above them. Man, but it felt good to cut it all loose, to see John rolling in the dust, laughing like a kid. "John?"

"Yeah?"

"Nothing." Whatever he had been about to say evaporated. There were no words to describe the last hour—the last day—without sounding crazy. Everything was suddenly reduced to its most ridiculous form.

Chapter 15

Agnes was once again sitting on the porch of the Cuny Café. The sky was studded with clouds and the air shimmered like gray silk. She wished Bill Elk Boy would come back. She needed to talk to him. A cycle is closing on earth now. She felt it.

In the early days, she'd expected to marry Bill, have his babies, and live a good Lakota life hanging wash on a clothesline, growing vegetables out behind his cabin, resting her weary body beside his each night. But the Creator had had other plans for them. There had been no babies—well, except the little one who couldn't stay. And there had been no marriage. The spirits had told Bill they would need him—all of him—for the work ahead. And Bill had listened. They also needed Agnes.

She'd had her first vision when she was twenty. She and Bill were in a tent at one of the village pow wows. It was late summer. The night had been ripe, like this one, perhaps more so because it was summer. She was young and in love and hadn't expected what came. Bill had made sweet, sweet love to her body and to her spirit, and then something unseen, like a shadow, had entered the tent and snatched her soul. One minute she had been splendidly close to sleep, floating on a cloud of lover's relief, and the next she was in another place.

A beautiful old woman with white hair and white buckskin was beside her, and they were sitting on a bluff above the village. Below she saw the pow wow, the people milling around, their tent . . . and she saw a young woman in her lover's arms. She was Agnes—but not Agnes.

131

"Where are we?" she'd asked the woman. "What has happened?"

The woman said, "Just watch." Then she disappeared.

And Agnes did. Watch. That had been the beginning.

Never again had she fully entered the body of the young woman she had been. Instead, all her life she'd been forced to view herself and others from this high bluff above the mundane rituals of daily life.

How strange, to live your life in a human body but to feel your spirit constantly above watching—and how difficult it had been to feel that little one begin to grow within her and then, just as quickly, gone.

Much later, when she'd explained it to Bill, he had taken her again in his arms and explained how he experienced his life the same detached way, as though watching his body. "We don't know what the Creator has in mind for us, my love. And so we will make ourselves ready."

A year later, she'd opened the Cuny Café and let that be the false front of her spiritual activities. She fed their bodies—and she fed their souls as well.

Instead of resisting what had happened, she and Bill crafted a life around what the Creator asked of them—and the Creator asked a lot. It was often painful to watch the actions below with the eye of one above. Only rarely could she influence the outcome with a story—or a cup of tea. For decades they had ministered to the people, stealing only the late nights for each other. Her one regret was that she'd born no living child from this body. To ease the pain she considered Danny as her son—and that would have to be enough.

That, too, had been part of the Creator's request, taking care of Danny. That task had not been hard—to nourish that boy, to see him grow tall and strong, to see him become a leader to his people was all she wanted.

And Terra, the young woman Bill had pointed out to her the night before, the one who arrived from nowhere just as she had seen in her vision. She would take her as daughter when this time was done.

And Bill. She was suddenly filled with a feeling of thanksgiving, of *Wopila*, that the Creator had given her this difficult life—but had not asked her to walk it alone. When Bill had taken Danny into his house, both of their lives had been about preparing for this potent moment. And now it was here.

I must be getting old and maudlin, she thought. I imagine myself to be the fairy godmother, the one who turns pumpkins into coaches, rats into footmen, ordinary humans into great beings. In truth, I only work for the grand woman, the grandmother, *Unci Makah*.

We certainly need her help now.

Agnes got up, went into her back bedroom, got the grandmother pipe and took it out of its bag. Except for the bowl, it looked more like a flute than a pipe. There were small notches placed where holes would be in a flute. Otherwise, the wood was smooth and polished as though a thousand hands had prayed with it. It had been polished with prayer. She touched the pipe to her forehead and slipped it back into the bag. From her closet she took out a small duffle bag and put in a warm sweater and a couple of bottles of water. Back out front, she jotted a note to Danny and taped it to the front door of the Café. She did not lock the door. She had never locked the door.

It was time to go.

Chapter 16

After Danny headed back in the direction of the trailer, John sat back down on the cottonwood stump to think. Wrestling with Danny had recharged his dead battery. He felt better; but his mind was all over the place, tumbling like a load of laundry.

It was ironic that the first woman to catch his interest in over three years would turn out to be, he couldn't even bring himself to say it, some Badlands sprite, a diva materialized out of a puff of smoke who would, most likely, disappear just as quickly. Talk about bad luck with women.

But last night under a pale, slivered moon, he'd felt so alive. And watching his two sons dance to her hidden, feminine melodies only made the ache more acute. His sons needed a woman, a mother. He needed a woman—a wife—but he didn't need this woman. He didn't know what to think of Danny's proclamation. Terra, an ambassador from the other realm? Unbelievable.

It was time to head for town but he couldn't move. He felt fused to the woody stump and wished he had a cup of Agnes's tea to clear his head. A few minutes later he heard truck doors slamming and a vehicle drive off. Then he smelled deep woods, pine needles composting, leaves wet with rain.

He looked up. Terra came around the end of the trailer and walked toward him. The urge to run was powerful, but he didn't know if it should be toward her— or away. He sat on the stump. She even looks like a wisp of smoke, he thought, her pale, shoulder-length hair swinging as she walked, her whole being no more substantial than dust or clouds.

She sat down on Danny's stump and said, "Hi."

"Where is Danny off to?" asked John.

"He said to tell you the scamps were anxious to get going, so he loaded their stuff and headed back to town. Said he had some things to do and they could help. Said he'd be at your house around 6:00 this evening. For supper."

He smiled. "That man is always planning ahead—to his next meal." He also knew Danny had conveniently arranged to heist his boys and force him to face the woman alone. Traitor.

Terra curled her body over her knees and looked at him. "Your boys are great. So is Danny. What are you doing?"

"Thinking." He didn't mean the words to sound so brusque. He stared straight ahead pretending to follow the dusty trail left by Danny's truck.

"Thinking? Or brooding?" she asked.

"What's the difference?"

"Big difference. I need to know what you think about Danny's theory," she said.

"It doesn't matter what I think."

"Stop being such a victim, John. You walk around as if your clothing is lined with lead. Thinking is half your problem."

"Don't dissect me. I mean, what are we talking about here with this big mysterious event? Are we talking Armageddon, a day of reckoning, a natural disaster?"

"Lighten up, John."

She sounded like Pete, and the idea that his youngest son was rubbing off on the mystery woman lightened his mood. Pete had a knack for lifting any mood.

Terra went on talking. "Do you always have such a bleak world view? Expecting only the bad? Do I look like a tornado? Or an earthquake? Come on."

He suddenly saw himself through her eyes, a thirty-nine year old man with a bad attitude. "Sorry. Sometimes life sucks."

"I'm not sure you'd know a good thing if it broadsided you."

"What the hell do you want from me?"

"How about, for starters, I need your trust and your help. And . . . ," she hesitated, "I need your boys."

Her words awakened something wild and catlike in him. "Leave my boys out of this circus."

"I can't."

"What do you mean you can't?"

"We need their pipes. They're like brand new pipes. When you peer inside, they shine with a kind of innocence and wonder. Don't you see? They shine with all the qualities adults have lost. Those are the qualities we need. Danny told me about meeting his grandfather, his idea that we are supposed to work with the spirits here to bring about a change. If we hope to pipe that kind of change into the world, we have to start with clean conduit. That's Pete. And Jed."

It was dark, this thing grabbing him, this terrible fear. "Those boys are my life, Terra." He said it and then let the words hang in the air between them. "I can't risk it."

She was quiet, staring at him, her eyes wide and unblinking. "That is a lot to put on the shoulders of two young boys. You ask them for more than I do."

He hated this twisted tangle of grief and fear, and regret—and yes, guilt. Those boys deserved not to have to be anything for him. He hadn't seen it before she said it. Those boys are my life. Those were the words he'd used. Not much of a life if you have to live it through two children.

The silence around them grew. He raised his head and saw the white bluffs behind them, the dark ridge of pine and the more distant hillsides that had burned in a fire a few years ago. The dead, charred trees looked like stick men living dry and twisted lives. Like his. He hated this view of his life but wasn't sure what to replace it with.

137

Finally, he admitted, "I can't wrap my mind around this spiritual stuff. I don't have a clue what's going on. I don't even know if there is a God or Creator or whatever name people give to the unknown."

"Nor do I, John. Nor do I."

He stared at her and could see that she was not playing a game here.

"It's true. I'm just conduit, too," she said. "So are you. I'm not sitting here with some blueprint for social change tucked into my pocket, ready to whip it out on the table and explain it. I'm like you—moving by gut instinct, feeling my way into things. You think you're confused?" She stood and walked a circle around the fire pit. "Try this one. Try waking up in a sandy bed in the middle of nowhere with two beautiful, brown-eyed Indian boys staring at you as if you were a lizard, with no idea what happened or what is about to happen. That's confusion. And then to have to fight against a wall of resistance offered by some bullheaded . . . man."

Her voice rose at the end. It was the closest he'd seen her come to anger. A vivid color painted her cheeks and her lower lip quivered.

She went on, her voice rising. "But you're so busy worrying about what you stand to lose—how to protect your limited territory of pain and self-pity—you can't see the suffering of any other person."

Clobbered. He felt clobbered by the truth. Images of Danny's grandfather and his broomstick lurched into his mind. He deserved to be clubbed. He silently added that to the list of his own flaws.

Had he given a single thought to her, to the woman who woke up in the Badlands with not a clue about who she is? Had he wondered at all what she must be feeling or thinking? She was right. He'd thought only of his own little territory. He looked at her now and liked the fire in her eyes and the fierce, determined look on her face as she stood there, hands on her hips. And he liked the pale hair, and the fact that, when she danced, luminous orbs danced with her. He liked the way she was with Jed and Pete. He

138

liked the ear lobes peeking out from beneath her hair. He liked her short fingers with their neatly trimmed nails. He liked that dip where her bones came together just below her throat. And he liked what was below. He really liked that.

He shook his head to divert the direction of his thoughts. For the first time since they began talking, he laughed. "Okay, you're right. I haven't been exactly helpful. So, we're on a mission? But how are we supposed to plan something when we have no idea what that something might be?"

Moments passed. Terra walked ten paces away and then came back and stood before him looking somewhat relieved. She said, "That puzzles me, too, except that it seems to be working. I seem to know what's next although, if I push too hard, the whole plan, if it could be called that, collapses around me." She sat down on another stump nearby.

The background and foreground around Terra disappeared, and he saw only her form. Damn, he thought, I want her. I want her head on my pillow, her feet walking beside my feet, her hand on Pete's head. He felt as if he was admitting to some crime, so long had he held his stony distance from life. He took a slow breath and said, "So, what does this moment dictate?"

He was suddenly swamped again with moist forest smells and tenderness and wanted to pull her onto his lap and kiss her. He felt like a lion stretched out in a sunny jungle meadow, all instinct and impulse. He stared at this stranger who had landed like a meteorite in the midst of their lives.

Terra watched him.

He felt his cheeks flush and his belly tighten.

She placed a finger on the small "vee" of his upper lip and traced his mouth. She slid off the stump and knelt in front of him and then leaned forward and kissed him softly, experimentally, like a girl kissing a boy for the very first time.

139

She said, "I've wanted to do that since the first time I saw you standing beside your truck looking so stern and fierce. I wanted to do that last night when you refused to remove your shoes. I've wanted to do that for at least ten thousand years."

"What are you doing?"

She smiled. "The next thing. This is the next thing I'm supposed to do."

Sensual energy flooded his being. He wanted, for once, not to let life move him any further than this early afternoon with the offspring of Earth herself before him. He wanted to stop time, stop memory and pain, stop thinking. He wanted only to stretch out on a sandy bluff and let the sun reach to the very bone of his being.

She pulled away from him and stood up. "Walk with me. Please?"

He stood up and followed her as she turned and walked toward the bluffs behind the trailer. His mind was vibrating from the twists and turns of the past few minutes. A lingering, stubborn part of him had no desire to go further with this wisp of a woman, yet another part couldn't resist the tug and pull of her. He felt stoned and lazy, thinking of cool mountain pools and smooth skin and sun-baked bodies. What the hell am I doing, he wondered.

Terra stopped on a small flat plate of land about half way up to the stone bowl. Her head was light and fuzzy. She felt John behind her like a wave of energy threatening to flood her. His need was great. So was hers. But she couldn't shake the feeling that each step ahead was being carefully choreographed.

Am I crazy, she wondered. What am I doing? Her moments of certainty were followed by blank uncertainty. She felt like flinging herself to the ground and weeping. Instead, she closed her eyes and steadied her breathing.

"Terra? What are you doing?"

"Shhh." She withdrew all attention from John, from her own body, and let the silence seep into her like water from a hidden spring. A moment passed and then many moments. She felt the outline of her body dissipate, blurring into something wider, greater than her physical being. Tears leaked out the corners of her eyes and ran down her cheeks until she tasted the salty, wetness of her own tears.

When she opened her eyes again, John stood beside her. He'd taken her hand and was holding it firmly in his own. She smiled at the sight of her pale hand wrapped in his. With hardly a shift, she leaned into his body. "It's about love, John. That's all I know. Whatever we are supposed to do or learn right now—it is about love."

He said nothing.

She went on, her voice a mere whisper. "Not sex or the meager love most of us know but a bigger love, a greater love, a love that stops time and turns it on its axis. Am I making any sense at all? You must think I'm a nut."

"No. I think I love you."

She looked at the emotions playing across his face, a man at war with his own soul. "No, you don't." She shook her head and held his hand more tightly. "When we love out of fear, John, that's fear not love. When we love out of need or desire that is only need or desire. Not love. Don't you see?" She could tell he didn't see.

He said, "Sometimes love is expensive, Terra. I loved Mae Jo. It cost me a lot. Cost my boys a lot."

"Don't do that, John. You wouldn't have those boys if not for that love. It cost you nothing and gave you everything. If more people on earth discovered great love, it would change the world."

She thought a moment and said. "Even if you love out of instinct, like you love your boys, it's still instinct, not love. Don't you see? Great love has its own greatness embedded within it. That's what we need to discover. What is great love? Love for its own sake." She again pulled away and turned back to the path. "I want to show you what we did."

"Terra, wait."

She turned and looked at him.

"I would like that," he said.

141

"What?"

"To love again, to trust again, to give my boys a mother again. But damn, it's hard." He paused. "I'm afraid. Afraid you'll disappear the same way you appeared. Poof, gone."

"See what I mean? That's fear, not love. Great love can't be lost, John. Great love is not in the one who is loved—but in the lover. It would be in you. Come on. I'll show you some of the great lovers."

John had not walked up this slope for many years. Instead he tended to bury his head in work and bills and getting along and caring for the boys and not bothering to probe his own ignored sense of wonder and curiosity about the world. At least the work got him out of his truck and into the nooks and crannies of the earth's most remote and beautiful places.

Terra took him to the stone bowl and showed him the swirling wheel of objects the boys had collected. She said nothing about how they had come to choose each one, and he didn't ask the question. They were strangely beautiful, like found art. He saw the old discarded hubcap and thought of Stonehenge and ancient rock altars. He saw the glint of brown glass and thought of spectacles and prophets and seers of the future. He desperately wanted to peer into that piece of broken glass as if it were able to tell the future. He saw the dried, fragile plant placed carefully across the center with the bit of pink quartz looking precariously close to the center hole of the hubcap, and he thought of Mae Jo.

John reached deep into the pocket of his jeans and pulled out the rough chunk of rose quartz that he'd carried with him for over a year. He'd picked it up one day at the base of Harney Peak while hiking—while trying to outdistance his own loneliness. He'd paused to catch his breath when suddenly the small stone, like a pink lady, had danced off a stony ledge and landed at his feet. At the time, he'd even imagined a girlish voice begging him to take her along, assuring him that he would not be alone

142

forever. The foolish fantasy had only deepened his loneliness.

Rubbing the stone a last time, he chose a spot outside the circumference of arranged objects and laid it down. When he stood back, it looked as if the pink stone had lined up with the other objects like hands on a clock or like the pointer on a compass, a life finder, a directional stone—and it was pointing at Terra.

She blushed, tipped her head slightly, and smiled.

His heart thumped and chugged in the thick sludge of his chest. His body stirred even more strongly with a desire he'd not felt for a long, long time.

Chapter 17

Jed stared at Danny. They were in his black Chevy truck driving toward Rapid City. He and Pete called the truck "the beast." Today, he thought Danny looked like a warrior riding the beast. When Danny had told them to grab their gear and get in the truck, he'd felt torn between leaving and staying, afraid he'd miss something either way. Danny hadn't given him a choice. He just said, "Trust me, Jed. I need your help."

Ten miles down the road, Pete, sitting between them, rolled over and fell asleep in his lap. Jed felt old and fatherly holding his little brother while he slept. Outside the window, the land changed from rolling hills to the harsh cutaways of the Badlands. This empty land always made him feel strange and alone. It had no buildings or people—hardly even a decent road; only the cows and buffalo looked at home out there, yet it always made his heart hurt and his throat tight.

"Penny for your thoughts, son?" The voice startled him, and he looked over at Danny. Next to his father and Pete, Uncle Danny was the most important person in the world to him. Danny and Carol weren't really related to him, but they insisted he call them uncle and auntie. "Pete's asleep."

"I see that. He's a tired guy—up half the night at the celebration and then out calling the spirits this morning. Hard work for such a young one, I'd say."

Jed knew Danny was making a way for him to talk about everything, but he was having trouble organizing what it was he wanted to say. His mind buzzed with a million questions about Terra and ghosts and old land and

145

old spirits coming back. When he finally opened his mouth, what came out was not what he expected.

"Did you know my mom very well? She died when I was ten."

Danny nodded. "You know I did. I knew her real well."

"I don't get it. One day she was there and then she was just gone. At first, Dad tried to make me think she'd be right back, like she had just gone to the store or to visit somebody. Maybe he wanted to think that himself, but he knew, didn't he? He knew she was gone."

"Yeah. He knew."

Always, when Jed thought of his mom, his jaw wanted to jerk and stretch like a horse's mouth. He resisted the weird urge, bothered by the way his body wanted to do things he didn't think were right. He thought about how he'd said, "I miss you" to her—and the urge went away. *Mom, I miss you*, he repeated again silently, keeping his eyes on the highway and his hand on Pete's damp head.

"What's really on your mind, boy?" Danny asked him.

He looked at the floor. "What I want to know, I guess, is . . . ." The words wouldn't come. He tried again. "Did I do something to make her want to leave? That's what I want to know. Did I . . . make her want to die?"

Danny took his arm and said in a fierce tone, "Jed, look at me, son."

Startled, he turned and looked at Danny.

"Listen to me. There isn't anything a boy could do to cause his mamma to want to die. Nothing. It was just an accident or fate or just plain old mystery why some die so young. Something might have called her spirit away; but it's a mystery. You didn't cause it." His grip loosened and he stroked Jed's arm. "It wasn't you, son."

Jed's throat tightened and his eyes watered. He nodded silently.

Danny went on. "You're a good, strong, brave boy. She loved you. It must have been terribly hard for her to leave you."

146

The cab of the truck was silent except for the road noise humming beneath the wheels. The world was whipping by like they were riding the wind instead of a truck. Jed swallowed and tried to blink back his tears. It hurt to talk about it, but Danny's words made it hurt less. He petted the top of Pete's sleeping head gently. "Pete hardly remembers her. That's sad, don't you think?"

"It's real sad, son."

He told Danny about how Terra had made them say aloud that they missed her. "I try to do things for Pete, like when he has a bad dream or needs help with his homework. I pretend I'm her or I tell him what she would have said or done. I figure maybe I can put my memories into Pete's head and make them stick there. Super Glue, that's me." Admitting this embarrassed him. He'd never told anybody this before. "Yesterday," he went on, "when we found Terra and she called him Petey, it was strange. At first I thought maybe she was my mom; but she isn't, of course, being a white woman and all. But at first it made me mad when Pete was so friendly with her."

Danny nodded. "You were protecting your mom's place. But Terra won't push her out of her place. And she can't take your place with Pete, either. Pete only has one big brother and you're it, lucky for him. But I'll tell you a secret. The heart is a big place—bigger than the Civic Center, bigger than the Badlands."

Talking like this to Danny made Jed feel older. "Yeah, I figured that. It isn't about losing something—it is about getting something else."

"You're smart. Even though we don't know much about Terra, we do know she's coming straight out of that big place in the heart. I mean, even Skid likes her—and Skid is probably smarter than any of us."

"You got that right."

Danny laughed, "Sure I do. Animals and small children recognize those heart people. I guess both Skid and Pete would marry her if they could."

Jed laughed softly at the idea. "Yeah, that'd be quite a wedding. Pete could ride on Skid's back—it'd make him a little taller, don't you think?" The movie formed in his head. "Or Skid could wear a suit and ride on Pete's shoulders." He laughed louder at the ridiculous image and Pete stirred, swatting a hand out as if annoyed by an insect. Jed lowered his voice and looked at Danny. "I'm waking him up—guess the little bridegroom needs his sleep."

Still smiling, Danny nodded and then leaned forward and switched on KILI FM Radio. The sound of a drum group pounded out of the speaker. The sun was bright but not hot. and in spite of the loud drumming, Jed felt drowsy. Telling Danny about his mom felt like he'd chased off a ghost or two. He guessed if people could call a ghost to them, they ought to be able to chase off a few, too.

Jed watched Danny drive in silence for a while, maneuvering the road. Every spring the thin layer of asphalt broke up in places. Hard on trucks, Danny had told him once. The sun was dropping and the distant hills looked like they'd been drawn onto the sky with a dark crayon. He loved the Black Hills in winter, spring, or any other season.

Danny must have been thinking the same thing because he jabbed a finger toward the windshield and said, "There's Harney Peak. That's where the Grandfathers took Black Elk when he had his great vision."

Jed nodded. He wondered if the fire in the stone bowl the night before had been a vision—or real. How did you know? After his mom died, he'd gotten more interested in spirits. He even dreamed about being a medicine man when he grew up. Danny wore a small gold stud in one ear. Jed wanted his ear pierced, too, but was afraid to tell his dad. He rested his head against the cool glass, thinking about being carried off by great warriors to the top of a mountain. "How old do you have to be to have a vision?"

"No rules about that, Jed. A person doesn't need to be any particular age to pray or have a vision."

"Hmm." Jed murmured, thinking of Terra at the Stone Bowl talking about the soft spot in the Earth's body or how, every time they climbed Harney Peak, he felt

148

something in his chest flutter. Nothing could top standing in that old lookout house on the top of the world feeling the magic and seeing out for miles and miles.

Danny had told him about all the sacred sites in the Black Hills. He said many tribes of Indian people used to travel from every direction to do the spring rituals and to tell stories. During the past year, Danny and his dad had taken him to several of the sacred sites: Wind Cave, Harney Peak, the Badlands, Bear Butte. He even loved the names. He thought about Terra talking about Earth's body. Now he imagined these sacred places were like body parts: head, hand, heart, eye, and shoulder to the world. He leaned his cheek against the cold glass of the car window and listened to the drum group still playing on the radio, feeling the weight of Pete's head in his lap.

He thought of his mom sitting in the stone bowl with two old drummers. She seemed like a pretty ghost now and thinking of her didn't hurt as much. Maybe she really is peeking around a curtain. On the edge of sleep, he felt a warm, swirling sensation fill his body as if she'd patted his head and said, "I love you." He thought of Terra; and again the warm, swirling feeling washed through him as if his mom were saying, "It's okay, son. You may love her, too. The heart really is a giant place."

Danny passed Rockyford and felt a powerful urge to stop at the Cuny Café. The light over the land looked soft near the horizon and when he came to the turnoff to The White River Visitor Center, he turned left. "I'm going to run up to Cuny Table. It won't take long. I need to see Agnes for a few minutes."

"Sure, Danny," Jed said sleepily.

Within two miles, the boy was asleep, his head rolling loosely on his neck. Danny turned down the radio and pulled a car blanket from behind the seat, rolled it into a ball and pushed it under the older boy's head for a pillow. He finished Jed's orange soda and drove, letting his mind wander freely.

149

When he pulled up in front of the Café, a strange silence once again engulfed the land. He was beginning to pay attention to that odd silence, almost a sound in itself. He got out and left the door open slightly with the engine running so the boys would stay asleep.

There was not another car or truck in front of the Café. Danny felt a sudden jab of fear that something had happened to Agnes. It was quiet . . . too quiet. He took the steps up the porch two at a time and was about to enter when he saw a note taped to the door. The note had no name on it, but Danny knew it was written to him. It said, "Take the boys to the Butte. Bring your drum and this bag of tea. You'll need it. No questions, boy, just go."

He tugged the note off the door along with the zip-lock bag filled with weedy looking tea. A sudden tingling, tangible energy suffused his body, as if small insects were running up and down his limbs. He wanted to go inside, find the old woman and force her to tell him what was going on—and to make sure she was all right—but his hand froze on the door handle. The sense of urgency intensified. He turned, got back into the truck, and drove to Uncle Bill's cabin. Nobody here either, he thought, just the damned silence.

Inside, he stopped only long enough to grab the large drum sitting in the center of his uncle's living room and a handful of drumsticks from the bureau drawer. He and Bill had crafted the drum from a chunk of cottonwood when Danny was twenty years old. It had sat in this central place ever since.

He wrapped the drum in the worn star quilt that was always draped across the back of Bill's couch, the gift of some long past giveaway. He tucked the wrapped drum in a large plastic bag and carried it to the truck, setting it down on the ground first in order to clear the truck bed of the tumbleweeds and trash collected the day before at the cemetery. It didn't seem right to put the drum in with the trash. In less than ten minutes he was driving back down the road with two sleeping boys, a pow wow drum, and a lot of crazy unanswered questions.

150

Bear Butte? Agnes's directions were specific. Danny had no other thought but to follow them. Bear Butte was sacred to the Lakota and other plains tribes—Cathedral to the Plains Indians, as it was often called. Excitement hummed through his body.

Jed stirred, pulled up his head and asked, "Where we going, Danny?"

"I don't know what's up, son, but we're on our way to Bear Butte, I guess."

"Hum, okay," murmured Jed. "It's a good place. If Terra called them all to come there, they would come for sure."

Danny said nothing but thought, you got that right, boy. Ah, the wisdom of youth. Jed had not so much as mentioned the strange web of events catching them all off guard; and yet, here he was, half asleep, popping off about Terra calling the Great Ones to Bear Butte.

He loved these boys. Grief tugged deep at his heart. He and Carol had had two sons, too. One lived a month, the other left in the eighth month of gestation. When the second son left, Carol had nearly gone with him. All her determination to walk the Good Red Road had shattered on an alcoholic rock. It had taken four years to bring her back to him, sober, much subdued . . . but alive. Thank the Creator, alive.

This was the hardest part of being a medicine man, feeling as though he were walking upstream in a river raging out of control. The reservation was a hard place to be. He'd lost two brothers, three uncles, countless cousins, and both parents—all dead. Not a single one lived to be fifty years old. He was forty-four.

Every day he watched the people soak themselves in alcohol or fight or cry or pull all manner of diseases into their bodies. Such endless pain was like an echo between canyon walls, a sound we can't seem to escape. Slowly, very slowly, though, things were changing.

He looked across at Jed with Pete asleep on his big brother's lap. They are my sons, too. He'd claimed them even before John had asked him and Carol to be their godparents—or parents—should anything ever happen to John. It was a privilege beyond words, to be entrusted with these two boys

Hopefully, spirit willing, they'd have a child of their own. Carol's journey into the dark abyss had changed her in some deep, fundamental way. When she had come out of it after those painful years, she was walking stronger. Now, maybe for the first time, she stood firmly beside him, present at all the ceremonies, supporting his work with her own bright energy. He was anxious to get home and tell her of all that had happened since last night. Had it really been only one day? He needed her with him now. He'd stop by the house, hook up the camper, grab Carol, and head to Bear Butte.

"Shee-it," he whispered aloud in the truck, glancing again at Jed, his head wobbling against the blanket, his face slack and his mouth hanging open. He smiled. Bear Butte. They were going to the Cathedral.

Chapter 18

Bill Elk Boy felt restless as an old coyote. No matter which chair he took or what chore he picked up, his mind was somewhere else. His bones had ached all day the way they did sometimes when a storm was brewing—but the air was smooth as a baby's behind and the sky was clear. He saw the big drum was gone and that disturbed him. That old drum never left the house except for special occasions. Danny must have taken it, he thought. No other explanation.

In fact, there was no explanation for last night or this morning either—or the restless feeling. Something was afoot.

For seventy years, he'd lived in this simple cabin. He'd had no need for more. Long ago he'd accepted that his lot in life was to tend to his people, teach his nephew, and help Agnes. In the small kitchen, he peeled a few potatoes and put a buffalo steak on for supper. At least he still had his own teeth. Without a good buffalo steak, he'd have left long ago.

Something to do with Danny and those two boys he thought . . . and that woman.

He cut an onion, tossed it in with the steak, and stirred it with a spatula. No sense fretting about it. Life had a way of dealing the cards and then playing the game.

Out the window he saw Agnes walking across the mesa with a small bundle under her arm and a backpack on her back. How many times had this scene replayed itself, he wondered. He looked at her short, firm steps, the look of intention about her, the beauty of her. He smiled. Of course not many would consider Agnes a beauty—but he did. For the better part of five decades, he and Agnes had loved each other from across this mesa, day after day, with him walking to her, her walking to him. It was almost a ritual. He would like to have married her, but . . .

No, not much sense in taking that trail again. It was hard to explain, but it was like those Catholic nuns who were married to Jesus. He and Agnes were in similar service, offering their time and spirit to others—and then refilling the tank with each other.

He went to the door and waited until she had walked the last three hundred yards to his front door. Besides, all that walking between the two places probably kept them young and slim. He grinned. A few years ago, when Agnes couldn't pass the vision test at the Driver's License place, the young guy had pulled her license. Lucky the poor fellow didn't lose his precious parts. Agnes was a force unto herself. Her eyes may be going bad, but there was nothing at all wrong with her sight.

No, he would change nothing about her, not a hair on her head, not a year they had spent together.

She reached the front door of his cabin, saw him looking out, and smiled. "Hello Bill. Got the coffee on?"

"Even better—I got a steak cooking with some potatoes. We need to talk."

"You got that right," she said.

Agnes thumped up the steps and came into the cabin. She pulled off her backpack and set it down, gave him a wry smile, then walked over and kissed him on the lips.

He smiled, amazed as always at what this plain-looking woman could do to him. "What was that for?"

"Don't ask. It's this darned wind blowing through. Got me feeling like a young miss again." She laughed and went to the stovetop and sniffed the steak and potatoes. "Smells good."

"Sit down. I'll fix us a plate. I'm feeling a bit coltish myself today."

"Sure you are. More like a horse's ass." But she smiled and crossed the space to kiss him again. "Come on and dish me up some of that food. We have a lot of work to do before this day is over."

They ate together in companionable silence with the sun outside giving a final nod to the day before slipping below the horizon. When they finished, Agnes took the pack and said, "Let's sit outside. I can't seem to stay indoors lately. I need to tell you what I see."

Chapter 19

John pulled into his driveway with Terra about five o'clock. He lived in a fifty-year-old home in the Canyon Lake area of Rapid City. The neighborhood had once been an apple orchard surrounded by summer cabins and his property included three of the original trees. He pointed the large trees out to her. "Every fall, we have to pick up truckloads of apples. The boys and I haul them out to the woods for the deer." In truth, he despised housing developments where you could walk into any single house and know exactly where the bathroom was. Not the case in this neighborhood with its odd collection of houses and remodeled cabins.

Terra got out of the car and looked around. "It's nice."

What was she thinking, he wondered. After their weighty conversation about great love, and his impulsive declaration of love, they had skirted around any real discussion on the way back to town. He felt as if the words—the possibilities—hung between them like ripe fruit.

There was no sign of the boys or Danny. When he got in the house he checked his messages. There was one from Danny that said only, "Took the camper and the scamps and Carol to Bear Butte. Come early tomorrow morning. Dress warm and bring food."

He turned to Terra and laughed, "Typical Danny. Hijacks my boys and then tells me to bring food besides." He didn't say it, but he also knew Danny was not impulsive—and the cryptic message puzzled him. Bear Butte was obviously where Act Three of their little play of

157

events was to take place. No doubt, Danny was there preparing already.

He gave Terra the ten-cent tour of his house. It wasn't much. He watched her wander around, poking into corners. Up in the boys' room, a converted sunroom above the garage, she opened a small door and discovered the cubby. "Oh, a cubby hole. I bet the boys love this." She peeked her head around the wall at the top of the stairs and smiled. "Everybody needs a cave to call their own."

"Yeah, I thought it would be the place to store winter stuff, latex paint and things, but the cubby belongs to them."

Rough, bold lettering on the ceiling and scattered toys, blankets, pillows, and the inevitable "Keep Out" and "No Girls Allowed" signs underscored this fact. Terra walked down into the living room and went to the window. Mature trees lined the street. "It's so light. I can see why you like this house."

"The place was a mess when I bought it—ratty green carpet, awful kitchen—but I saw this window with the sky and those trees coming right into the room and had to have it. There've been moments of regret—it needs a lot of care—but we like it."

"It looks good now," she said, glancing around at the high ceilings, the soft blue walls, and the clean, white trim.

"It has two rental units, a little house over on the corner and a downstairs apartment. The money helps me out financially. I'm not sure I could work as an independent if I didn't have that edge. Half of the little house is my studio, too, so no office rent."

He took her around the rest of the house, out to his studio, and then into the backyard that was sliced in two by an old, rock-lined irrigation ditch that was still dry this time of year.

Terra gazed across the long stretch of tilled yard still buried beneath a bed of leaves. "You are a gardener." It was more of a statement than a question.

"Yeah, sort of. Jed is more of a gardener than I am. He takes a personal interest in it. We just grow the vegetables we like the best—chard, some green beans, lots of tomatoes—and pumpkins. Pete loves the pumpkins. Last year the plants nearly took over the whole garden and the back yard. The cottonwoods cause a shade problem, but every time a tree in the neighborhood goes down under the chain saw, it breaks our hearts."

Terra stared in awe at the cottonwood stretching high overhead in the neighbor's backyard. "Wow, it's huge—a giant gentleman."

"It is."

"Cutting that old guy down would be criminal."

John laughed. "I probably won't think that when it comes down on my roof." To himself he thought, I feel like a realtor. Why the hell are we talking about a cottonwood tree—avoiding what is so thick and sweet between us. He watched as Terra tipped her face to the sky to admire the giant tree. The curve of her neck fascinated him—and the place where her sweater nearly touched her ear lobes. He resisted the urge to rub his thumb along her chin.

Since the moment on the bluff above Danny's trailer, he'd been living in another universe, swamped with sensation, alive with need and an over-the-top sexual urge. I'm off my rocker, he thought, shaking himself out of a trance for the tenth time. He said, "I hired somebody else to film the reunion concert tonight, and Danny has the boys. What would you like to do?"

Terra tugged at a low branch of the apple tree outside his back door. "Well, food would be good." She held her arms out away from her body. "Also, Danny said to dress warm, but I seem to have stumbled into this adventure without luggage. I can't wear Jed's sweats or this same pair of jeans and sweater forever, but I seem to have little in the way of resources. You know—money."

He laughed, noticing the boyish clothing for the first time, "You are right about me being stuck in my own stuff. I didn't think about it." There was also the little matter of the missing luggage, the missing history, the missing answers, the need to call the authorities, but he shook his head and gave up that line of thinking for the moment.

"Let's swing out to the mall and pick up a few things. I have an empty charge card just begging to be used." He reached over his head and took hold of one of the larger branches and smiled down at Terra. "You're not, like, invisible if you look in the mirror or anything, are you?"

She poked his arm. "I'm not a ghost, for goodness sake. Or a vampire. Flesh and blood, buddy, believe me, every inch flesh . . . and blood."

The words made his gut go soft and warm again. The evening sun cut deep shadows across the backyard, and the leafless apple tree looked forlorn, waiting for its fruit. Leaning closer, he sniffed her scent. "Flesh and blood huh? Looks real—but I don't know what to believe anymore. It may require further research. You are beautiful, you know, even in Jed's sweats." He kissed her then, pushing beyond the earlier boyish kiss, wanting her to feel the intensity, the greatness that had come to him in the past hours. She kissed him back, leaning into his body; and he felt the perfect fit of a man and a woman. Never had he felt quite so sweet or tender, not even with Mae Jo, he thought with a quicksilver flash of guilt. No, with Terra he felt as though they were two interlocking puzzle pieces, bits of sky the same shade of blue, something larger than either could be alone. He felt foolish, almost poetic. "I may not know about great love; but I think I'm learning." He shook his head. "I can't believe I'm even saying this."

She laughed. "Yes, there may be hope for you yet, Mr. John Forrest."

Chapter 20

(Prayer posted at the base of Bear Butte)

Great Spirit, I invoke the peace pipe with reverence and gratitude of thy vast Creation, of which I am a part of. To the life giving of thy servant, the Sun and all Heavenly Bodies. The blue sky, the great everlasting rocks, the magnificent mountains with their fragrant forests, pure streams, and the animal kingdom. We thank thee for all these gifts.

To the North and its Guard, the White Eagle, keep us pure and clean of mind. Thoughts as white as Thy blanket, the snow. Make us hardy.

To the East and thy Sentry, the Red Eagle, and have better understanding with everyone.

To the South and thy Sentinel, the Brown Eagle, the beautiful one, grant us warmth of heart love and kindness to all.

To the West and the Thunderbird, who flies over the universe hidden in a cloak of rain clouds and cleans off the filth, cleanse our bodies and souls of all evil things.

To Mother Earth, we came from thee and will return to thee, keep us in plenty that our days be long with thee.

Great Spirit, we thank thee and appreciate all these wonderful gifts to us. Have pity on us.

By the time Danny arrived at Bear Butte with his entourage, it was after five o'clock, but there was still enough light left to make camp. He had picked Carol up on his way out and she had simply gotten the supplies they needed and jumped in the truck. He smiled to himself at the way she allowed him to do what was needed.

161

Legally, they could not set up the old pop-up tent camper on the lower asphalt lot down by the ceremonial grounds, but he knew the ranger who lived west of the Butte. Frank Wright respected him and turned away whenever he did something unorthodox. The ranger's skin is white—but his heart is Lakota—was Danny's grateful summary.

Fortunately the combined, if meager, clout of the plains tribes had blocked any major tourist development of the sacred site. It remained relatively pristine with only a small visitor's center down at the entrance. At the base of the mountain, a modest timber shelter with a plastic-covered signboard posted the rules and a Lakota prayer. There was also a picnic gazebo with crude plank benches and the trail leading up, always up.

This time of the year the grounds were deserted. Danny had recently joined a group from Sturgis attempting to block the construction of a gun range within earshot of Bear Butte. The native people had again fought one more threat to their sacred site and won. He bypassed the upper level and pulled the pop-up down to the lower parking lot.

The two boys, refreshed and eager from their earlier naps, begged to be allowed to explore. Carol waved them off with a simple warning, "Stay on the Ceremonial Trail and come back before the light is gone."

They headed down the trail, but Jed hesitated and ran back. "Do you have any cloth, Uncle Danny?"

He studied the boy for a moment. Jed was becoming a young man. That he would ask for prayer cloth stunned him. "I do. Let me get you some."

Strips of cloth in the six sacred colors and tiny tobacco pouches hang on tree branches all over Bear Butte, representative of the many prayers and offerings of the people. Danny walked to the truck and pulled the cloth from behind his seat and tore off strips of red, yellow, black, white, blue, and green, wondering with each rend of the cloth about Jed's prayer—and Pete's. Jed stood silent behind him. He wanted the boys to have whatever they

162

prayed for. He handed the strips to Jed along with some tobacco ties.

Jed looked up at him, his eyes wide. "Thanks, Uncle Danny."

He nodded and watched Jed turn and run back to Pete, feeling as though the simple action had initiated some larger action. The boys scurried off up the trail with the offerings clutched carefully in their fingers.

When he walked back to Carol, a smile softened the strong features of her face. He loved her face. The commercial images of Indian women with their pudgy cheeks, pouting little mouths, and submissive eyes were way off base. The movies and doll makers needed to model Carol if they wanted the real deal. She could have been fashioned from stone and earth.

Carol taught junior-high English and was a school counselor. Her whole life was about children, Indian or white, any color, size, or shape. Danny threw his own prayer to the top of the Butte that sometime, soon, they would have a child of their own.

"We won't see them again until dark," she said. "I can't blame them. This place always makes me want to dance up the trails and play with the squirrels."

They unlatched the pop-up camper, throwing up canvas walls against the fading light. His work took place all over Indian country and the little camper was his answer to ending up anywhere and being comfortable. Just hitch it to the truck and go. They'd recently restocked it with canned goods, plenty of blankets, a first aid kit, lanterns, and other supplies.

He helped her haul out the canvas camp chairs and Coleman stove and smiled as she began carving a kitchen for herself out of the late afternoon air. She set up the chairs and pulled the card table from the floor of the camper and arranged the stove with a small basket of coffee supplies, condiments, and other easy-to-reach items.

When she finished, she turned to him and said, "Okay, big guy. Are you going to tell me what we're doing here setting up camp on the last day of February—on the edge of winter? The young ears are way up the trail by now. We can talk."

He'd waited to tell her of the unusual events of the past day until he could do so in private. Now, he didn't know what to say. "I have been asked to assist a medicine woman with a healing ceremony." He almost laughed at how simple and logical he made it sound. It didn't in any way reflect the massive tangle of confusion bundling his brain these past twenty-four hours.

"Who is it for?" she asked.

He knew Carol had been patiently waiting for information since he had arrived at the apartment with the boys in tow and hustled them all off on this adventure. When he hesitated, he saw a flash of fear cross her face.

"It's not Jed? Or Pete?" she asked.

"No. Relax, baby. They're fine. It's just, they've been asked to assist."

"The boys? You mean they're going to participate, don't you? What do you mean assist? Danny, what's going on?"

Feeling scolded, and rightly so, he laughed. "Can't sneak anything past you, can I?" He pulled the two chairs to the table where Carol was already starting the camp coffee. "Sit down, sweetheart. I'll tell you the whole story."

She threw a few handfuls of coffee grounds into the pan of water heating above the dancing flame and stirred. "Talk, Danny. I can listen while I'm finishing this."

He began by describing his first meeting with Terra, the unusually light attitude of the reunion, and the late night vision of his Grandfather. Carol had been the one to point out the small dancing lights above Terra's head and body at the pow wow, so she didn't seem surprised.

She poured the coffee, handed him a cup, and then sat down on one of the stools and nodded for him to continue.

For twenty minutes, they sat in the quiet evening sipping coffee as he listed the string of events one by one, beginning with the horrible dreams and visions, his confusing talk with Agnes, the mixed salad of information

164

from the boys about the Stone Bowl, and ending with his theory. "I believe we're being guided to perform a renewal ceremony for the earth, and Terra is here to help." He let Carol absorb his words for a moment while he poured them each a second cup.

"Thanks." She clutched the cup between her two hands. "Wow. And all along I thought it was only a nice little pow wow and we were just taking a winter camping trip. You should visit my creative writing class—this story would be a big hit with those kids."

He laughed. "You got that right."

"It gives me the shivers."

"Me, too."

"So what are we doing here, Danny?" she asked seriously.

"I'm not sure. The plan, if you could call it that, is revealing itself piece by piece. Even Terra doesn't know exactly what is supposed to happen. Today, on my way back to Rapid City with the boys, I stopped up at Cuny Table. I thought Agnes would have some idea of what's happening. All I found was a note telling me to bring the boys and the drum here." He pulled the bag of tea out of his pocket and gave it to Carol. "And this—a bag of *Unci's* tea. Go figure."

He grew serious again and said, "I feel them all around us, Carol, just like Terra said. But the only image I saw in my prayers this morning was my Grandfather sitting alone in front of a drum down here in the meadow, beating the drum real slow . . . so slow. When I tried to add or change the image, it wouldn't shift. I saw Grandfather, and the drum . . . in this place. That's all I can tell you. I brought the drum." He looked at her and shrugged his shoulders.

"How do you think the boys figure into this?" she asked.

"I don't know, baby. I just don't know enough. I have the vague feeling I'm supposed to make them ready. In fact, my first thought was to do a sweat, but a sweat is for cleansing and purifying." He laughed. "There isn't much in

165

those two young boys that needs to be cleansed. They squeak as it is." Setting down his mug, he stood up and walked the space. Walking helped him think. "I suspect the Spirits are getting a kick out of this. I can sense it, like a big game is about to begin; and they all have the rules and the prizes in mind but they aren't telling. Even Grandfather was trying not to crack a smile."

She laughed. "He would love something like this, wouldn't he? And he would certainly not put up with being left out of it." They'd married young, almost twenty-five years earlier. Carol had gotten to know and love his Grandfather before he died.

He imagined his Grandfather on the other side arguing with Mother Earth, Herself. "That's the truth."

"Well, I'm sure supper must be the next step, especially when those two hungry guys come tumbling down that hill."

When she stood up, he embraced her, taking her loose ponytail in his hand and fanning it across his cheek. "Do you know how much I love you?" He tickled the back of her neck with the tip of the tail.

"Will you build a fire?" she asked.

You didn't answer me, but yes, I am sure I could build a nice, hot fire."

She gave him a coy smile. "I'm not even going there. You have that certain lecherous look in your eye, and I have a supper to build."

He patted her backside, and gave in. "Okay. What can I do to help?"

"Well, I can do veggies on the Coleman; but let's cook the burgers on an open fire. They're so much better that way."

"Right. Do you want buffalo burger? I could jog on down to Frank's meadow and see what's hoofing around down there." The ranger raised a herd of buffalo on several acres surrounding the Butte.

"The mighty hunter, hey? I bet Frank would love you hauling off one of his prize buffalo for our supper."

"Ah, Frank's a good guy. He wouldn't mind. Much."

166

While Carol prepared supper, he built a fire for the burgers. They said little but worked together in companion-able silence. As the evening light dimmed, the world grew still and silent, not even a breeze stirred around them. He caught himself looking up at the sky, watching the horizon as though expecting a storm . . . or company.

Jed was practically running up the slope as if trying to get away from a mountain lion. Ever since they had arrived at Bear Butte, the hair on his arms had been standing straight up, and it wasn't from the cool air. Danny and Carol were acting like they were just there for a picnic— but something told him it was more, much more.

"Wait up, Jed. I can't run that fast," Pete said.

He'd almost forgotten Pete was behind him. For some reason he felt an urgent need to get to the first lookout on Bear Butte. He really wanted to go straight to the top but knew it would be dark before they could get back down. "Hurry, Pete."

"What? You got a girlfriend waiting for you up there or something? Why are you in such a hurry?"

Jed reached the first lookout and turned to stare out at the empty land below him. He couldn't see the camper, but he knew right where it was. A small puff of smoke— Danny must be building a fire. He squinted, searching and searching through the trees.

Pete came up beside him, panting from the race up the mountain. "What are you looking for?"

All the racing energy in his body suddenly stopped as he realized what he'd been hoping to see—a couple of old Indians, a fire burning in a stone circle, a woman in white buckskin . . . .   A crush of disappointment suddenly pressed down on his chest. He flopped to the ground, crossed his legs, and then dropped his head into his hands. He felt like crying.

Pete sat down beside him. "Jed," he said quietly.

"Not now."

"But . . ."

"I said not now, Pete."

167

"Jed. Look. It's them. They're here."

The note of urgency in Pete's voice pulled him out of his dark disappointment. He looked up and felt a tingle in his upper lip. A buzzing hum began in his ears and it reminded him of the time his dad had taken them to a party and he'd snuck a beer and drank it all in one gulp. "Who's here?"

"The ones we called with Terra—I see them."

He looked out and saw nothing but a strange evening sky filled with thin wisps of clouds in a dozen sunset colors. It was pretty but nothing special. "It's just clouds, Pete."

"No. It's them."

Jed looked again and had to admit these were the oddest clouds he'd ever seen; they were moving in small spirals like colored tornados only slow and lazy, not fierce and fast. One spiral met another and they seemed to dance a minute and then blend and move toward another spiral. They were coming from the southwest in lazy twirls. He had no idea why Pete thought these clouds had anything to do with the rocks and sticks and bones they'd laid in a circle around the hubcap. "What makes you think it's them?"

"I don't know. Just know it is."

Jed looked at Pete—his eyes were wide and full of tears. "Why are you crying?"

Pete seemed to gulp back the tears, but his dripping nose gave him away. "I'm not."

The strong, protective feeling Jed had felt for his brother earlier in Danny's truck came back. "Pete?"

Nothing.

"Tell me, Pete. I'm your brother."

As if he could no longer hold back, Pete burst into tears. He hid his face but the tears came anyway. Pete cried so hard he finally bent over as if he had a bad belly ache. In all the years since their mother died, Jed had never seen Pete cry this way. He was afraid to touch him, afraid his little brother would fly into a million pieces and float up to join the colored wisps sailing across the sky. Finally, he had

168

to do something so, without a word, he reached over and tipped Pete's curled body into his lap. His own eyes were wet now, but he put his ear next to Pete's finally and said, "I saw her."

Pete went still. The shuddering stopped, and he whispered, "Who?"

"Mom. I saw her."

Pete raised his head. "Here?"

"No. Last night. Up at the stone bowl."

Giant big tears slid from Pete's eyes and a lump the size of a rock formed in Jed's throat—but he swallowed, swallowed again, and then he straightened his spine and said, "But she came here with the others." He couldn't believe he was saying this. "She's here, Pete. I can feel her. Remember what Terra said about Mom seeing us sad and unhappy. Look up, Pete. Look up."

As Pete brought his head up and looked out, the spiraling clouds chose that moment to open in the center and form a perfect circle around the lowering sun. "Shee-it," whispered Pete.

Jed laughed and said, "Watch your mouth, little brother. She might hear you. Come on, let's hang the flags and tobacco. This has to be the right place." He handed Pete one each of the yellow, white, and red flags, and he took the others. They walked around tying each piece of cloth to the lower branches and adding a tobacco tie when it seemed right.

Chapter 21

John hated shopping malls—hated shopping, period, unless it was for a new camera or microphone—and yet here he was wandering the Rushmore Mall with Terra. For an hour they roamed the stores. Terra shopped for warm and practical while he had the overwhelming urge to drape her in silk, throw garlands of fresh gardenias over her head, and buy exotic oils to dab between her toes.

She refused all of the outlandish items he suggested. Instead they bought jeans, two sweatshirts, a turtleneck, and a pair of walking shoes with practical wool socks and an ugly brown stocking cap from a winter clearance bin. Only when they passed the lingerie section in JC Penney's did she stand aside and let him show her a long, form-fitting aqua gown, a color so fluid a person could drown in its folds.

She resisted for a moment. "John, be practical."

"This isn't extravagant," he chided. "Strictly practical. After all, you do need something to sleep in besides my t-shirt."

But he lied. He wanted to see her wearing this gown. Thinking about it made his belly heat up. "Besides, it's beautiful—like you." Holding the gown against her body, he saw the same deep lake-tones in the scattered flecks of her eyes. He shivered and tucked the gown under his arm. "If you don't want it, I'll wear it," he teased and carried his prize to the sales counter.

In the parking lot, when they were again folded into the comfortable darkness of the truck's interior, Terra said, "Tell me about Mae Jo."

To his surprise, there was no clutch of emotion this time, no pain jabbing his heart. "We met out east in Sioux Falls. Mae Jo's family was from Pine Ridge. I was in college at Vermillion, and she was at a weekend workshop, a writing workshop. She really wanted to write, but it's like your version of great love. Wanting to write and writing are two totally different things."

His thoughts swirled, and he waited until they formed more fully. "Mae Jo liked the idea of something but not necessarily the thing itself. She loved the idea of marriage, of children, of homemaking—but, the truth was, she was never quite present with any of it. It's hard to explain—like part of her lived somewhere else. I never could figure out where." Stunned at how easily he could speak of these things now, he went on. "We were married almost fourteen years. I loved her, Terra. Lord knows I was not always easy to live with either. And then she went to the store one winter night and never came back. It was awful. I thought I'd die, too. And the boys . . . well, there were no words—I didn't know how to tell them . . . ." He stretched his hand out to feel the warm air coming from the heater.

"I'm sorry, John. That must have been terrible."

He put the truck in drive and pulled out. "Her great grandfather died in the Wounded Knee Massacre. Mae Jo—and the boys, too—are descended from survivors. There's always been something about Wounded Knee that draws me."

Terra nodded. "It's a powerful place."

"I've wondered if marrying Mae Jo was my way of getting closer to the culture. My mother had friends out there, so we spent a lot of time on Pine Ridge. I fell in love with the Lakota people—and the culture. Danny keeps pushing me to get involved with Lakota traditional life; but, honestly, I don't fit in there." Silence settled around them and, oddly, he noticed the residual anger and hurt of Mae Jo's death was just that, a residue, like ashes from a long-dead fire. "So, that was my marriage. And Jed and Pete were two great results."

Terra slid closer and rested her head against his shoulder. "Change is never easy. In fact, I'm not sure we ever really change. Maybe we just get closer to who we were all along."

"You seem so sure, so wise in a way. I wish I knew more about you."

She smiled wistfully, "So do I, John. So do I."

Chapter 22

On Cuny Table, Bill had called two of his young male helpers to build a fire and heat stones for an *Inipi* ceremony. The trampled site buzzed with activity as they stacked the wood over the stones and quickly had a fire burning west of the opening to the sweat lodge; the men were careful not to cross between the door and the blazing fire.

Agnes sat on a low bench nearby watching them. One of them was a young man she'd pulled from a car wreck ten years ago. The poor kid had been drunk as a skunk and nearly died. He'd been sober ever since and was never far from Bill's side.

She was waiting for a sign, a signal, a way to see into this pregnant night. In truth, she'd felt this night coming for half a century and, most of all, she was waiting for this moment to be over. She stared out across the sleeping land and saw that, tonight, there were no dreams. After the flashing, flickering day all the people rested, their sleep devoid of naked longing or aching images.

No sight, no scent, no sound. Just silence.

She closed her eyes and saw them, pale wisps of light in pink and soft green and cream—all the colors of the spectrum—moving. They numbered in the thousands, maybe hundreds of thousands. Agnes hummed low—*we are traveling, traveling* and felt them all around, the spirits. Like whirring street cleaners, these whisperers-in-the-night were moving through South Dakota and beyond sweeping away all negativity, all sadness and anger and replacing it all with . . . silence.

Chapter 23

Danny flipped the burgers over the fire, and when the boys came tumbling down the mountain, they were ready for them. Carol fixed the plates and poured them each a glass of juice. They ate, sitting in chairs around the tiny fire.

"What a magnificent night," Carol said. "It's so warm for this time of year."

He nodded, feeling distracted and edgy. It didn't take a magician to know that those boys had done more than take a late afternoon romp. Both Jed and Pete looked on fire, their cheeks blotched red, and their eyes glittering. The meal seemed to pull them back into their bodies and they relaxed and were laughing and playing around again. For some reason, he didn't quiz them about what had happened up the slope.

After they finished eating he told the boys to help Carol put the food away. He listened to their friendly laughter and chatter but heard it as if from a distance. He left the dim circle of light from the campfire and paced the dark circumference beyond the firelight.

I don't know what's next, he thought, feeling tortured, weighed down with the significance of something he couldn't see, couldn't hear, and couldn't touch. An urgent, panicky feeling clutched his chest. He walked further out into the clearing and prayed that the stillness of this night would find its way into his own heart and lead the way. "It will be well," he said aloud. "It will be exactly as it's supposed to be. I am not alone." He turned and went back to the boys and Carol.

She looked at his worried face and said, "Let's make some hot chocolate. It's getting chilly out here." She filled the pot with water and set it over the glowing coals. Minutes later she was passing mugs of hot chocolate out, dropping a few marshmallows into each cup.

He took the cup and smiled at her. "I'm fine," he told her, seeing the intense way she was looking at him. Jed and Pete, too, were all wide-eyed and waiting. He sat down and said, "Did I ever tell you about the time I saw a nation gather?"

"No. Tell us, Danny," said Pete.

"It was the nation of hawks. I was staying at my friend Lonny's house out on Rosebud. We'd done a ceremony the night before, and the next morning he ran into the house and practically jerked me out of the door. We went behind his house and there they were—the entire hawk nation, perched everywhere, hardly making a sound. The birds were all different colors, sizes, shapes—big ones, small ones, from many different tribes—but all hawks. I tried to count them but couldn't. There were hundreds of them."

"Wow," said Jed. "What do you suppose it meant? What were they doing?"

"I wondered that myself. It looked like they were having a meeting. Lonny said his grandfather saw the owl nation gather once. His grandfather told him that all nations must gather every so often to strengthen the tribe, to build relationships—said it's necessary for their continued survival. I thought it was the damnedest . . . . "

"Danny," Carol cautioned him on his language.

"Oh, Aunt Carol, we don't care if he cusses," said Jed.

"Jed Forrest!" She scolded.

Danny laughed. "Come to think of it, I've heard Jed use a word or two that wouldn't pass his teacher's ears unnoticed. They're only words, Carol."

Pete clutched his hot chocolate, a sleepy look in his eyes. "Tell us another story."

"Well, let me think . . . ."

As the darkness thickened like pudding around them, he added sticks of wood to the fire one by one and told them stories of Lakota leaders; Black Elk, Crazy Horse and Red Shirt. He spoke of the Cheyenne prophet, Sweet Medicine, who was given the sacred arrows in a cave right here on this very butte. He included the great stories of all people, not just the Lakotas. Besides the plains people, he told stories of Jesus, Buddha, Shiva, and John the Baptist—or any he had recognized in the great river the previous night.

For nearly an hour he spoke. The boys listened in complete silence and stillness. Danny's voice became a drone, a hypnotist's watch swinging before their eyes, entrancing them. As if hooked to hidden wire, their spines pulled toward the stars until their bodies stayed upright even when their eyelids drooped with weariness.

Finally, as if an inner alarm had gone off inside, Danny got off his campstool, went to the truck, and pulled the drum from the bed. He went back and looked at Jed and Pete. "It's time for you to be introduced to the drum."

Carol was watching him again, and he almost laughed. He didn't know how to tell her that he had no idea what he was doing or why. He shook his head at her as if to say, don't worry—and don't ask.

"This is a very special honor, boys," he explained. "Not to be taken lightly."

Jed and Pete nodded at him. He gave them each a small pinch of tobacco and told them to offer it to the drum, to lay their hands on the wide skin to let the drum know that they were friends, approaching it with only pure intention. Their eyes were wide and dark as they made the offering.

Following an inner impulse, he then sang four songs over the drum, letting his voice lift and whirl and travel around in the dark night. When the final song was finished, he sensed that the long invocation had brought a pinpoint of energy to this place. It was knife-sharp and spiraling out from him and the drum. He was calling them

179

to come, just as Terra had called them to the center of the stone bowl.

He turned to Carol and said quietly, "Can you tuck these boys into a warm sleeping bag for now? They're like little potatoes looking for a warm oven."

She smiled weakly, nodded, and helped the half-asleep boys gain their feet, then guided them off into the darkness. He watched a moment, and then picked up the drum again.

The night draped around them like cloth. Nothing stirred except the subtle, ever-present breezes of Bear Butte.

Chapter 24

John took Terra's hand as they walked into the bookstore. He felt almost normal, just like the other people milling around, reading magazines, and pawing the books stacked on tables and shelves. He soaked in the calming energy.

The past thirty-six hours had seemed more like a month—or six months—and he wanted to relax his grip for a minute. In the back of his mind, he knew this was just an illusion, this feeling of being like everyone else. There was nothing normal about this night. He felt it humming in the background, had felt it since he held the aqua gown up to catch the color of her eyes.

He smiled to himself. Danny was a sorcerer. How convenient to take the boys and leave him alone with this stranger—and with his own thoughts, and with his own body that had not known a woman for far too many years. As if reading his mind, Terra asked, "What are you thinking about?"

"You don't want to know." He pulled her a little closer. "I was thinking of Danny doing his disappearing act. And leaving us alone."

"Oh." She smiled.

"Come on. I'll buy you a coffee."

Terra had a stack of magazines in her arm, and when they had bought two Lattes', they sat down at a table. She flipped open one of the magazines.

"I want to check the newspapers, see what kind of coverage the reunion is getting. I'll be right back."

Terra nodded, sipping the coffee, her nose already buried in a magazine.

He walked around to the low shelf of newspapers. He felt slow and lazy, as if he had a lifetime to move to the next place. The article on the Four Directions Walk was in the middle section of the Rapid City Journal. He'd hoped for front-page coverage. Next he picked up the Sioux Falls Argus Leader to see if, by chance, the article had made it to the eastern part of the state.

He was idly flipping pages when his eye stopped on a small story, just two column inches, with a headline that read, "Autistic Woman Missing from Yankton State Hospital." The words wobbled in front of his eyes. He pulled the page closer and looked into the smudged photo and read the opening lines.

"Theresa Bennington, age twenty-six, has been missing from the Yankton State Hospital since Tuesday, February 25th."

John stopped breathing. All the tender, wide-awake sensations of the past day tumbled like an avalanche and buried him. "Terra."

Stillness. Disbelief. A moment of disappointment so deep it cut. A dim voice berated him for trusting that anything could be sweet and different.

He read the article and the words swam together. "Ms. Bennington has been hospitalized since age six for severe autism . . . unable to communicate . . . highly intelligent . . . an avid reader . . . disappeared while on a shopping outing with a caregiver . . . not known whether she was taken against her will or is lost . . . call authorities immediately if you have any information . . . .

Damn. He needed to breathe, needed to run, needed to be anywhere but here. He flopped down in a black chair near the newspapers, forcing the air into his lungs, still holding the newspaper in his hands. A woman stopped, stared at him, and then asked, concern in her voice, "Sir, are you all right?"

He nodded, "Fine. I'm fine." She eyed him again and then walked on. "What the hell?" he whispered aloud. "How could I believe . . . ." He berated himself again for allowing this crazy tumble into pure fairy tale—great rivers of love, and happily-ever-after, and great beings—what a fool he was.

Five minutes later, he was still sitting there, newspaper in hand, when Terra came around the last row of magazine shelves and saw him. "John? What is it?" She took the chair next to him, but all he could do was slide the paper over onto her lap and say, "Theresa."

Confusion wrinkled her brow as she looked from his face to the newspaper in his lap.

"Read it," he said. "Just read it."

She looked where he pointed and her mouth formed a small 'o' as she eyed the image and then read the article. She took a long time reading, and rereading, each word. "What are you thinking?" she whispered.

"I was nearly right," he said sadly. "when I thought you were some poor schizophrenic lost in the Badlands. How did you get here all the way from Yankton, Terra? That's clear on the other side of the state. And why didn't you tell me?"

"It's not what you think. You have to believe me. That may or may not be me in that picture, but I'm somebody else, too. I know it."

"What do you know, Terra? Or Theresa? Just exactly what do you know?"

"Oh, John."

"It's you. Damn it, don't you see? It's you."

"You don't know that for sure. It's fuzzy, and you can't—"

"I have to get out of here." He stood, refusing to look at her. He took the newspaper over to the checkout counter, paid for it, and then headed toward the door feeling fifty years older since picking up that damned newspaper. Oddly, it was not anger but a deep, bone-weary sadness that occupied his body.

At the door he turned again, finally looking her in the eyes. "We'll have to call the authorities." He had visions of men in white coats arriving at his front door, giant hypodermic needles in hand. And, sadly, he thought of his earlier full-blown fantasy of Terra wearing a gown of aqua and turquoise, long and silky, colored like a stormy sea, a tempest. What a damn fool I am.

Terra followed him out the door and across the parking lot to his truck. She said nothing. When the truck was running and the heat began to fill the cab, John shuddered, feeling cold to the bone.

She rested her hand on his arm and said, "Don't do this. Don't toss it all away just because what we thought was real appears to be something else. Please don't."

He fought the sudden urge to lash out at her, realizing again that the fuel of his anger was really grief . . . and regret. "Leave it be." The inner war raged on as he drove the nearly empty streets toward home. He oscillated between cutting self-criticism and the tender feelings he'd acquired in the past day—and not knowing if he could give those tender feelings up again. How the hell could he leave it be? Some caged creature had been set free, and he didn't have the heart to push it back into confinement. To Terra, he said nothing but drove across town and into his driveway in total silence.

"Go on in," he said. "I'll get the packages."

Terra went into the house. He grabbed the bags out of the back and followed her in. She stood in the kitchen staring at him with a look of sadness so deep it shook him to the core. He couldn't stand it. "Don't look at me like that, Terra. None of this is my doing."

"Please don't send me away . . . not yet . . . not until we finish whatever we're supposed to do here."

"Listen to you. My God. What are you talking about? There is nothing to finish."

"Yes. There is. You have to trust me. I know what this looks like to you. Maybe my body has been sitting in that hospital for twenty years, but I was not there."

"Terra, honey," he said softly. "They're looking for you. You're family thinks you were abducted, maybe killed." The thought that she had family sitting somewhere out in eastern South Dakota who at this moment might be huddled together in worry and fear cut a new wound into his heart. "We have to call the authorities so they can contact your family."

"In the morning. Please, just give me one more night."

She was growing hysterical, and he felt like a monster. He found himself unable to deny her urgent request. Christ, he felt like a cracked pot anyway so what could one more night matter? "Okay. It's late and we're both exhausted—but in the morning—we call the authorities. You can sleep upstairs in Jed's bedroom. Go now and get some sleep, please? I need some time to myself."

She nodded, picked up the shopping bags, and carried them slowly up the steps.

Terra looked around the room and felt like wailing aloud. Not fair. This is not fair. She saw Jed and Pete's things tossed all over the place like friendly litter. No. I won't believe it. It just isn't possible that this whole numinous unfolding event had been some kind of perverted cosmic joke. And Jed and Pete? Not to be with them? Not to see them grow and change and become handsome young men? No.

Darkness threatened to dim her vision, to shut down her breath, to stop her heart from beating. She stood in the center of the room and said aloud, "It can't be." She didn't know what was going on, but the center of her being knew with utter certainty she was not—not—some sick, lost woman from Yankton. No matter the evidence, no matter the blurry picture and bold black headlines, no matter John's collapse into believing that crap.

Standing on the brink of disaster, a fierce determination grew within her. She'd been pulled by the nose into this strange event—but she was not going to become its victim. Who she was before or how she got here was an unknown, and it could remain an unknown as far as she was concerned.

No, she thought, what is real is this house, those boys, that man downstairs with his wounded eyes, his wounded heart . . . and the way he touched her as if thirsting for what only she could give. Only that could be real. Shock and disbelief at what had transpired during the past hour slid over, and in its place, a collage of images flooded in—of every single moment since two boys had found her asleep in the sand. She thought of the barefoot walk, the calling of spirits, Danny . . . and the boys, so hurt in their hearts, calling out to their mother. She felt again John's body beside hers, his warmth, the touch of his lips. No, no, no. Only this can be real. And only I can make it real.

She moved as if in a trance, putting the shopping bags on the Spiderman comforter, opening them, stripping off Jed's sweats, and pulling the gown from the bag. She sniffed its store-bought scent but smelled musk and water, green forest and moss. It was a wet thing. Life had to be wet and flowing. It had to be. She slipped the gown over her naked body and loved the feel of the slinky, cool fabric, felt her body come alive in a way that even last night's fancy dance—or John's kisses—hadn't accomplished. Shivering with determination and something much more ripe and alive, she smoothed the fabric over breast and ribs, over thighs and hips, and went to the door of the bedroom.

John heated water for tea and moved like a robot in the kitchen. Terra had gone upstairs clutching her new clothing and looking like a scared little girl. He felt like an ogre.

The water came to a boil and he prepared his tea, his thoughts a million miles away—or more like 350 miles away—with a family who had misplaced a severely disturbed daughter.

He was sitting at the kitchen table sipping the hot cup of lemon tea when Terra appeared in the doorway of the kitchen wearing the long, aqua gown, her hair brushed and shining, her eyes wide and wet. The girl clutching her packages had fled; in her place was a woman, a full-grown woman. She said nothing but crossed the small space and stood before him.

He felt his heart speed up. My God, he thought, she looks like myth and legend, like a goddess awake beside a mountain pool, eyes wide open on the world. "What are you doing?"

"What I was built to do," she said softly.

"Damn it, Terra. This is no game we're playing."

"I know that. I know it better than you do. It was never a game." She swayed her hips slightly and the folds of the gown swirled and swam around her.

Powerless to stop himself, he reached out his hands, pulled the silky lake of her to him, and buried his head in her belly. "Oh, I want you to be real. Don't you see? I want this--I want it all."

"Then don't be a fool. Trust yourself enough to believe in what is real."

It was not a choice, not anymore. Energy vibrated through his body like wind on water. Unthinking, moving purely with his soul, he pulled her to his lap. She did not speak. He planted small, feathery kisses on her neck and arms until she was trembling with need. He tasted her skin and tasted oceans and forests. Time seemed to slow, even stop, as he slid a hand beneath the aqua folds and found her calves, her thighs, and the deep well of her being. Terra moaned and he knew all was lost—his sanity, his logic, his armor and, most dangerously, his heart.

When he took her to his bed, he slid the aqua gown from her body and it pooled on the sheets, he felt as though he'd discovered a deep pure well within the earth's core. Perhaps it was the pool where life first formed, where a single cell split and then turned to see its twin; and where life—magnificent life—began, the cells doubling, and tripling until all of earth teamed with life.

Her body was pale and soft, so soft. He was aware of nothing but her, as if a gentle animal had swallowed the whole world outside while they made love; when he joined her, she took not just a part of his body but his entire soul. For hours he whispered to her, and she to him, in a language of love as ancient as time itself.

Later, much later, with the moon bathing the bed with gentle light, John kissed her again and pulled her close beside him. "We still have to call them. We'll take it from there, Terra. Whatever it was that caught you in its net, it is gone. You seem fine now."

She laughed softly. "What an understatement. I am as fine as silver thread. Thank you, John, for trusting me. For trusting yourself."

And then she slept.

John rose from his bed and left Terra asleep in the silent house. He needed to think. It felt like a lifetime, a century, since Jed had stood bare-chested in Danny's trailer house kitchen early that morning worrying about ghosts, and looking so much the man, a young warrior.

The house was too still, too empty without the boys. A strange loneliness overcame him. It shocked him that even with the way humans beings carry on, building friendships, having parents, being parents, bearing and caring for children, we are still, in the sharpest sense, alone inside our own skins. He went and stood at the huge picture window in his living room and stared out. The streets were empty, the silence pervasive.

In the stillness, John Forrest suddenly saw the universe, the descending sky, as the great, black velvet robe of the Creator. And somewhere, woven into the threads and stitches of the underside of that cloak, was himself. He realized this was the first time he'd not thought of himself as separate from God, not separate . . . but sewn right into the cloth of the Creator.

His breathing slowed. His mind wandered through the great teachings he'd studied always from afar like a watcher but never entering a single teaching wholly. He thought of the great wide-open lands of the prairie, the Badlands—so much a part of his soul—and he saw that a single teaspoon of that sand was still a part of the whole. Even the smallest portion belonged to the greater body of earth. Something in his understanding splintered in that quiet moment as he stood in the black outline of his own living room window.

Great love.

This feeling, this sensation, this understanding—was great love.

He fanned ten fingers on the cool glass of the window. There was no need for further words, no need to continue grasping toward unobtainable goals. All had arrived in the deep silence of this night. And it was perfect.

Yes, the authorities would have to be called. Life would twist on its trunk like a sapling once again. Beyond that he knew only that he knew nothing about the mysteries, the puzzles, and the subtle energies fueling the world—but he wanted to know.

Chapter 25

Bill Elk Boy crawled out of the sweat lodge and stood. He looked at the empty dish Agnes had filled with spirit food before the *Inipi* ceremony. Dripping with sweat, he took his towel and mopped his face. The night air was scented with wood smoke and a hint of cedar. He emptied his *cannunpa* and slid the pipe back in the beaded bag. He felt stunned into silence by this night and what had just happened in the *Inipi*.

At supper, he and Agnes had decided they would do the ceremony alone, a way to support Danny and this night's task, but a half hour before they were ready to start, the others came. He always figured it was the smoke from his fire that let the locals know there would be a sweat, but not tonight. Only the old ones came. Five men and two women Elders had pulled up next to the sweat lodge, got out of their cars and trucks, and circled the fire without speaking. They'd come from all over the reservation. Nobody spoke as the young men hauled in the rocks—they just waited, and then stooped and crawled into the lodge.

An hour later Agnes came out of the sweat lodge wearing her calico Inipi dress, her hair hanging down her back in a long braid. She looks like a girl, he thought, amazed once again at how deeply this woman was lodged into his spirit.

With quick, firm steps she went up the slope to the cabin and a few minutes later came back with a platter full of sandwiches, a jug of iced tea swinging from the other hand. One of the helpers followed behind with cups and napkins. "Here. Eat before you go, boys. You, too, ladies."

191

Bill smiled to himself. Agnes called them all boys, even the ones who looked old enough to be in the grave. They dug into the plates of food. Agnes had been feeding them all for decades, body and soul, himself included.

After the men had eaten and drifted off into the night, Bill took one of his helpers aside. "Did you do as I asked?"

"I did, Uncle."

"And?"

"Didn't see much during the first and second round but during the third round I saw what looked like wisps of smoke or light darting above the sweat lodge. There were hundreds of them. And they flew in and out of the lodge."

He nodded. "Good. You did good, son."

"Uncle, why did you want me to watch?"

"Just a hunch. I figured since you went to death's doorway during that car accident, maybe you would be able to see them."

The young man grew still. "What were they?"

"The spirits."

"Oh." The young man's eyes looked luminous and awed. "They left during the fourth round."

"Tell me what you saw."

"During the fourth round, they pulled together in what looked almost like a pale cloud and then whoosh, they moved off going west and north."

Bill smiled. "They went to Bear Butte. They must have heard it. Put that fire out now and then head out. You did a good thing, nephew."

"Thank you, Uncle."

Agnes had stood with her backside to the fire while he talked to his helper. When they were done, she walked over to him. The young man took a shovel and began to cover the fire with dirt. Agnes took Bill's arm and pulled him into the shadows and asked him, "You done here?"

"Soon as he puts out the fire. Come, I'll take you home."

"No, Bill. I'm staying here tonight. With you."

192

"You feeling okay?" He'd tried for decades to get her to stay at his cabin with him. She always refused to spend the night.

Agnes smiled. "I'm fine. It's almost done, Bill. I want to be with you tonight."

Chapter 26

Carol sat in the dim light of the campfire huddled beneath a blanket and staring across the fire at the shadowy form of her husband. She tried to pray, really wanted to pray, but all she could do was clutch her middle, look at her watch, and wonder how much longer this already everlasting night could be. Not ever in twenty years had she seen Danny in such a perilous state; she feared he might be dying.

She was not cold but her hands shook. It had been at least two hours since she'd led each boy to his bag and tucked him in, planting a firm kiss to each forehead, each kiss a bright shield to protect them from this night. It was not that the night felt dangerous or evil—it was just too acute, too pregnant and ripe for comfort.

She recalled the earlier, innocent scene of those two boys, eyes wide as owls, staring with solemn expressions as Danny told stories and sang and drummed. At one point she had scooted into the camper and snatched two blankets to drape around their shoulders to protect them against the growing chill. They hadn't even blinked when she touched them.

The moment she had tucked in the boys, she heard Danny hit the first beat of the drum, the beat that was continuing on through this night. Tum. Da tum. Tum. Da tum. There was a painfully long pause between each double beat, so much slower than the beat of her own heart that it gave her an uneasy feeling, and she wanted to urge him to speed up.

This is a lonely thing he does, she realized. Her presence wasn't needed.

195

She went back to the camper and crawled into a sleeping bag to try and rest. She was tired, but the drum was too present. It was well past midnight, but sleep eluded her. She felt oddly bereft, aware as never before, that her husband traveled to places she could not follow.

Tum. Da tum.

These places he traveled were not places on a map that said Rosebud or Martin or Eagle Butte. No, they were places only his years of study as a medicine man had ticketed him to enter. He seldom spoke of the *Yuwipi* or healing ceremonies done for those who came to the house. Often she was unexpectedly required to feed or house great numbers of people without being included in any of their undertakings.

Tum. Da tum.

Tonight, Danny and his drum confirmed this. "I travel alone to these places I must go."

She understood. She'd been to her own private places and back. Now that she was sober and standing strong in life again, she didn't mind serving his greater purposes.

She stroked her belly slowly, meditatively, cherishing the belief that, once again, a tiny life had embedded itself into her womb like a microscopic jewel. Six weeks since her last period—but a cautious fear forced her to quell all hope and play, instead, a most painful game of wait and see. Don't get your hopes up, she reminded herself. Still she stroked and petted, repeating over and over again in her mind like a mantra, *you are welcome here.*

Tum. Da tum.

Soon, she'd have to tell Danny. He would be afraid for her, for their unborn child, and what might happen should the child leave—like the others had.

Yes, she also traveled to places he could not follow. Perhaps here, buried in her womb was the greatest mystery of all, the spark of human life, the beginning of future generations.

Later, she realized her whispered welcome and the strokes to her belly had unconsciously synchronized themselves with the slow beating of her husband's drum.

Sliding out from the sleeping bag, careful not to disturb the sleeping boys, she left the camper and walked over to the fire.

Only a dim glow remained. The fire was dying.

She glanced at her watch, surprised that it was nearly three o'clock. Danny had not shifted his position or the beat of his drum for over three hours. It was cold now, and a flash of fear, and then guilt, slid through her as she scurried to build up the dying fire to warm her husband.

When the dry wood caught and the light flared up forming a dusky halo around the site, she turned to study him. She knew better than to speak or intrude, and yet the sight of him worried her. His body, though as full and well built as ever, looked like a shell, like an insect that had fled leaving only the most fragile, transparent casing behind. His face was pallid, his eyes glazed and unseeing. She moved nearer the fire, but not even a flicker of movement in his eyes signaled any awareness of her.

Fear ignited within her, overwhelming earlier efforts to comfort her own uneasiness. She desperately wanted to call his name, to call him back or, at the very least, take his hand and help him to do whatever it was that he must do. She did none of these things. She was as terrified of interrupting his trance as she was of not interrupting it. What if his spirit had fled to the furthest reaches of the world and disturbing him would make his spirit unable to return?

With sudden urgency, she moved away from the fire to search for a sprig of ground sage. She hurried to the truck, rummaged for a flashlight, and began a close scrutiny of the dry grass in search of the sacred plant. Grabbing wildly at the first cluster, she apologized to the plant for the late hour and her haste. Twisting the sprigs of sage into a hasty rope, she lit the end in the campfire, and watched until a full inch and a half flamed away to near dust. Then she blew out the flame and smudged herself, wrapping her head and shoulders in the sweet, calming scent. Moving quietly behind Danny, she smudged him, raising the sacred smoke high and low, waving her hand

197

until the smoke engulfed his whole body. The simple action soothed her, and she moved back by the fire to wait. The mantra of earlier circled her mind again and her hand went to her belly. "You are welcome here," she whispered aloud.

After a while, she felt as though the welcome extended beyond her womb to the night beings. Something joined her in that space, reassuring her that nothing—nothing—would chase the seed from her womb or prevent her husband from finding his way back. Trembling with cold and exhaustion, she sat down by the fire to wait.

Jed smelled sage burning and the smell finally made his body relax. For what felt like hours he'd lain in the camper bed as rigid as a tree limb. He felt numb from the stiffness. The camper was pitch black except for one tiny red dot on the smoke alarm, and he'd not taken his eyes from that tiny light in like forever.

What was Danny doing out there? Every slow thump of the drum echoed in his brain until the next came, and the next. And each slow thump brought images—so many images. He couldn't even close his eyes for fear he would miss one. All the stories Danny had told them that night were replaying in his head like movies.

He'd wanted to call out to Carol when she left but even his voice wouldn't work. But the sage was melting the stiffness away. Finally, he sat up slowly and rubbed his arms to bring the life back. Pete was sound asleep and the familiar little snore also brought back the life to his own limbs. He crossed his legs and smiled, no longer frozen, no longer afraid, no longer lonely, and with that he stretched out beside his brother and fell instantly asleep.

From the half world of sleep, John heard a voice, so close and afraid, so insistent. He'd been dreaming of silver and pink-hued fish swimming in a waterless world, but then he heard the voice as if from a long tunnel.

198

"John. John, wake up," it urged. "We have to go. It's time."

Disoriented, his first thought was that the voice was Mae Jo's telling him the baby was coming, and he had to wake up to take her to the hospital. "Honey?" he murmured.

"It's me, Terra. Wake up, John. We need to go."

His mind cleared and he saw Terra, fully dressed, shaking him gently she said, "I already put the food in the truck."

He sat up, his head spinning from lack of sleep and the residue of his dream. "What time is it?"

"It's three o'clock."

"Terra, it's the middle of the night. Danny said early but not this early."

She sat on the edge of the bed and took one of his hands in her own. "John, I heard them, the drumming, it's been going on all night, getting slower and slower until I fear it might stop completely. We have to get over there right now."

Suddenly, he remembered all that had unfolded the night before . . . Theresa Bennington, severe autism, twenty years institutionalized . . . and deep aqua pools, and loving her loving him. He shook his head. "Terra, nothing is going on. It's all in your mind, honey, remember? Theresa Bennington?"

"No. You don't understand. "Oh," she whispered, her voice rough with frustration, "how can I convince you?"

From the far corner of the room there was a sudden crash, the sound of breaking glass. Thinking some kid had tossed a rock through the window, He got up and flipped on a light and saw it. The crystal tree Mae Jo had given him years ago as a wedding present lay on the floor, shattered into a dozen pieces. When he'd cleared out Mae Jo's things from the bedroom after her death, this was the one thing he could not bear to part with. "My crystal clear forest," she'd crooned, laughing and kissing his ear. "I can always see through the trees in this forest."

199

The memory pierced him. He bent and picked up a small piece of broken glass. It felt warm to his touch.

"What is it?" Terra asked.

He stared at the glass, picked up a second chunk and cradled it in his hands. Her wish-fulfilling tree, Mae Jo had called it. Why, he wondered, at this moment, for no reason, did it tumble off the shelf and land at his feet? There was no logical explanation, except . . . . "Never mind. Let's go."

He dressed quickly in warm clothes and they went out into the dark night, climbed into the cold truck, and drove toward Bear Butte.

At three o'clock Agnes sat straight up in bed, her blank, unseeing eyes focused on the far wall. Bill, asleep beside her, awoke and jerked upright. He reached over and flicked on the lamp near the bed and stared at her. "Agnes? What is it, my girl?"

Nothing.

He touched her arm softly, not wanting to make any sudden moves. Her skin was cold. He saw a small shiver begin in her lower torso and travel up to her head. Gently, very gently, he lowered her down onto the bed and then wrapped her in his arms to ease the chill from her limbs. Outwardly, her body was rigid as a stone but, when he pulled her close, he could feel the trembling deep inside, as if from some inner force. "It's okay, dear one. All is well. The end is near, and all will be well."

Chapter 27

At 3:45 a.m. Carol saw the flash of headlights leap over the hill and a truck crawl down into the camp. She stood up, her legs weak and numb from sitting, and went to meet John and Terra. Inside, she trembled with relief. Thank God, she thought, this long night was coming to a close.

John emerged out of the shadow and came to her. "Carol," he said, kissing her cheek.

All the tension and weight of this night overwhelmed her and she began to cry. "Oh John, I am so glad to see you."

He pulled her close in his arms and held her. "What's the matter? Carol, are you all right? Is everything . . . ."

She leaned against him, grateful for his warmth and comfort. With a sniff she calmed her rolling emotions and then pulled away. "I'm all right. So are the boys. It's Danny I'm worried about."

Carol saw Terra come up behind John and she impulsively turned and gave her a hug. "You must be Terra. I'm so glad you came early." She turned to John. "I've been so worried. He's been drumming in front of the fire all night. He doesn't see or hear me."

Terra turned in Danny's direction, in the direction of the drum. An odd look came into her eyes, distant and glazed. "It was him?"

She watched the younger woman study her husband. "Terra?"

"I heard him. It woke me up." Terra stared, wide-eyed. "Somebody had to keep the rhythm—or it will all collapse."

"What did you say?" John said.

Terra touched his arm. "Don't you feel it? It was all removed. All the existing rhythms and vibrations—but the beat had to be maintained so the entire field would not collapse in on itself. Come on, we have to go to him right away." She turned and strode toward the fire.

Carol thought of Terra dancing beneath flashing orbs of light, her hair whirling around her head the night before. And she thought about all Danny had told her, about the coming of the great ones, and the ceremony, and suddenly she understood. They were all serving some greater purpose, in the dark, maybe, both literally and figuratively, but serving all the same. She smiled and turned to John. "I think your friend knows more than we do about this. I suggest we follow her lead." The dark hood of the sky felt like a tent around them as she took John's hand and followed Terra into the camp.

Carol stood beside John as Terra went to the edge of the fire and watched Danny drumming. She seemed to study his face, his posture, and the movement of his hand carefully. Finally Terra turned away and said quietly, "Carol, can you get a pot of water heating? He'll need some tea or broth, something warm, but not too hot, close to body temperature."

Relieved to have somebody taking charge, she said, "Agnes gave him a bag of tea today. I'll brew some of that."

Terra gave her a quick hug. "We'll bring him back, my dear. He may look awful right now, but we will bring him back. Go now. You'll know what he needs."

John helped Carol bank the fire and set the grillwork over it for the pot. The water on the bottom of the pot sizzled as they set it on the grill. The scent of wood smoke was heavy but rising straight up.

Through it all, Danny continued his rhythmic stroking of the drum, oblivious to the activity flowing around him. Tum. Da. Tum. Carol wondered how he could keep such a steady, slow thrumming when he didn't even look conscious. The sky was gathering light on the

202

eastern edges, the darkness silky and sheer now. The trees looked ghostly, and the stones jutted out of the earth as if alive. When the water was heating, she sat down and waited with one eye on her husband, always on her husband.

Terra felt as though she had crawled out of a cocoon, tugging at the paper shell and emerging into this night. Gone were the bleary lines of her world, gone the doubt and fear, gone the wondering and waiting—it was all about this moment right now. Excitement burned through her body. She saw pale shimmering wisps of light all around her. She couldn't believe she and John had been sleeping right through this like a pair of lions, all tangled up in each other's arms and legs. But that, too, was part of the shimmer.

She sat down on a campstool to watch the horizon, every cell of her body activated, humming with energy until she thought she might explode. When John took a stool and sat down beside her, she jumped.

He whispered, "Please tell me what the hell is happening here."

"I can't explain it right now. We had no idea how perilous this night has been. I had no idea." She didn't look at him. For some reason she couldn't take her eyes off Danny. "Please, you have to just trust me and do as I ask. When the sun is almost ready to break over the horizon, get the boys up and bring them to me. In fact, get them up a little earlier so they can eat some of the food we brought."

"No," he said firmly. "I don't know what is going on here, but it will have to go on without my boys being involved." John glanced at Danny. "I'm afraid for them. Afraid for him."

She did turn to face him now, breaking her connection with Danny for a moment. "Oh John. Don't back up now. Please? There isn't time, and we can't go forward without Jed and Pete. Don't you see? It's all about Jed and Pete, about all of them, all of the children. It's for them."

She curled her fingers around his arms, and waited for his response.

"I can't do this. I won't lose them, too."

"You can't lose them, John. You don't own them. They have their own place in the world—can't you see that? You just have to trust it. Accept whatever fate or the Creator has in store for them." She waited, watching him, sensing deep within that all the world was poised with her, on this pinpoint of a moment, on this man, on his ability to reach deep inside and find that ember of belief, of longing, of trust . . . of great love. To love or not to love?

He looked intensely into her eyes. A shudder passed through his body, and then he said, "I'll wake the boys up at dawn."

The shimmering energy suffused her entire being and tears fell from her eyes, tears wet with life and belief and love and trust. There was no need to say the words, "I love you." She leaned over and kissed his lips. "I'll keep them safe. I promise you." And then she stood up and went to sit beside Danny.

John turned and whispered aloud, "I must be as crazy as the rest of them." He thought back to his intimate joining with Terra and wondered how it all fit together. Fear tweaked his mind, fear that Terra would evaporate at first light, or that his buddy Danny would not return, or that his sons' spirits would wander off over the butte and dive into the great river. Overall, they were messing with night forces they knew nothing about. He wanted Danny to speed up the drumming to match the racing of his own heart. He went back and sat down by the fire.

He watched the horizon. He watched Terra. She had taken a canvas camp chair and pulled it up on Danny's right. At first she just sat as still as a stone, staring intently at the of top the unpainted drum. Danny's drumstick was adorned with tiny glass beads that caught the firelight and flashed outward toward the dark sky. She wore the ugly brown stocking cap they had bought at the mall. Her hair was tucked beneath it, and her pale face was lit only by the fire. Her image was ageless, without form or sex, without race. He thought she looked like stone and tree and water. The smoke drifting into the haze of morning added to the surreal landscape of their camp.

He watched as Terra mirrored Danny's posture. Then her right arm began to move, following his up stroke, his down, the short up and down of the second beat in a soundless parody like a mime practicing her art—but this was not theater.

He remembered the big picture window of his living room and the dark, draping skirt of the universe, the tiny hemstitches tying them all together. The campstool was too confining, so he got up and sat down cross-legged on the cool, damp earth near the fire with Terra directly across from him. Her eyes were already glazed and unseeing. Carol came and sat across from Danny, and together they waited and watched.

The night felt like a heavy blanket on John's shoulders, no sound but the crackling fire and the beating drum, no scent but the wood smoke and the damp morning soon to unfold. In the dark stillness, he felt the presence of others around them, all others. He narrowed his eyes to slits, defocused, and could almost see them— pale shimmering particle-forms with the suggestion of colors, of lavender, yellow, and green. He held his breath. His body tingled with an unfamiliar energy.

It made sense to him now, in some illogical way, the whisper at the back of his mind that said, "You will not be alone. You are never alone." His fear was gone completely.

When he looked up, Terra was gazing at him, tears pooling in her eyes, and the softest, expression adorning her face. Somehow, without knowing how, he understood that they had just received the blessings of these most powerful beings of the night. He lowered his gaze, humbled to tears himself, wanting to touch his forehead to the ground and pay his respects. When he looked back up at Terra, she was once again lost in her trance, traveling out and away in search of Danny's spirit.

Without warning, the tingling sensation in his limbs intensified. The sensation ran up his arms and legs, and moved to his ears with an audible buzzing and whirring. His breath nearly stopped. He glanced at Carol. She, too, was tense and wide-eyed, her head turned slightly to the left as if listening.

A loud crack exploded the quiet night like the sound of a branch splitting off from the main trunk of a tree. Terra moved quickly, reaching over to Danny, and in one quick Olympian moment, she had transferred the drumstick from his right hand to hers, like the pass of the wand as the runners surge forward. Terra was on the drum now, and Danny rolled off his chair and landed in a huddle on the cold ground, his body curled into itself like a fetus. Before John could react, Carol jumped to Danny's side.

He stared at Terra now sitting where Danny had sat through the long night. All was well. Whatever Terra had needed to do, she had done it. Only now it was her hand drumming the beat. He turned to Carol, "Is he all right?"

"Get the tea," she whispered urgently. "It's right where I was sitting,"

He grabbed the heavy mug and handed it to her. She pulled Danny out of his curl and brought his head to her lap. Tears streamed down her face, and she was whispering in rapid, staccato words. "I love you, Danny Elk Boy. Please come back. I love you. I want you back with me now. You are mine and I will not let you go with them. Here, Danny, here I am." It was as if she fought wildly to overwhelm the slow pace of the drum and her husband's dim heartbeat with her racing words.

"Give him the tea," John whispered. Her head came up like a startled animal. She took a deep, hitching breath and appeared to calm herself. She forced the cup to Danny's lips, and he responded, drinking in the warm draught of Agnes's tea. His body appeared to relax. He sipped again.

John watched as Carol began rocking, an ancient and instinctual rhythm, the rhythm of mothers and wives from the beginning of time, of sex, and birth, and comfort.

Danny, too, must have felt the new rhythm, so altered from the beat he'd carried through the night. It seemed to pull him finally, fully, from the drum's world and back to his wife and her warm, welcoming body.

Danny's eyelids flickered, opened, and then came to rest on Carol's face. He pulled in great gasps of air as his lungs filled and emptied, and filled again, never taking his eyes off of his wife. Another sip of the tea and then great, bulging tears slipped from his eyes and coursed down his cheeks. He spoke, his voice little more than a croak, "Oh Carol, baby, I saw her. She came to me and, damn, she was so beautiful. Just like you." With that he sobbed, gulping and shuddering.

Carol tightened her grip on him. "Who? Who came to you?"

John watched Danny breathe in again and then pull himself upright. Shuddering off the remains of the night's ordeal, he grinned at Carol, and laid his palms over her stomach. She looked confused. "I saw our daughter. This one. The one resting right here, right now, waiting for her own long night to be over."

John felt like an intruder. He got up and walked a few feet away, unwilling to get very far from Terra until it was time to get the boys. He knew Danny and Carol had tried, unsuccessfully, to have a child.

He heard Carol gasp, "A daughter?" His own throat tightened with emotion.

"Yes, she came to tell me," Danny laughed quietly. "not to worry. She has no intention of going anywhere but into our home and our lives." He shook his head. "Oh, Lord. I'm afraid she's going to be a handful. Grandfather was grinning as he waved her off toward us. She'll be headstrong, whoee."

Carol started to cry and then hugged herself and hugged Danny, and then she jumped up and was hugging John. He fully expected nobody would be safe from her hugging—not for a long time.

John leaned over to Danny. "A daughter, huh? Thought you wanted a son."

207

"Are you kidding? Nobody could refuse this girl . . . I mean nobody." Danny laughed again and leaned over to whisper into his ear only. "Besides, Grandfather told me there would be a son as well." Danny sat up and pulled Carol to him. "Man, but I am powerfully tired. Bone tired."

"Come on. I'll help you to the camper," said Carol.

Danny shook his head. "No, this isn't done yet. I can't leave yet. She may need me." He pointed to Terra who was now looking like his twin of the night, pale and drumming and unmoving except for the right arm. "Damn, never have I had a harder task. It was like trying to drum in mud, thick mud, with resistance from all sides." He said to Carol, "Can you just get me a blanket and a pillow? I'll rest here. Keep an eye on things. But I sense the worst is almost over. Dawn is coming."

Dawn. Terra had said to awaken the boys just before dawn. John knew the Elders thought it was in the space before dawn when the balance between life and death was most tenuously held, a time when the membrane between the world is thinnest and all is exposed and unsteady. He felt it now, the morning forces gaining power, drawing around the camp like stone guards.

Carol went to the camper and came back with a pillow for Danny. Within minutes he was snoring, with Carol safe in the crook of her husband's strong right arm, and between them, a daughter nestled deep in a world of tissue, fluid, and darkness . . . waiting.

Sighing, John resumed his position across from Terra and waited for morning.

He watched the sky. He watched Terra. He watched the shadows. He thought of the boys asleep in the camper and found his mind wondering simple things, mundane things, ridiculous things when held against the backdrop of the extraordinary events of the past two days. Will she be my wife? Will she be mother to Jed and Pete, help them with math problems, stand beside them when they are hurt or angry? Will we grow vegetables?

And what of a family in the eastern part of the state looking for their lost daughter?

What of it? All his life he'd slept with the stinging scorpions of fear and sadness, letting them bite him over and over again. No longer.

At last the gray, silken sky began to lighten. He rose, went to his truck, pulled the small cooler from the back and carried it into the camper. A fierce urge to haul his boys to the truck and drive the hell away from this place came over him, the urge to shield them from whatever would come next, but suddenly he recognized it as the urge to freeze, to stop time and movement itself, and he resisted.

He loved Jed and Pete. Without batting an eye, he would die or kill another to protect them. It was a spear point of self-knowledge, but Terra was right . . . he did not own them.

John nuzzled each boy in turn until they stirred from slumber and, like typical children, were instantly up, instantly on.

"Dad!" Pete sat up on his sleeping bag and threw his arms around John.

"You looked pretty comfortable. I hated to wake you up."

"What's happening?" Jed asked.

"I'm not sure yet. Get up and eat, and then we'll go find out." He lit the lantern, spread bagels with cream cheese and strawberry jam, opened bananas and poured apple juice. Jed and Pete whispered together as they ate, telling him about Danny's drum songs and the long tales that, Pete said, were like ghost stories.

Jed ate his bagel, excitement shimmering in his eyes. When he was finished, he said, "I heard the drum all night long. Even in my dreams. What are we doing, Dad?"

"I'm really not sure, but we aren't finished with these doings yet. I'm on Terra's orders."

Jed smiled at him in the lamplight. "Yeah, she can be like that sometimes, can't she?"

Pete grew quiet, as though his mind was somewhere else. He'd hardly touched his food. "Pete? How are you doing?" John asked. "Are you okay?"

"Sure. It's just . . . I had the weirdest dream."

"Tell me about it." It was the right thing to say but for some reason he wasn't sure he wanted to hear anymore about dream worlds.

Pete began. "Uncle Danny was going up to the top of Bear Butte and I decided to follow him. I ran but couldn't catch up. When I got to the top I couldn't see him. He'd disappeared. And then I saw this big river flowing down the hill. Dad, there isn't a river here, is there?"

John shook his head. "No, there isn't, but this was a dream, remember? Anything can happen in a dream."

Pete nodded. "I wanted to jump right into that great river—it was sparkling and full of fishes. I never saw so many shiny fishes, not in my whole life. But I remembered how you are about rivers and lakes. I knew I better not jump in with those fishes or you'd be mighty mad. So, I came back." There was a sad, tearful tone in his voice.

John felt an unseen cold thing touch his back. "I'm glad you came back, Pete. But . . . why so sad?"

Pete gulped back his tears. "It was those fish, Dad. I really wanted to swim with the fishes, but now I won't get to. I should have just jumped in. I should have."

"No, you did right. The fish will be there. So will the river. When it's time, you will get to swim with them, son."

"Maybe it was like Danny told us," Pete said. "A nation gathering. This was a nation of fish."

John again fought the urge to grab his boys and skip out. "What nation?"

Jed cut in. "It was one of the stories Danny told, about how he saw a gathering of the hawk nation. He said all the creatures need to gather sometimes with their own kind."

A gathering of the hawk nation. Powerful image, he thought. John pulled Pete close and studied his young face, noticing the way his shirt hung loosely on his thin frame. Sometime in the past year or two, the baby fat had burned off. "I'm glad you didn't go," he whispered, kissing the top of Pete's head. "Come on and get dressed now. Terra wants us out there before the sun breaks. Did you eat enough?"

They nodded, then hustled into jeans, sweatshirts, and jackets. John planted a woolly cap on each head and then eyed them for a moment. "Well, men, are you ready?"

They smiled and stood a little taller, as though proud to be called men. As they stepped out into the morning, Jed stopped and looked at him. "You know, Dad, everything will be all right. It's a good thing."

The pale light of the coming sun struck Jed's face and illuminated the sharpening lines of his face. How easy it is, John thought, to see these young ones as lacking wisdom or knowledge. But they know . . . they know so much. He rested an arm across Jed's shoulder and nodded. "I know, son."

They walked into the peach-colored morning and turned in the direction of the dying fire and the constantly thrumming drum.

Jed saw Danny and Carol curled up near the fire fast asleep, and Terra sitting like a ghost drummer on the canvas chair, "What is she doing?" he asked.

"Danny kept the drum all night long. It was part of what needed doing, I guess. Terra took over when we got here."

Jed nodded. "He must be really tired."

Suddenly he understood what Terra had meant about needing the clean pipes of a child.

Chapter 28

Terra felt the change. She'd been at the drum holding the beat for what must have been close to an hour now. Although her eyes were fixed on the drum, her sphere of awareness expanded to take in the entire camp. It was as if she could see and hear everything around her although her physical body was occupied with the drumming. Around her, the sky was brightening, the light pushing away the curtain of night one more time. The air smelled freshly washed. She took a deep breath and extended her awareness out even further.

She saw Carol stir, open her eyes, and roll away from Danny as if trying not to awaken him. Danny had ceased his rattling snores, and Terra could feel his breath moving in and out of his body. She saw John approach with the boys—and Carol go and sit beside Pete, gathering him close to her and asking, "Have you guys eaten?"

Behind her own breastbone, she felt the beating heart of those two boys, excited and alert as they nodded to Carol.

Carol looked at John. "What now?"

As if on cue, Danny sat up and was wide-awake. Surveying the site, he saw her still on the drum, the boys up and dressed, everybody waiting.

Her sphere of awareness widened further, and in her mind she heard Danny ask, *what next, Terra?*

Although he'd not spoken, she heard him. Her entire being was focused on the drum and on everything and the next step emerged. *Prepare the boys for the drum, Danny.*

He nodded. She realized he was in this interior place of the spirit, this place of the greater voice. *I'm fine,* she thought in his direction, *but it is almost time*. Danny nodded again. She took another breath, and another, realizing he understood and would do what was necessary.

Danny stood, stretched, and moved to the camper returning with two additional drumsticks. He held them up before Jed and Pete and said, "Pick which one is yours." With scarcely a thought, each boy reached for a stick. Danny nodded. "Fine, real fine. Pete, you go sit on Terra's left and Jed, you take the right."

Yes, Terra sent the thought to Danny. *That's right*.

The boys picked up campstools and quietly took their places beside her. Both Jed and Pete wore solemn expressions and sat tall, as though sensing the significance of this moment.

Danny watched her, watched the drum, closed his eyes and took a breath. "Now, listen close boys," he whispered. "It's been a very long night in the world, probably the longest night ever. But likewise, it's going to be a long morning, too. And you boys get to help set the new rhythm for the world. It's a warrior thing you are being asked to do, and it has never been done like this before. This is the very first time."

The boys straightened their backs and sat even taller.

Terra wanted to smile and cheer but the trance was too thick. All she could do was bring her hand down on the drum and again feel the peculiar widening of her sensory field. She felt, more than saw, John lean forward. She felt the fear cutting his being, and she felt Danny's calming presence wash the fear out, as if saying to John, trust me in this.

When John turned to look at her, she managed a tiny smile through the trance, a way to let him know he also was a warrior, to allow his boys to take up the drumsticks. In her mind she reassured him. *Trust me, John. No harm will come to Jed and Pete.*

Danny went on talking to the boys in a serious, whispered tone of voice, "Trust your inner selves and it will come. And don't worry—you can't do it wrong, boys. Do you hear me? Years from now, people will probably

214

sing songs about Jed and Pete Forrest and their great action." He smiled at them.

Terra felt her mind send another arrow of thought to Danny. *Funny man.*

You know it, came back to her.

And just when she was thinking this form of communication was rather fun, the greater voice took over completely and she lost all conscious thought. The silence of this interior space stunned her, made her gasp, grab for breath, an edge of panic overtaking her.

Danny felt the change. Whatever communication had been flowing between them now came to him directly. He glanced at Terra sitting at the drum and felt the panicky edge in her. He'd felt the same panic just before she took the drum from him.

Now. It was now.

Pete started to ask a question, but Danny stopped him. "No, keep silent, Pete. I'll explain as we go along." He waited only a moment, and the clarity shone through like the early sun. Danny said, "First, just follow Terra's beat, softly. Let the drum talk to you. The drum will tell you what to do next. Listen only to the drum. Once you start, I'll not speak again, but I'll be protecting you from all sides. Follow the drum, boys. Follow the drum. Go on now. Raise your sticks. You'll know what to do next."

Jed and Pete looked at each other, confusion playing across their young faces, but they nodded. White-knuckling their sticks, they began tapping the rhythm along with Terra. She nodded her approval.

They beat the drum tentatively, at first, and then their faces grew still and the pupils of their eyes narrowed into pinpoints, all excess light shuttered. The drum whispered. Hands relaxed. Breathing slowed. Slowed again. Danny watched, and listened deeply within.

He knew Terra saw and felt every movement, the way an eagle sees across a vast landscape. Across the butte and out into the early morning, the drum dominated all. Creatures, sentient and insentient, took their direction

215

from the drum. Twittering birds ceased their twittering. Constantly moving breezes stilled. Trees stood silent sentry as two small boys found their way into the drum world.

Danny reached for the mug of now-chilly tea and downed it thirstily as they sat and watched Terra drumming along with the boys. They couldn't see the sun top the far horizon but they all knew the moment it rose. With a small shiver and a blink of her eyes, Terra emerged from the trance and looked straight at Danny.

He nodded at her. Terra smiled, her hand still drumming. She was back, her body once again under her command. She turned to Jed and Pete and asked, "Does the drum speak?"

Both boys nodded.

"Clearly?"

They nodded again.

"And can you hear your heart?"

Again, the silent nods.

"Good. Very good." Her voice was so soft it barely entered the silence surrounding the beating drum. She looked at Danny. He nodded and said silently, *Go girl.* Whatever lines of communication had opened, they were open still. Danny was alert, poised, ready to step into the breach should she falter.

Terra continued. "All is well, boys. Soon I'll stop speaking and fall off the drum and leave it to you. There is a rhythm in your hearts. The drum already hears it. It has been waiting for you. When I'm off the drum, you are to follow whatever rhythm comes from inside you, from this great friendship between the drum and your own hearts. You'll know it, Jed . . . Pete . . . in fact, you already hear it."

Both boys nodded, their eyes glazing over as they concentrated.

Her voice was like a lyrical whisper, an ancient sound, hers but not hers. "This will be a new rhythm you discover. It is important to beat it like you mean it. Beat it hard and steady and make it sound out. Remember, you can only do right. Go on now. Listen. Find that new rhythm."

With those final words, Terra's beat on the drum grew softer and softer and, as she withdrew, the boys' pattern grew stronger.

She seemed to watch them until a shiver of understanding, of special hearing and energy, shimmered on each small face. Only then did she cease her hand.

For many moments the painfully slow rhythm continued and then, in unison, the boy warriors at last changed the beat.

Just as he had done earlier, Terra tumbled out of her chair as if thrown off and fell to the earth. John was beside her in a flash, mug of warm tea in hand, arms curling around her, pulling her next to his body. She drank the warm tea, never taking her eyes off the two boys on the drum. Danny sent her a final thought. *It is done. Leave it to the boys. All is well.*

She blinked, stood up, took John's warm hand in her own, and together they sat down to watch over Jed and Pete.

The four adults said nothing, only watched and listened in awe to the drumming boys. They heard water rippling, stones rolling, and thunder pounding; they heard dance rhythms, and song rhythms, and birth rhythms, and rhythms that spoke of joy and curiosity and love. They heard the rhythm of a small boy throwing rocks against a barn, the click of a stick in chain link, a skip, a hop, a bop, and a roll down a grassy hill; and they heard the whisper of a mother at bedtime, leaning over the little one and saying, sleep well, my precious one, sleep well. They heard all of these rhythms and more.

Nobody was surprised when a soft keening sound issued from Jed's mouth followed by Pete's response, the call of one brother to another. It was a sound beyond language, a drum sound with voice added, and it became a living thing, the first language, the first song, the first music, a rhythm that straightened the spine of the Earth and pulled its inhabitants into alignment around one drum, one rhythm.

Pleasure seeped into the listeners, deep abiding pleasure, the kind of pleasure generally found only on the birth bed or the marriage bed, the kind of pleasure issuing from the soul when nothing more is wanted from the perfected moment.

When the drum had carried Jed and Pete in, out, and around the new songs of the world, the drum grew light. It grew so light that Jed feared it might float upward, carrying them with it. He looked over at Pete, who stared back, eyes wide as plates. He was still bringing the stick down, but looking panicky and foolish. The sudden floating lightness of the drum broke the hold it had on Jed and he couldn't help it—he giggled. He tried to firm his hand but the laughter took over his mouth and throat. Pete grinned, too, trying to contain what bubbled up in his own belly, and then he burst out laughing. When Pete's nose started dripping, Jed lost it completely.

Within two minutes both boys had fallen off the drum and were helplessly laughing and rolling on the ground, bopping each other with their sticks. Pete screeched, "Stop, Jed. I got to pee. Stop it."

Jed jumped on Pete and started tickling him, "The pee monster is coming. The pee monster is coming." Pete laughed so hard he couldn't get out from under Jed.

Then, simultaneously, the boys realized what they had done. They scurried up from the ground, shame-faced before the four adults. "Sheesh, we're sorry," said Jed. "It just got so funny. The drum was tickling me. And then Pete's nose started to drip . . . ," Jed giggled again, trying desperately to contain the laughter. Pete looked ready to burst into tears but he, too, burst into a fresh fit of giggles. They were helpless, caught in a loop of trying to apologize, but unable to hold back the laughter.

Terra broke into one of her own fluted laughs. The boys stared at her, relief pouring from their bodies like little-boy cologne. "It's okay, guys. Really it is," she told them. "That old drum threw you off. You didn't quit." She shot a mock defiant look at the drum and laughed again. "Besides, the deed is done." Terra hugged them both and whispered something in Pete's ear. He ran off into the bushes like a snake was after him. Jed blushed when Terra planted a kiss on the top of his head, and said, "Good work, man."

Then, as if on cue, the world began to twitter and buzz and hum once again. A fresh breeze blew into camp, and the first rays of the morning sun touched the people gathered at the base of Bear Butte. One chubby squirrel came and sat, watching them intently. The serious scrutiny of such a small creature threw them all into laughter again. Pete took a crust of bagel and walked over to give the squirrel a chunk.

Danny said at last, patting his stomach. "I don't know about the rest of you, but I'm famished."

As if one body, the whole crew began searching every corner of camper and truck for food and drink. Carol pulled a large terry tablecloth out and laid it on the ground near the drum, arranging fruit, jams, fresh brown rolls, and small cartons of juice. She prepared a plate with small bits of all the food they were about to eat, a spirit plate, and gently set it near the drum. Terra took the coffeepot and soon had it brewing. In minutes, all were elbow deep in the breakfast picnic. They ate and talked, but not a single one referred to the long, unusual night that had just passed into day. The drum sat like a royal guest of honor in the midst of their picnic. No one, not even Pete, so much as approached the head of it with a juice carton, crumbling donut, or steaming mug of coffee.

Chapter 29

Bill Elk Boy laced his coffee with milk and sugar and drank it down. He couldn't awaken Agnes. She was sleeping like the dead, and he didn't know why. All night long he'd held her trembling body, but there was no fever, no other sign of illness, just a shudder deep within her body. He gulped the rest of the coffee and went back into the bedroom. He lay down beside her. For decades his life had revolved around this woman. It was impossible to consider going on without her.

With one forefinger, he traced the deep lines of her face, the place where the skin folded over itself like a newborn's. He loved every line, every wrinkle, every fold. He kissed her, and when he did, she opened her eyes and smiled up at him.

"What? You think you're some kind of Prince Charming or something? Or are you taking advantage of me when I'm asleep?"

He laughed and said, "I would never."

"Sure you wouldn't. And I'm a young girl again."

"You had me worried, Agnes."

"Some kind of night, huh? I'm bone tired." She sat up and rubbed her face with both hands.

"Can you tell me about it?" Over the past few days he'd known that whatever was taking place was in her territory and not his. He had accepted, that but he was now ready to hear more of what was going on and not just to serve blindly.

Agnes looked up at him and smiled. "You have been patient while we women worked. I thank you for this."

221

"Women's work?" He laughed. "I can't wait to hear more."

"In time, my friend. But right now, you smell like coffee and I could sure use a cup."

"Coming, my girl. Coming." He planted a kiss on her forehead and watched as she lay her head back down and closed her eyes, a slight smile on her lips.

Chapter 30

During the drive back to Rapid City along Interstate 90, John let the truck practically drive itself while he followed his soaring thoughts. He was tired. They were all tired. Moments after climbing into the truck, Terra had rested her head against the door and fallen fast asleep. The boys were not far behind.

The hum of the engine lulled his senses. He fought the urge to doze and forced himself to concentrate on the road ahead. He drove through the Piedmont Valley loving the gentle, scooping land even though it was now filled with housing developments and trailer sales lots with not much grazing land left for cattle. Long ago, during the gold rush years, the valley had been just a train stop called Spring Valley Station.

Peeking through the housing developments and sales lots, he could still see the strip of red soil. Lakota Elders claim it was burned red during the great race between all the creatures of Earth to see who would rule. The winner would have the primary care of the earth. The racetrack, as it was called, circled the entire Black Hills.

John considered all the old Lakota legends and realized that, most likely, the old stories contained chunks of truth that could only be known by the heart and soul, not the mind.

What exactly had happened out there beneath the wide night sky?

Fighting sleep, he was relieved to get back into town. He maneuvered the final three blocks and pulled into the haven of home, the long night behind them at last. As soon as he shut off the engine, the boys were up and

223

rubbing their eyes. He opened his door and eased them out his side in order to let Terra sleep. He handed off the bags, packs, and cooler from the truck bed into the waiting arms of Jed and Pete, and they carried the load into the house. When he walked back out to the truck he looked at Terra, her head wobbling against the truck window. Her face looked deathly pale, almost gray.

His palms went damp and his breath quickened. He opened her door gently so as not to startle her from sleep. Her head rolled gently back onto the headrest.

"Terra? Terra, honey, we're home."

He touched her arm but she felt cold, the kind of cold that crept from her skin to his instantly. He shivered. "Terra, wake up." She was unresponsive. In a panic now, he slipped an arm behind her knees and the other beneath her shoulders and lifted her out of the truck. She weighs nothing, he thought, like air. He carried her limp body into the house, struggling to open the lower door, listening for her breathing at the same time. Inside, he laid her on the couch, fear boiling in his throat.

No, he thought, please, don't leave me.

Jed came out of the kitchen. "Dad?"

"Son, get a wet cloth, quick. I can't wake her up. Hurry." Jed stared a moment and then jumped into action.

Pete came down the steps from the sunroom to find his father bent over Terra's still body. "Dad, what's wrong with her? Is she okay?"

"I'm not sure, Pete. I can't wake her." A grayish sheen had formed around her mouth, and her breathing was shallow. He was afraid, more afraid than he ever remembered being. The night was back. The damned long, dark night was back. He searched for her pulse . . . weak and hard to locate. Her chest moved ever-so-slightly up and down. He wanted to snatch the air from his own lungs to give her more breath.

By the time Jed brought the wet cloth back, he was frantic but didn't want to panic the boys. Calmly he said, "I have to call Danny. Wipe her forehead with that, Jed, her whole face, and talk to her. You too, Pete, come and talk to her."

"Talk about what, Dad?" Jed was already applying the cool cloth to her head.

"I don't know. Tell her . . . I don't know . . . tell her to come back, tell her you want to grow squash and pumpkins with her, tell her you want her to help you with math. Tell her stories . . . whatever . . . just talk to her, do you understand, boys? We can't let her leave us. Not now."

Jed and Pete perched on their knees by the couch and began talking, their voices trembling with fear, tears leaking out of the corners of their eyes. When he walked into the kitchen and turned back, the boys looked like they were on their knees praying. He found the phone and dialed Danny's number, his hand trembling, hoping they had gone straight home from Bear Butte. They had a little house out in Rapid Valley only fifteen minutes away. The phone rang. And rang. And rang.

At last he heard a click and Danny's voice. "Yeah?"

"Danny, it's John."

"Hey, little brother, we just now walked in the door. What's up?"

"It's Terra. She fell asleep in the car on the way home. When we got here, I couldn't wake her up. I think she's in a coma or something." He thought of Theresa Bennington; twenty years silent, but he clamped the fear like a bleeding artery. "She looks bad, Danny. What should I do? Call an ambulance?"

"No, just hang on. I'll be right there. Don't do anything except make sure she's breathing." He heard an abrupt click. John held the phone out as if it were a dead thing.

Taking a big breath to stay calm, he went back into the living room. Jed and Pete were rolling over each other now in their efforts to tell Terra all the things they wanted to do with her. He was slammed to the core by the crashing needs and desires emerging from the poor, stunted spirits of his two sons. The list rolled on in wave after wave. They wanted to play ball with her, go

225

swimming with her, camp, pow wow, tell bedtime stories, make s'mores over an open fire, draw pictures, decorate the Christmas tree—all crisp little promises and requests, solemnly offered, solemnly asked. You'll be so happy with us, they told her; we'll buy you candles, and pick flowers and, and, and . . . .

They want her as badly as I do, he thought. He fought an urge to weep. Danny was right. The boys needed more than he alone could give them. They needed Terra to stay and be with them and make what was broken whole again. Damn. He wanted to fight back somehow against whatever unseen thing had followed them from Bear Butte. Damn it.

No, he thought, I will not let the black thoughts hide what I have seen. Terra—she'd told him that great love is in the lover, not the beloved.

He walked into the living room and knelt beside his sons. They stared at him with damp, wide eyes and kept on talking while he took the cloth and patted Terra's cheeks, her chin, and the place where her neck met her shoulders. He thought again of her body draped in aqua satin and forced that sweet energy to move outward and dissolve all of his fears. He joined his own silent prayers and promises to those of the boys. We will live a great love. We will pour water from small cups to wash each other's pain away. In his mind he whispered about the children they would have, future brothers and sisters to Jed and Pete; he told her about Mae Jo, how she'd smashed the little tree to let him know that she wanted Terra to care for her boys and take a place beside him.

Finally, he lifted Terra up, pulled off her coat, and said, "Here, let me put her on the bed. Danny is on his way. He'll know what to do." He carried her to his bedroom. Out the window, a giant flowering crab tree, still skeletal from winter, guarded the room. He hoped the powerful energy of that tree would spring her back to him.

"Great love," he whispered softly to her. "Terra, you have to stay so I can learn more about great love. Please come back. We need you more than they do. Tell them.

Tell them you want to stay." He couldn't believe he was insisting she make demands to the Creator, the Great Spirits—to *Unci Makah*. Not a single action in his entire life had ever confirmed his buried belief in a divine presence as much as this single plea. He kissed each eyelid and smiled. "Open your eyes, Terra. Open them." He waited. Nothing happened.

The boys trailed into the bedroom, helpless and frightened. He didn't want to scare them. Taking a deep breath, he sat on the edge of the bed, pulled Pete onto his lap, and patted the space next to him. Jed lumbered up and crossed his legs.

He told them, "Sing 'Ten Little Indians' to her, like you guys did in the truck the first day she came."

Pete grinned. "Yeah, that was her idea. She said that song is okay because all the Indians don't disappear—not the way she sings it. They just get more and more." Pete started singing, his voice quavering. "Ten little, twenty little, thirty little Indians . . . ."

Jed sang along. Not knowing what else to do, John joined his voice to that of his sons.

That was how Danny and Carol found them, sitting and singing around Terra as if she were a campfire and they needed to warm themselves. Danny grinned at the picture they made. "All right guys, out. I need to be alone with Terra so I can find out what's going on. Come on."

The boys scooted toward the door. John got up off the bed and stood there, waiting; Danny waved him out as well. John hated to leave her side even for a moment, but he trusted Danny to bring her back.

When he went into the kitchen, Carol had quickly taken over that end of the house in her quiet, efficient way. She was heating water in the teapot, taking cups and spoons and plates out of the cupboards and setting the table. She had even managed to find cookies in a remote cupboard. The boys planted themselves at the table, chins resting in the palms of their hands.

He told Carol briefly what had happened.

"Don't worry, John," she said, glancing at Jed and Pete. "He'll bring her back."

"Thanks for coming so quickly," he said, touching her arm.

The cookies disappeared rapidly, so Carol made mountains of toast and the boys were soon dipping the corners into steaming cups of hot chocolate. She located a small bag of dried-out marshmallows and plopped them into their cups. John sipped the warm cocoa but felt as though his throat was closing, and he'd never eat or drink again.

Finally, Danny appeared at the kitchen door and motioned him into the living room. They stood at the picture window looking out. The sky was gray, overcast, a pall shadowing the land. Danny said, "I don't know what it is, John. On the way over here, all I could think of was that I," his voice caught, "I didn't introduce her to the drum. And last night, that drum was probably the most powerful force in the whole universe. It almost took me out. I don't know. I just don't know. I get the feeling she's off in council with them, with her relatives. Damn it, man, it confuses me."

"I think I know what it is," said John.

There had been no time to tell Danny about his discovery of the missing Theresa Bennington. He told him now about the article. "The newspaper said she'd not communicated directly with anyone for twenty years, that she lived in a world of her own making."

Danny looked thoughtful. "In the early days of our culture, the Elders believed the mentally ill were directly connected to the spirit world. They were respected—and a little bit feared. In fact, we didn't even have a word for mental illness."

The words "mentally ill" hit John with a force of their own. He told Danny, "But it doesn't add up. Except while she was drumming, there has been no withdrawal from us. I told her last night we'd have to call the authorities—her family is looking for her. She begged me to wait until this morning. And then we . . . we made love." He nearly

228

choked on his own words, unable to believe he could lose her now, after all they had done, to this thing called "autism."

Danny put his arm around him. "Maybe we better call the authorities."

"No."

"John?"

"Damn it. This can't be real. You said she was from Grandmother Earth. You told me that." He laughed a bitter, harsh laugh. "I can't accept this. I can't accept that after all this she is some sick girl who wandered off from a hospital. And I can't accept that the spirits dropped her out of the sky to do the good deed, and now that it's done, what? They drag her back again? What am I supposed to believe here, Danny? Either way, it sucks." A red rage washed through him and his breathing grew rough and raspy. "Hell, is this some kind of cosmic joke? What?"

"Easy, buddy. I'm not the enemy here. Neither is she. We just don't have the whole picture yet. It's still shrouded—but, whatever happened out on the Butte last night, it was real. You have to believe that."

"That's what kicks me in the ass the hardest. I do believe it. Me—John Forrest—skeptic to the max and yet, I do believe. What I can't believe is that men in frigging white coats from Yankton are going to show up and take her away from me. And from my boys. They need her. I need her." He felt like smashing his fist through a wall, to see if it was real or if his hand would float right through it. Instead, he sat down on the couch and looked up at Danny. "So what do we do?"

"Let's wait a bit and see. She's fighting it. Her pulse is strong and her color came back. Could be the drumming drained her energy and she needs to fill her tank. Hell, I don't know."

John shook his head, "We're still in the dark here, aren't we?"

Danny nodded and sat down beside him. "I think I'll call Uncle Bill. We need his help. And Agnes's. Somehow they're connected to this. That's why I took Jed and Pete to Bear Butte."

"What do you mean?" John asked.

"I stopped at Cuny Table before I left for town. There was a note on Agnes's door that said to get the drum, take the tea, take the boys, and go to the Butte."

"I didn't know that."

"No, everything happened so fast, there was no chance to tell you."

Instead of confusing John further, knowing Agnes and Bill were linked into this event actually comforted him. "Okay. You call Bill. I'm going downtown to talk to the sheriff, at least tell him about Terra. The boys don't know anything about this. Man, I hate to think of her family sitting there worried sick about her."

"Go then. I'll call Bill and keep an eye on things here."

John hesitated. "I don't want to do this."

"I know that. But go, it is the right thing. Somehow this is going to work out, buddy. Trust me."

John almost laughed aloud. How many times had he heard those words over the past few days . . . trust me. He nodded but said, "I don't know how the hell it can work out."

Chapter 31

After John left, Danny wandered the room scratching his jaw, trying to figure out what was happening. Something didn't feel right. When everything should be rising like yeast bread, it had suddenly, and inexplicably, gone flat. It didn't make any sense. He thought about John, the years of watching his buddy struggle to cope with losing Mae Jo. He wanted the damn bread to rise. People should be able to live happily ever after. Of course, this wasn't a movie with perfectly placed camera angles and characters as deep as your thumbnail. He couldn't help but smile. It was beginning to feel like a movie—what with the heroine in a coma, the hero racing off to do the right thing, and two boys motherless once again. Maybe John had it right—a cosmic joke.

He planted his bulky form on the too-soft couch, crossed his legs at the ankles, and stared at the toes of his cowboy boots. Man, I'm tired, he thought, closing his eyes. A sleep as deep as a coma wouldn't be such a bad thing.

A movie. More comedy than tragedy, he realized. The Creator was at play in the wily world. What's going on, Grandfather, he asked to the living room ceiling. He saw the image of his grandfather bopping old George on the head, only it wasn't George getting clobbered, it was himself. Trust me, he heard far back in his mind, all is well. It sounded like Terra's voice, the hidden voice she had used to communicate during the drumming time. It also sounded like his grandfather's voice. In a flash, Danny realized that they had most certainly not been alone on

Bear Butte last night . . . and they were not alone now. So what was the problem?

The confusing, clenching uncertainty fled, and he grinned. And then he laughed. When Carol and the boys came in to see what he was laughing about, he only laughed harder.

Then, in the middle of his laughing fit, Terra walked out of the bedroom looking confused and left out. "What's so funny?" she asked.

Danny stopped laughing. They were stunned into silence by her sudden appearance.

"What's so funny?" she asked again.

Danny stared at her and began laughing again so hard he had to hold his sides. The others looked at Danny, and then at Terra.

Then, in a flurry of sudden motion, the two boys railroaded Terra like two small trains colliding on her track. They bounced her to the floor, tickling and rolling around until she was breathless, and they were all laughing. When she caught her breath and said, "I'm hungry," a fresh round of giggles ensued.

As the hilarity subsided and food was again being laid before them by Carol's competent hands, it was Pete who pointed to the fact that John was not among them. "Dad thought you were leaving us for good, Terra. He said to tell you all the things we wanted to do with you so you wouldn't go away."

"Yes. I heard some of that. Something about s'mores and camping?"

Pete grinned. "Well—they are awfully good."

"Sure—good for the dentists." Terra turned to Danny. "Where did John go?"

"He went downtown to talk to someone. Come on, let's take a little walk."

She gave him a puzzled look but nodded and reached for her jacket. Danny looked at Carol and the boys and reassured them, "We'll be right back. I promise." They went out the front door and turned left toward the park. He finally broke the silence. "John was out of his head,

232

Terra. When he realized you might not come out of it, he nearly lost it. He told me about the woman missing from Yankton. He went downtown to talk to the sheriff."

Terra stopped walking and stared down the quiet street. "She is not me, Danny. That woman is not me, I know it. I still don't understand what is happening, but I know that isn't me."

"What do you remember?" he asked.

"Not much. It was so strange, where I was. One minute I was in the truck with John and the boys heading back to Rapid, and then I was simply somewhere else." She took his hand and gave him a soft look. "I could hear what was going on, but I couldn't open my eyes or speak. I had no control over my body. It was as if I was suspended in some thick fluid that glued all my senses shut. At the same time, I was back with Grandmother, telling her how things went and telling her all the reasons I needed to stay here . . . with you guys." Terra smiled and stopped walking. She turned to him. "I kept offering more and more reasons and explanations. She laughed, said I was trying to sell her a potato peeler when she already had three. 'You love him,' she said finally. I said, "Yes, I love them all." Then she nodded and said, "I put you in a woman's form—so it's no surprise that you would act like a woman."

"The old woman does have a sense of humor, doesn't she?" He shook his head, his mind reeling with all she had told him.

"I called her Unci. I didn't know the word actually meant grandmother. She used to make us hot tea made from plants she gathered twice a year. That tea is all she serves. She gave me some while I was out. It made my lips buzz and that's what woke me up."

Danny thought he was beyond being shocked by the rare events unfolding over the past couple of days, but Terra's words made his head spin anew. Unci? Agnes? No sense even going there, he wouldn't understand anyway; but early tomorrow morning he planned to head down to Cuny Table to have a nice long talk with Agnes. He had more than a few questions—and he sure could use a cup of her tea—or maybe one of her stories. He had the fleeting urge to quiz Terra further, especially about the other side, but he shrugged it off, realizing he didn't care to know more than he already did. Not until it was time. Not until he had obtained enough good marks as a human being to deserve a greater glimpse.

"I am so tired, though," she said finally, looking at him again. "You must be, too. That was something . . . holding the drum. And you held it most of the night. If you don't mind, I think I'll go crawl back into that bed and rest. Don't worry. I won't go any further than the normal dream boundary. I'm content with here and now."

Her smile touched his spirit, and he reached out and hugged her. His mind was whirring as they walked back in silence. So much to consider—and nothing to consider. It was done, all done. Somehow he felt that in his gut. And there were many questions that would never have answers, not in this realm anyways. It didn't matter what John discovered about Terra's origins. She would stay with them and be a part of the next chapter and the next. It was done.

When they walked back into the house, Terra yawned, gave Jed and Pete a quick, reassuring hug, then she wandered into the kitchen, stood in front of Carol and looked at her, one woman to another. "Thank you," Terra said.

He stared at them and felt the intense energy of two women in deep contact with one another, one thanking the other for what, he didn't even know, for the care of each other, for the care of the boys, for the role each had played? Terra placed a hand tenderly on Carol's womb, smiled, and then left the room.

He felt like going to his knees then, to offer thanks for the daughter embedded there, to Carol, for being his wife, and for all women who risked their lives to give birth to the next generation—or the next age on Earth. He went to Carol and wrapped his arms around her and held her close, a sense of the sacred in his heart. "I love you," he said.

She turned her shining face to his and said, "I love you, too. Always."

Jed and Pete came into the kitchen carrying their sweatshirts and backpacks. They grinned at the older couple kissing in the kitchen. Danny cocked one eye in their direction and asked, "What? What do you guys want?"

Carol laughed and pulled away. "While you were walking with Terra, the guys decided they want to make good on a few of their promises right away. We're off to buy candles and pretty flowers. Pete thinks plastic flowers would be good—they last longer, you know." She grinned and winked at him. "They've decided today is Terra's official birthday, so we are going to have a party later."

"Good idea." He was anxious for John to return and realized that Carol was intentionally taking the boys off before he came back. "Terra will probably sleep awhile," he said, handing her the keys to the truck. She and the boys were out the door in a buzz of excitement. Again he felt his own bone-weariness and was about to seek the couch when the door opened, and Jed came back in.

"They're waiting for me out in the truck, but I just needed to ask you something, Uncle Danny."

"What is it?"

"I was wondering if you would teach me?"

"Teach you?"

"To be Lakota."

"Jed, you are Lakota. I don't need to teach you to be what you already are."

"No, I mean teach me about the drum, the songs . . . and the medicine."

Jed's breathing was shallow and tense, his face so, so serious. "You want to do things Lakota way?" Danny asked.

The young man nodded.

"It won't be an easy path."

Jed nodded. "I think I know that."

"Of course you do. And yes, I'd be mighty proud to teach you." He stuck his hand out. Jed grabbed it, shook it softly, and then went out the door.

What a day, Danny thought, every moment a sacred moment.

Fifteen minutes later Danny was half asleep on the living room couch when John walked in drinking coffee from a paper cup and looking confused.

He shook himself and sat up. "You're back. What happened?"

"Nothing."

"What did the sheriff say?"

John sat down on the couch. "It isn't Terra. She isn't Theresa Bennington"

"What?" Danny said simply.

"It looked like her, but the sheriff said the woman was found the same day just a few blocks away having a Coke in a café."

"Shee-it. Really." Danny laughed. "Go figure. By the way, she's awake."

"What? Why the hell didn't you say so?"

"You didn't ask. Besides, she's sleeping again."

"What?"

If John hadn't looked so confounded, Danny would have liked to wrestle him to the ground again. He laughed and said, "Jesus, man, you sound like a broken record. She is just sleeping. She was tired." He told John how he had started laughing at the ridiculousness of it all and how Terra had simply walked into the living room to see what he was laughing about.

John snickered, "Some medicine man. I figured I'd come back and find you burning strange roots or praying and pulling wicked things from her body. Turns out, you laughed her out of a coma."

"Can't argue with what works, my friend. Actually, if people laughed more, my work would be a whole lot easier. At any rate, she's back and, it seems, intent on staying. She can tell you herself what happened and about the meeting with her grandmother."

"Where are the boys?" John asked.

"They declared this day Terra's official birthday and went to buy her presents. Seems they made a lot of promises while they were jabbering away at her."

John sobered. "You were right, Danny. Those boys need more than I can give them. I need more. In fact," he smiled, "I made a few promises myself—and I plan to keep them." His face grew serious. He kept his eyes on Danny for a long moment. "Do you think it's over?"

"I don't know, John. It's never really over, is it? No guarantees in life except death—and whatever's on the other side of death."

John nodded, smiling. "I still don't know who she is."

"I think you should go and talk to her."

John walked into the bedroom where Terra was sleeping. He resisted the urge to bow or wave sage and cedar to the spirits. God, but she is beautiful, he thought. Her deep steady breathing reassured him, and the earlier gray pallor was now replaced with the heated pink of sleep. He crossed the room and stretched out alongside her, curling his body toward hers like the bend of a shield. Terra's eyes flickered, opened on his face, and she smiled. "Hi, you."

"Hi, yourself," he said.

"I thought you went to see the sheriff."

"I did. Theresa Bennington is back in Yankton. She isn't you. As Pete would say, go figure."

Terra laughed softly. "I knew that."

"Right." He leaned toward her and kissed her soft mouth. "You scared me, Terra, real bad."

"No, you scared yourself. My Grandmother has a weird sense of humor, but she's not cruel. Never cruel. She understands—better than anyone—about great love." Terra flattened her palm on his chest, fanning her fingers as if to feel the strength there. "You never were abandoned, you know. Not for a single moment."

"Yeah, I'm starting to understand that. Just starting."

"Where is everybody?"

"Carol took the boys shopping. Seems they are planning a big party."

Terra's eyes widened and she groaned. "Oh no, not a party, please."

"It's a party for you. They've declared today your birthday. They also made a list of promises as long as my arm while you were out cold. It may take them most of their lives to get through the list. You up for that?"

"Up for what? For staying to watch two gorgeous, sweet boys grow up to be strong young men? Or should I say three gorgeous men? Or to stay and watch the way the world turns from this weekend's events? Or," she leaned toward him, and kissed his lips. "Maybe you're saying to stay and live great love with a handsome man as my husband, maybe to write poetry, and go to pow wows and dance and cuddle next to my Grandmother's heart in these Black Hills as long as I live? Is that what you are asking?"

"Yeah, something like that."

"Hmm . . . let me think about it."

Chapter 32

Danny dozed on the couch in the quiet living room waiting for Carol and the boys to return from their shopping spree. His body, though exhausted, felt alive and rejuvenated. It was not even noon yet but what a day this had been. He could recall little of his own long night on the drum but felt deeply satisfied. After dozing for half an hour, he pulled himself upright, yawned, and used the remote to turn on the television.

On the screen, a perky young woman was standing in the parking lot at the Sylvan Lake Campground giving a live remote report. She said, "An astounding and unexplained phenomenon is occurring here at the base of the tallest mountain in the Black Hills, Harney Peak, on this first day of March. Since sunrise, people have been arriving in great numbers to climb this mountain, considered sacred by the Lakota People . . . ."

He stared at the television in disbelief as the camera panned the area to show dozens of people trudging through the parking lot and campground at the base of Harney Peak. Others were already starting up the hiking trail, a hike that takes several hours to reach the stone forestry building on top.

He jumped off the couch, hurried down the hall, and knocked on John's door. "Come here. You have to see this."

A few minutes later John and Terra, looking barely awake, came out of the bedroom. "What is it?"

When they came into the living room, he pointed at the television and said, "Look at this."

They watched as the reporter held a microphone in front of a couple just starting up the trail. "From what I understand, there was no special event or walk-a-thon planned for this Sunday morning, and yet, here are you, along with dozens of others." The newswoman shook her head in amazement. "What are you all doing here?"

The couple smiled and moved aside to let others get around them while they talked to the reporter. The woman said, "We don't know. When we woke up this morning, we just started putting on our hiking boots and tossing lunch into our backpacks, and here we are. We even had other plans for the day. It was very spontaneous."

Her husband nodded, grinning. "Had no idea there would be such a crowd."

John didn't wait to hear another word. "Come on. Let's go. We can catch up with Carol and the boys at Baken Park. We have to get up there."

They squeezed into John's small truck and drove to the shopping center. Within minutes, they located Carol and the boys, their arms laden with bags and packages. Pete, when he spotted Terra, yelled happily, "Gosh Terra, you should see what we got you! It's your birthday today, did you know that?" Terra widened her arms to include Pete and all his packages in her embrace.

John tousled Pete's head and said, "Well, come on then, let's go have a birthday party." They loaded into Danny's truck because it had a second seat and drove south on Mount Rushmore Road.

Forty-five minutes later they joined the growing crowd gathering at the campground. Terra couldn't contain her excitement and was out of the truck in an instant. "Look at this. I can't believe it. There must be hundreds of people here."

The whole area was jammed with people arriving in cars, trucks, and motorcycles with more pulling in every minute. Cars were parking across the lake at the store and lining the sides of the road leading to the Needles Highway.

Danny parked on the grass, and they walked up the road and across the campground to join the line of people moving up the trailhead. In spite of the great numbers, the trail was quiet, serene, as if everyone was entering a great cathedral, the service about to begin.

Only Jed and Pete seemed unable to contain the jubilant energy dancing in their bodies. The adults had to hurry to keep pace with them. Pete sang "Happy Birthday To You" at the top of his lungs while Jed dogged his heels trying to hush him up, obviously embarrassed at the attention and smiles Pete drew from the quiet hikers.

By three-thirty, breathless from the hike, they began the final climb up the stone steps to the lookout. Harney Peak was like a busy anthill, jam-packed with other people. The sun was setting in the western sky and the air seemed to shimmer with color.

Pete moved to Terra's side and took her hand, as if he couldn't wait to get to the top and show Terra the world according to Pete Forrest. "Hurry, Ter. We need to get up there."

"I'm trying, big guy. What's the hurry?"

"Don't know . . . just know we got to get up there, fast." Suddenly Pete stopped on a step and turned to look for Jed. He motioned for his brother and the others to come near.

The Black Hills spread out like ancient, granite-helmeted warriors before them. John noticed the bright, wide-eyed look on his youngest son's face and looked around, trying to see what Pete was looking at. "What is it, Pete?"

"It's those fishes, Dad, like in my dream. I know this isn't a lake or anything, but the fishes . . . see . . . there . . . and there."

John strained his eyes and scanned the vast overlook. "What fish, son? What are you talking about?"

Even as he questioned Pete, the crowd all along the mountaintop grew still as they watched the air shimmer with color and form, an inexplicable presence settling on the mountaintop, a phenomenon of barely perceptible light and color. Terra, John, Danny, Carol, and Jed all circled around Pete and stared.

A collective "ahh" rose from the throats and lips of the people gathered there watching the stupendous, unnatural sight. There was still too much day for northern lights and no electrical storm for St. Elmo's fire. The crowd grew silent and then, just as quickly as it had occurred, the wash of light and color was gone.

"What was it?" Carol hadn't said a word until now, but the awe in her voice clearly indicated she'd seen what just happened.

Pete cried, "It was the fishes, those silver and pink fishes! Holy cow, they were here and now they left, they just swam right away again!" He turned to his dad, "Remember my dream, Dad? I told you about those pretty fishes. It was them."

"Shhh, son. You can tell me in a moment." John felt enveloped in the sweet wash of the gentle goodbye from the spirits up on this holy mountain.

Terra moved close to John and rested her head on his shoulder. "Good-bye," she mouthed aloud his inner thoughts, "good-bye, and thank you!"

Chapter 33

As above, so below the ancient Lakota Elders say. Agnes and Bill watched the five-o'clock news that Sunday afternoon. The newscaster reported odd stories from around the country. All of the ancient places of prayer had been hit with multitudes of people the way Harney Peak was that day: Medicine Wheel, Wyoming. Sedona, Arizona. Chaco Canyon, New Mexico. In the kivas, the cliffs, the canyons, even the cathedrals, all across the nation the people gathered.

Again and again they told reporters they didn't know why or for what purpose or who had led them to do so— but everyone who came had felt the call to come.

Agnes walked over to the television screen and touched some of the faces of the people being interviewed. She saw in them the renewal of hope, the flash of collective memory, of a time when great love was not a rare occurrence—but a way of being.

Bill smiled at her. "Do you think they can feel you touching them?"

She laughed. "I know they can. Or they wouldn't have come."

He walked up behind her and put his arms around her waist. He liked the strength and solidity of this woman's body, liked the feel of it beneath his hands. "You can put it away now."

"What."

"The pipe. Your hidden pipe—*Unci Makah's* pipe."

She turned to him and smiled, her eyes soft and wet. "She is so beautiful, this mother, this gentle mother."

"Yes, she is," said Bill.

"Come with me. So we can see the end."

Bill smiled and said, "Or is it the beginning?"

Agnes nodded, went out onto the rough-lumber porch of the Cuny Café, and sat down in the rocker. She slid the pipe a final time from her grandmother's bag. She fingered the notches, knowing that each notch tied her to the women behind her and the women behind them to the original woman, *Unci Makah*, the mother of all.

She lit the pipe, handed it to Bill, and together they watched as the sun went down over the Black Hills. The puffs of color, nearly invisible once again, hovered over Harney Peak.

Epilogue

Six Months Later

Terra was alone in the car driving along the empty highway that cut along the edge of the Badlands. That morning she had felt the baby kick for the first time. In a few months, Jed and Pete would have a little sister. She couldn't explain why she knew it was a girl—she just did, and without any help from modern technology.

Somehow that first limb pressing against her abdomen from within had spurred the lonely journey today. John was on a job in Spearfish, the boys off with Danny for the weekend. Terra needed to talk to Agnes. But first . . . .

She pulled up to her favorite overlook and got out of the car. It was hot—over 90 degrees already—so very different from a chilly February morning six months earlier. Had it really only been six months? She may not remember anything prior to that day, but every second, every minute, every lovely day since then was sharply cut into the prism of her life now—with them.

Oddly, the memory loss had not seemed to matter at all before, so why now, why since she discovered she was pregnant had it become more and more pressing to remember? She loved John and the boys but felt disconnected from all but this bit of Badlands—her birthplace, it would seem. She stood staring out across the carved land and took a deep breath, willing the land to restore all of her life to her now.

Nothing came to her as she walked the path leading down to the floor of the Badlands. She didn't go far—it was too hot and she didn't want to do anything to risk the health of her baby. It had been fun getting to know Carol better—and Danny. She and Carol were exchanging baby information on a daily basis now. The dangerous first trimester was long past for Carol, so there seemed little chance of a miscarriage. In fact, Carol's due date was September 6th. She'd also met Agnes and Bill and had felt deeply connected to them from the first minute. It was for this reason she wanted to see Agnes. That dear, sneaky, old woman was holding something back—she knew it.

Forty minutes later, she pulled up in front of the café on Cuny Table. Agnes was sitting alone on the porch, and Terra had the uncanny feeling that the old woman had been waiting for her. She got out, closed the door quietly, and walked over to the porch. "Hi, Agnes."

"You look good, my girl," Agnes said.

Terra patted her growing tummy and smiled. "I feel good. Better than good."

Agnes nodded. "Then all is well."

She climbed the steps and took the chair beside Agnes's old rocker. "I don't know, Agnes."

"What don't you know?"

"I don't know who I am . . . where I come from."

Agnes laughed. "That again? Why can't you just be con-tent with the life you have been given. It is what we all have to do. None of us really know."

"Please, Agnes. You know more than you say—I know you do. Can't you understand that I need to know. My baby deserves to know who her relatives are."

For a long moment Agnes was silent. She reached over and put her hand on Terra's growing belly and she closed her eyes. When she opened them again, they were damp with tears. "A granddaughter." She smiled.

"But Agnes, she is not your granddaughter. You are not my mother. I have no family."

Agnes gave her such a long and loving look that Terra almost felt guilty. Since arriving in this place, the old woman had acted exactly like she imagined a mother or grandmother would act. How could she be so ungrateful? "Talk to me. Please."

246

Agnes nodded. "There is so much we don't understand, but I will tell you a story. I can offer you no other proof than this."

Terra smiled. Stories and Agnes could not be separated. "I'm listening."

"When I was young, much younger than you are now, I conceived a child, a daughter I was sure. Bill and I were so young—and so in love. We had planned to get married immediately, but shortly after her conception I was also called away by the spirits. This made it impossible for my daughter to stay within my body. I knew this, and so I made an agreement with them. They could have me—and my child—until such a time when the world would need us both . . . here. And that is what happened. The women in my family have always been called—makes for an interesting life, it does." She laughed a little and then rested her hand on Terra's belly. "And more fun yet to come, if I am not mistaken."

Terra could scarcely take in what the woman was saying. "What? You are saying that you are my mother? And that Bill is my father? But . . . I don't understand. How could that be when I am white—and you are both Lakota? I really don't understand."

Agnes laughed. "You sound like Danny. He had the same reaction when I told him my theory. All I can say is that you had another mother, too—the Badlands—and you took on some of her beautiful coloring."

Terra began to shiver in spite of the heat of the day. A person doesn't just drop out of the sky—no matter what Agnes believed. It was just too . . .

And then she remembered the woman on the hillside, the voice she heard—and the woman, Unci, who had come to her during her coma and fed her tea . . . they were all Agnes—at different ages. Her mother. The explanation was so simple, and suddenly so easy for her to accept, that Terra burst into tears and wept. Months of wondering and not knowing, of feeling alone and frustrated shivered right out of her body. Agnes did not try to comfort her. The old woman simply waited until her shivering and tears had

247

ceased, and then laid a hand on her head. Terra felt like all that had just shivered out of her body was filled in again with that one hand laid upon her head. Finally, Terra took a deep breath, and said, "Does Uncle Bill know?"

Agnes smiled and said, "Why don't you ask him?" She pointed up behind her. Terra looked up and saw Bill framed in the doorway of the café. He was smiling, his cheeks wet with tears. She didn't say a word but got up slowly and faced him. Bill opened the screen door, stepped out, and closed it softly behind him, never taking his eyes from her face. He waited. She took a step toward him, and the next minute she was wrapped in his arms and they were both crying. He was whispering to her, "There, there now, my girl. You have come home to us. It is over. We have finished it now."

His body felt like a sturdy tree next to her body. For the first time since arriving here, she felt herself grow roots, hers winding themselves around his—and all fear and not knowing and loneliness fled. Bill reached out around her and took Agnes' hand and it was complete.

And I saw that the sacred hoop of my people was one of many hoops that made one circle, wide as daylight and as starlight, and in the center grew one mighty flowering tree to shelter all the children of one mother and one father. And I saw that it was holy.

~~From Black Elk Speaks by J. Neihardt

About the Author

Patricia "Jamie" Lee has traveled extensively into Indian Country with her husband, Milt Lee, an enrolled member of the Cheyenne River Sioux Tribe. Together they have produced over seventy public radio documentaries including the 52-part native series, *Oyate Ta Olowan—The Songs of the People*. Their work has aired internationally and received six Golden Reel Awards from the National Federation of Community Broadcasters with major funding from The Corporation for Public Broadcasting and The National Endowment for the Arts. Jamie also taught at Oglala Lakota College on the Pine Ridge Reservation in South Dakota.

In 2007 Lee's first novel, *Washaka—The Bear Dreamer*, was a finalist in the PEN USA Literary Awards. Her short fiction has been published in *The South Dakota Review, Winds of Change Magazine, Heartlands Magazine, Byline* and others.

Lee has an MA in Human Development and has studied and taught workshops in NLP, Family Constellation Work, Core Communications and currently is offering personal development retreats called, Life by Design. She grew up on The Leech Lake Reservation in northern Minnesota. In 2010, Jamie and her husband, producer Milt Lee bought land in her home territory in northern Minnesota and have built a straw bale house and studio.

To learn more about the Earth Songs series or Jamie Lee, visit her blog, *No Ordinary Life* at www.jamieleeonline.com

Made in the USA
San Bernardino, CA
17 March 2016